VAMPIRE SLAYERS

VAMPIRE SLAYERS

Stories of Those Who Dare to Take Back the Night

THE SLAYERS SERIES

Edited by
Martin H. Greenberg
and
Elizabeth Ann Scarborough

CUMBERLAND HOUSE
Nashville, Tennessee

Published by Cumberland House Publishing, Inc., 431 Harding Industrial Drive, Nashville, TN 37211-3160.

Cover design by Becky Brauner
Interior design by Julie Pitkin

Library of Congress Cataloging-in-Publication Data is available.
ISBN: 1-58182-036-4

Printed in the United States of America
1 2 3 4 5 6 7 — 03 02 01 00 99

Contents

Introduction

It's amazing how times change; how human perception can alter even over the course of a few decades. Take the stereotypical vampire, for example. For a while it had seemed that the image of the traditional evil bloodsucker preying on helpless humans had gotten a fairly extensive update. Gone were the cloak-draped men with thick eastern European accents living in seclusion in their forlorn castles high in the mountain ranges of obscure European principalities. With the advent of novels by Anne Rice, reading audiences now encountered handsomely morose dilettantes who spent decades of their unlife bemoaning their fate instead of getting down to what they were supposed to be doing, which was being the personification of evil. *Bram Stoker's Dracula*, as interpreted by Francis Ford Coppola, made the mythic archetypal figure a doomed hero, cursed by God and trapped by his love for Mina Harker, which no doubt had Mr. Stoker spinning in his grave. There was even a television miniseries called *Vampire: The Masquerade*, about the trials and tribulations of the day-to-day life of modern-day vampires. It seemed that the vampire had pulled his greatest trick yet—that of becoming sympathetic.

Fortunately, with the advent of new movies (e.g. *John Carpenter's Vampires* and *Blade*), television shows (*Buffy the Vampire Slayer*), and authors such as Laurell K. Hamilton, the pendulum has swung the other way once again, and vampires top the list of monsters we love to hate. Cunning, existing only to satisfy their thirst for blood, these vampires deserve not our pity, but only the sharp end of a wooden stake.

Luckily for the rest of us, there is a small percentage of people who, once they discover what is lurking among the world's population, are only too anxious to put an end to these minions of darkness.

From Professor von Helsing and Jonathan Harker to Blade and Buffy, a new generation of hunters are rising to take back the night from these insidious undead. Armed with the power of religion, or more often a good old-fashioned stake or arrow, these vampire slayers will go to any lengths to find and bring down their prey.

And that is what we've gathered here for you: eleven stories of those fearless, or perhaps crazy, people who hunt down and kill these inhuman creatures of the night. Tales of those who can see the monsters for what they are and are willing to do whatever it takes to destroy them. From a hunter who deals with a very special kind of vampire in Ed Gorman's "Duty" to a clash between vampires and the congregation of a small parish in F. Paul Wilson's "Midnight Mass," these stories prove that it's not just the vampires who are out for blood anymore. So turn the page, and take up the torch and cross, and step into the twilight world of the vampire slayer . . .

VAMPIRE SLAYERS

THE LAST GRAVE
OF LILL WARRAN

Manly Wade Wellman

The side road became a rutted track through the pines, and the track became a trail. John Thunstone reflected that he might have known his car would not be able to travel the full distance, and in any case a car seemed out of place in these ancient and uncombed woods. A lumber wagon would be more in keeping, or riding a mule, if John Thunstone were smaller and lighter, a fair load for a mule. He got out of the car, rolled up the windows, and locked the door. Ahead of him a path snaked through the thickets, narrow but well marked by the feet of nobody knew how many years of tramping.

He set his own big feet upon it. His giant body moved with silent grace. John Thunstone was at home in woods, or in wilder places.

He had dressed roughly for this expedition. He had no intention of appearing before the Sandhill woods people as a tailored and foreign invader. So he wore corduroys, a leather jacket that had been cut for him from deer hides of his own shooting and a shabby felt hat. His strong-boned, trim-mustached face was sober and watchful. It did not betray excitement, or any advance on the wonder he expected to feel when he finished his quest. In his big right hand he carried a walking stick of old dark wood.

"Yep, yep," the courthouse loafers at the town back on the paved road had answered his questions. "Lill Warran—that's her

11

name, Lill, not Lily. Not much lily about her, nothin' so sweet and pure. She was a witch, all right, mister. Sure she was dug out of her grave. Nope, we wasn't there, we just heard about the thing. She was buried, appears like, in Beaver Dam churchyard. And somebody or several somebodies, done dug her up outta there and flung her body clear of the place. Old-time folks believe it's poison bad luck to bury a witch in church ground. You do that and leave her, you might's well forget the church 'cause it won't be blessed no more. Ain't saying we believe that personal; it's country belief."

But the courthouse loafers had not denied the belief in the necessity of digging up a witch. One or two of them contributed tales of Lill Warran. How she was no dry, stooped, gnarled old crone, but a "well-growed" woman, tall and fully and finely made, with a heavy massive wealth of black hair. She wore it knotted into a great loaf at her nape, they said, and that hair shone like fresh-melted tar. Her eyes, they said, were green as green glass, in a brown face, and her mouth—

"Huh!" they'd agreed to Thunstone. "You've come a far piece, and it's like you seen a many fine-looking women. But, mister, ain't no possible argument, you seen Lill Warran and that red mouth she had on her, you'd slap a mortgage on your immortal soul to get a kiss of it."

And the inference was, more than one man had mortgaged his immortal soul for a kiss of Lill Warran's mouth. She was dead now. How? Bullet, some said. Accident, said others. But she was dead, and she'd been buried twice over, and dug up the both times.

Gathering this and other information, John Thunstone was on the trail of the end of the story. For it has been John Thunstone's study and career to follow such stories to their end. His story-searches have brought him into adventures of which only the tenth part has been told, and that tenth part the simplest and most believable. His experiences in most cases he has kept to himself. Those experiences have helped, perhaps, to sprinkle gray in his smooth black hair, to make somber his calm, strong face.

THE TRAIL WOUND, AND climbed. Here the wooded land sloped upward. And brush of a spiny species grew under the pines, encroaching so that John Thunstone had to force his way through, like a bull in a swamp. The spines plucked at his leather-clad arms and flanks, like little detaining fingers.

At the top of the slope was the clearing he sought.

It was a clearing in the strictest sense of the word. The tall pines had been axed away, undoubtedly their strong, straight trunks had gone to the building of the log house at the center. And cypress, from some swamp near by, had been split for the heavy shingles on the roof. All around the house was bare sand. Not a spear of grass, not a tuft of weed, grew there. It was as naked as a beach by the sea. Nobody moved in that naked yard, but from behind the house came a noise. *Plink, plink,* rhythmically. *Plink, plink.* Blows of metal on something solid, like stone or masonry.

Moving silently as an Indian, John Thunstone rounded the corner of the log house, paused to make sure of what was beyond, then moved toward it.

A man knelt there, of a height to match John Thunstone's own, but lean and spare, after the fashion of Sandhills brush dwellers. He wore a shabby checked shirt and blue dungaree pants, worn and frayed and washed out to the blue of a robin's egg. His sleeves were rolled to the biceps, showing gaunt, pallid arms with sharp elbows and knotty hands. His back was toward Thunstone. 'Me crown of his tow head was beginning to be bald. Before him on the ground lay a flat rectangle of liver-colored stone. He held a short-handled, heavy-headed hammer in his right hand, and in his left a narrow-pointed wedge, such as is used to split sections of log into fire wood. The point of the wedge he held set against the face of the stone, and with the hammer he tapped the wedge butt. *Plink, plink.* He moved the point. *Plink.*

Still silent as a drifting cloud, Thunstone edged up behind him. He could see what the gaunt man was chiseling upon the stone. The last letter of a series of words, the letters irregular but deep and square:

HERE LIES
LILL WARREN
TWICE BURIED AND TWICE DUG UP
BY FOOLS AND COWARDS
NOW SHE MAY
REST IN PEACE
SHE WAS A ROSE OF SHARON
A LILY OF THE VALLEY

John Thunstone bent to read the final word, and the bright afternoon sun threw his shadow upon the stone. Immediately the lean man was up and his whole body whipped erect and away on the other side of his work, swift and furtive as a weasel. He stood and stared at John Thunstone, the hammer lowered, the lean-pointed wedge lifted a trifle.

"Who you?" the gaunt man wheezed breathily. He had a sharp face, a nose that projected like a pointed-beak, with forehead and chin sloping back from it above and below. His eyes were dark, beady and close-set. His face was yellow and leathery, and even the whites of his eyes looked clouded, as with biliousness.

"My name is John Thunstone," Thunstone made reply, as casually as possible. "I'm looking for Mr. Parrell."

"That's me. Pos Parrell."

Pos . . . It was plain to see where the name suited the man. That lean, pointed snout, the meager chin and brow, the sharp eyes, looked like those of an opossum. A suspicious, angry, dangerous opossum.

"What can I do for you?" demanded Pos Parrell. He sounded as if he would like to do something violent.

"I want to ask about Miss Lill Warran," said Thunstone, still quietly, soothingly, as he might speak to a restive dog or horse. "I see you're making a gravestone for her." He pointed with his stick.

"And why not?" snapped Pos Parrell. His thin lips drew back from lean, strong teeth, like stained fangs. "Ain't she to be allowed to rest peacefully in her grave sometime?"

"I hope she will," said Thunstone. "I heard at the county seat about how she'd been dragged out of her grave at the churchyard."

Pos Parrell snorted. His hands tightened on hammer and wedge. "Now, mister, what almighty pick is it of yours? Listen, are you the law? If you are, you just trot your law back to the county seat. I'm not studying to hear any law. They won't let her stay buried at Beaver Dam, I've buried her here, and here she'll stay."

"No," Thunstone assured him. "I'm not the law."

"Then what are you? One of them reporters from the newspapers? Whatever you are, get off my place."

"Not until we've talked a bit, Mr. Parrell."

"I'll put you off. I got a right to put you off my place."

Thunstone smiled his most charming. "You do have the right. But could you put me off?"

Pos Parrell raked him with the beady eyes. "You about twice as big as me, but—"

He dropped the hammer. It struck the sand with a grim thud. He whipped the lean wedge over to his right hand, holding it daggerwise.

"Don't try that," warned Thunstone, and his walking stick lifted in his own hand.

Pos Parrell took a stamping stride forward. His left hand clutched at the tip of Thunstone's stick, the wedge lifted in his right.

But Thunstone drew back on the stick's handle. There was a metallic whisper. The lower part of the stick, clamped in Parrell's grasp, stripped away like the sheath of a sword, revealing a long, straight skewer of gleaming blade that set in the handle as in a heft. As Parrell drove forward with his wedge, Thunstone delicately flicked the point of his sword cane across the back of Parrell's fist. Parrell squeaked with pain, and the wedge fell beside the hammer. Next instant Parrell was backing away hurriedly. Thunstone moved lightly, calmly after him, the sword point quivering inches from Parrell's throat.

"Hey!" protested Parrell. "Hey!"

"I'm sorry, but you'll have to listen to me."

"Put that thing down. I quit!"

Thunstone lowered the point, and smiled.

"Let's both quit. Let's talk."

PARRELL SUBSIDED. HE STILL held the hollow lower length of the stick. Thunstone took it from him and sheathed his blade.

"You know what?" said Parrell, rather wearily. "That's about the curiousest place I ever seen a man carry a stab weapon."

"It's a sword cane," explained Thunstone, friendly again. "It was made hundreds of years ago. The man who gave it to me said it was made by Saint Dunstan."

"Who was that?"

"He was an Englishman."

"Foreigner, huh?"

"Saint Dunstan was a silversmith," Thunstone told Parrell. "This blade in my stick is made out of silver. Among other things, Saint Dunstan is said to have twisted the devil's nose."

"Lemme see that thing again," Parrell said, and again Thunstone cleared the blade. "Huh!" grunted Parrell. "It got words on it. I can't make 'em out."

Thunstone's big finger tapped the engraved lettering. *"Sic pereant omnes inimici tui, Domine,"* he read aloud. "That means, 'So perish all thine enemies, O God.' "

"Bible words or charm words?"

"Perhaps both," said Thunstone. "Now, Parrell, I want to be your friend. The people in town are pretty rough in their talk about you."

"And about Lill," said Parrell, so faintly that Thunstone could hardly hear. "But I loved her. Lots of men has loved her, but I reckon I was the only one loving her when she died."

"Tell me," urged Thunstone.

Parrell tramped back toward the cabin, and Thunstone followed. Parrell sat on the door sill and scuffed the dirt with his coarse shoes. He studied the back of his right hand, where Thunstone's skillful flick of the silver blade had raised a thin wale and shed a drop of blood.

"You know, you could have hurt me worse if you'd had a mind," he said.

"I didn't have a mind," Thunstone told him.

Again the shoes scuffed the sand. "I prized up my door stoop stone to make that marker for Lill's grave."

"It's a good one."

Parrell gestured to the edge of the clearing. There, in the shade of the pines, showed a mound of sand, dark with fresh digging, the size and shape of a body.

"I buried her there," he said, "and there she'll stay. At the last end, I reckon, she knowed I loved her and nothing could change it."

A rose of Sharon, a lily of the valley. Lill Warran had been no sweet lily, the courthouse loafers had insisted. Thunstone squatted on his heels.

"You know," he said, "you'll feel better if you talk about it to somebody who will listen."

"Reckon I will."

And Pos Parrell talked.

Later Thunstone wrote down Parrell's story from memory, as a most interesting record of belief in the supernatural, and also belief in a most beautiful and willful woman.

* * *

LILL WARRAN WAS CALLED a witch because her mother had been one, and her grandmother had been one. Folks said she could curse pigs thin, and curse hens out of laying, and make trees fall on men cutting them. They wouldn't hear of things like that happening by chance. The preacher at Beaver Dam had sworn she said the Lord's Prayer wrong—"Our Father, who *wert* in heaven." Which meant Satan, who'd fallen from the Pearly Gates, the way it says in the book of Isaiah. No, the preacher hadn't read Lill Warran out of church, but she stopped coming, and laughed at the people who mumbled. The old folks hated her, the children were afraid and the women suspicious. But the men!

"She could get any man," said Parrell. "She got practically all of them. A hunter would leave his gun, a drinker would leave his bottle of stump-hole whiskey, a farmer would leave his plough standing in the field. There was a many wives crying tears because their husbands were out at night, following after Lill Warran. And Nobe Filder hanged himself, everybody knows, because he was to meet Lill and she didn't come, but went that night to a square dance with Newton Henley. And Newton grew to hate her, but he took sick and when he was dying he called on her name."

Pos Parrell had just loved her. She never promised to meet him, she tossed him smiles and chance words, like so many table scraps to a dog. Maybe it was as well. Those who were lovers of Lill Warran worshiped her, then feared and hated her.

That, at least, was witch history as Thunstone had read it and researched it. The old books of the old scholars were full of evidence about such seductive enchantresses, all the way back to the goddesses of dark love—Ishtar, Astoreth, Astarte, various names for the same force, terrible in love as the God of War is terrible in battle. To Thunstone's mind came a fragment of the Epic of Gilgamesh, lettered on a Chaldean tablet of clay five millennia ago. Gilgamesh had taunted Ishtar's overtures:

> *Thou fellest in love with the herdsman*
> *Who ever scattered grain for thee,*
> *And daily slaughtered a kid for thee;*
> *Thou smotest him,*
> *Turned him into a wolf . . .*

"It didn't prove nothing," Parrell was protesting. "Only that she was easy to fall in love with and hard to keep."

"What did she live on?" asked Thunstone. "Did her family have anything?"

"Shucks, no. She was orphaned. She lived by herself—they've burned the cabin now. People said she knew spells, so she could witch meat out of smokehouses into her pot, witch meal out of pantries onto her table."

"I've heard of people suspecting that of witches," nodded Thunstone, careful to keep his manner sympathetic. "It's an easy story to make yourself believe."

"I never believed it, not even when—"

Parrell told the climax of the sorry, eerie tale. It had happened a week ago. It had to do with a silver bullet.

FOR SILVER BULLETS ARE sure death to demons, and this was known to a young man by the name of Taylor Howatt, the latest to flutter around the fascinating flame that was Lill Warran. His friends warned him about her, and he wouldn't listen. Not Taylor! Not until there was prowling around his cabin by something that whined and yelped like a beast-Varmint—a wolf, the old folks would say, except that wolves hadn't been seen in those parts since the old frontier days. And Taylor Howatt had glimpsed the thing once or twice by moonlight. It was shaggy, it had pointy ears and a pointy muzzle, but it stood up on its two legs, part of the time at least.

"The werewolf story," commented Thunstone, but Parrell continued.

Taylor Howatt knew what to do. He had an old, old deer rifle, the kind made by country gunsmiths as long back as the War with the North. He had the bullet mold, too, and he'd melted down half a silver dollar and cast him a bullet. He'd loaded the deer rifle ready, and listened for several nights to the howls. When the thing came peeking close to an open window, he caught its shape square against the rising moon and fired.

Next day, Lill Warran was found dead on the footpath leading to her own home, and her heart was shot through.

Of course, there'd been a sheriff deputy down. Taylor Howatt was able to claim it was accidental. The people had gathered at Lill's cabin, and there they'd found stuff, they said. One claimed a side of bacon he said had hung in his smokehouse. And another found a book.

"Book?" said John Thunstone quickly. For books are generally interesting properties in stories like the story of Lill Warran.

"I've been told about it by three folks who swore they seen it," replied Parrell. "Me myself, I didn't see it, so I hold I ain't called on to judge it."

"What did those people tell you about it?"

"Well—it was hairy like. The cover all hairy and dark, like the skin of a black bear. And inside it had three parts."

"The first part," said Thunstone, "was written with red ink on white paper. The second part, with black ink on red paper. And the third, black paper, written on with—"

"You been talking to them other folks!" accused Parrell, half starting up.

"No. Though I heard the book mentioned at the courthouse. It's just that I've heard of such books before. The third part of the book, black paper, is written on with white ink that will shine in the dark, so that it can be read without light."

"Then them folks mocking me heard what you heard about the like of the book. They made it up to vex my soul."

"Maybe," agreed Thunstone, though he doubted that the people of the Sandhills brush would have so much knowledge of classical and rare grimoires. "Go on."

The way Parrell had heard the book explained, the first part— red ink on white paper—was made up of rather simple charms, to cure rheumatism or sore eyes, with one or two more interesting spells that concerned the winning of love or the causing of a wearisome lover to depart. The second, the black ink on red, had the charm to bring food from the stores of neighbors, as well as something that purported to make the practitioner invisible, and something else that aided in the construction of a mirror in which one could see far away scenes and actions.

"And the black part of the book?" asked Thunstone, more calmly than he felt.

"Nobody got that far."

"Good," said Thunstone thankfully. He himself would have thought twice, and more than twice, before reading the shiny letters in the black third section of such a book.

"The preacher took it. Said he locked it in his desk. Next day it was gone. Folks think it went back to Satan himself."

Folks might not be far wrong, thought Thunstone, but did not say as much aloud.

PARRELL'S VOICE WAS WRETCHED as he finished his narrative. Lill Warran had had no kinsmen, none who would claim her body at least. So he, Parrell, had claimed it—bought a coffin and paid for a plot in Beaver Dam churchyard. He and an undertaker's helper had been alone at the burying of Lill Warran.

"Since nobody wanted to be Christian, nothing was said from the Bible at the burying," Parrell told Thunstone. "I did say a little verse of a song I remembered, I always remembered, when I thought of her. This is what it was."

He half-crooned the rhyme:

> *"The raven crow is a coal, coal black.*
> *The jay is a purple blue,*
> *If ever I forget my own fair love,*
> *Let my heart melt away like dew."*

Thunstone wondered how old the song was. "Then?" he prompted.

"You know the rest. The morning after, they tore her up out of the grave and flung her in my yard. I found her lying near to my doorstep, the one I just now cut for her gravestone." Parrell nodded toward where it lay. "I took her and buried her again. And this morning it was the same. There she lay. So let them all go curse. I buried her yonder, and yonder she'll stay, or if anybody says different I'll argue with something more than a law book. Did I do wrong, mister?"

"Not you," said Thunstone. "You did what your heart told you."

"Thanks. Thank you kindly. Like you said, I do feel better for talking it over." Parrell rose. "I'm going to set up that stone."

Thunstone helped him. The weight of the slab taxed their strength. Parrell drove it into the sand at the head of the grave. Then he looked to where the sun was sinking behind the pines.

"You won't be getting back away from here before it's dark and hard to pick the way. I'll be honored if you stopped here tonight. Not much of a bed or supper doings, but if you'll be so kind—"

"Thank you," said Thunstone, who had been wondering how to manage an overnight stay.

They entered the front room of the little cabin. Inside it was finished in boards, rough sawn but evenly fitted into place. There was an old table, old chairs, a very old cook stove, pans hanging to nails on the walls. Parrell beckoned Thunstone to where a picture was tacked to a wall.

"It's her," he said.

The photograph was cheap, and some slipshod studio artist had touched it up with colors. But Thunstone could see what sort of woman Lill Warran had been. The picture was half length, and she wore a snug dress with large flower figuring. She smiled into the camera, with the wide full mouth of which he had heard. Her eyes were slanting, mocking and lustrous. Her head was proud on fine shoulders. Round and deep was the bosom into which a silver bullet had been sent by the old deer rifle of Taylor Howatt.

"You see why I loved her," said Parrell.

"I see," Thunstone assured him.

PARRELL COOKED FOR THEM. There was corn bread and syrup, and a plate of rib meat, hearty fare. Despite his sorrow, Parrell ate well of his own cooking. When the meal was finished, Parrell bowed and mumbled an old country blessing. They went out into the yard. Parrell walked slowly to the grave of Lill Warran and gazed down at it. Thunstone moved in among the trees, saw something that grew, and stooped to gouge it out.

"What you gathering?" called Parrell.

"Just an odd little growth," Thunstone called back, and pulled another. They were the roots called throughout the south by the name of John the Conqueror, great specifics against enchantment. Thunstone filled his pockets with them, and walked back to join Parrell.

"I'm glad you came along, Mr. Thunstone," said Parrell. His opossum face was touched with a shy smile. "I've lived alone for two years, but never so lonely as the last week."

Together they entered the house, Parrell found and lighted an oil lamp, and immediately Thunstone felt the impact of eyes from across the room. Swiftly facing that way, he gazed into the face of the portrait of Lill Warran. The pictured smile seemed to taunt and defy him, and to invite him as well. What had the man leered at the court house? *You'd slap a mortgage on your immortal soul to get a kiss.* That picture was enough to convince Thunstone that better men than pitiful, spindling Pos Parrell could find Lill Warran herself irresistible.

"I'll make you up a pallet bed here," offered Parrell.

"You needn't bother for me," Thunstone said, but Parrell opened a battered old wooden chest and brought out a quilt, another. As he spread them out, Thunstone recognized the ancient and famous patterns of the quilt work. Kentucky Blazing Star, that was one of them. Another was True Love Fancy.

"My old mamma made them," Parrell informed him.

Parrell folded the quilts into a pallet along the wall. "Sure you'll be all right? You won't prefer to take my bed."

"I've slept a lot harder than what you're fixing for me," Thunstone quickly assured him.

They sat at a table and talked. Parrell's thoughts were still for his lost love. He spoke of her, earnestly, revealingly. Once or twice Thunstone suspected him of trying for poetic speech.

"I would look at her," said Parrell, "and it was like hearing, not seeing."

"Hearing what?"

"Hearing—well, more than anything else it was like the sound of a fiddle, played prettier than you ever heard. Prettier than I can ever play."

Thunstone had seen the battered fiddle-case on a handhewn shelf beside the door of the rear room which was apparently Parrell's sleeping quarters, but he had not mentioned it. "Suppose you play us something now," he suggested.

Parrell swallowed. "Play music? With her lying out there in her grave?"

"She wouldn't object, if she knew. Playing the fiddle gives you pleasure, doesn't it?"

Parrell seemed to need no more bidding. He rose, opened the case and brought out the fiddle. It was old and dark, and he turned it with fingers diffidently skillful. Thunstone looked at him. "Where did you get it? The fiddle, I mean."

"Oh, my granddaddy inherited it to me. I was the onliest grandboy he had cared to learn."

"Where did he get it?"

"I don't rightly know how to tell you that. I always heard a foreigner fellow—I mean a sure-enough foreigner from Europe or some place, not just somebody from some other part of the country—gave it to my granddaddy, or either traded it to him."

Thunstone knew something about violins, and judged that this one was worth a sum that would surprise Parrell, if no more than mentioned. Thunstone did not mention any sum. He only said, "Play something, why not?"

Parrell grinned, showing his lean teeth. He tucked the instrument against his jowl and played. He was erratic but vigorous; with training, he might have been brilliant. The music soared, wailed, thundered and died down. "That was interesting," said Thunstone. "What was it?"

"Just something I sort of figured out for myself," said Parrell apologetically. "I do that once in a while, but not lots. Folks would rather hear the old songs—things they know, like 'Arkansas Traveler' and 'Fire in the Mountains.' I generally play my own stuff to myself, alone here in the evenings." Parrell laid down the instrument. "My fiddle's kept me company, sometimes at night when I wished Lill was with me."

"Did you ever know," said Thunstone, "why we have so many fiddles in the American country localities?"

"Never heard that I recollect."

"In the beginnings of America," Thunstone told him, "frontier homes were lonely and there were wild beasts around. Wolves, mostly."

"Not now," put in Parrell. "Remember that crazy yarn Taylor Howatt told about shooting at a wolf, and there hasn't been a wolf around here since I don't know when."

"Maybe not now, but there were wolves in the old days. And the strains of fiddle music hurt the ears of the wolves and kept them away."

"There may be a lot in what you say," nodded Parrell, and put his instrument back into its box. "Listen, I'm tired. I've not slept fit for a dog these past six nights. But now, with you here, talking sense like you have—" Parrell paused, stretched and yawned. "If it's all right with you, I'll go sleep a while."

"Good night, Parrell," said Thunstone, and watched his host go into the rear room and close the door.

THEN THUNSTONE WENT OUTSIDE. It was quiet and starry, and the moon rose, half of its disk gleaming pale. He took from his pockets the roots of John the Conqueror, placing one on the sill above the door, another above the front window, and so on around the shanty. Returning, he entered the front room again, turned up the lamp a trifle and spread out a piece of paper. He produced a pen and began to write:

> My Dear de Grandin:
> I know your investigations kept you from coming here with me, but I wonder if this thing isn't more interesting, if not more important, than what you chose to stay and do in New Jersey.
> The rumors about Lill Warran, as outlined to you in the letter I wrote this morning, are mostly confirmed. Here, however, are the new items I've uncovered:
> *Strong evidence of the worst type of grimoire.* I refer to one with white, red and black sections. Since it's mentioned in this case, I incline to believe there was one—these country folk could hardly make up such a grimoire out of their heads. Lill Warran, it seems, had a copy, which later vanished from a locked drawer. Naturally! Or, supernaturally!
> *Presence of a werewolf.* One Taylor Howatt was sure enough to make himself a silver bullet, and to use it effectively. He fired at a hairy, point-eared monster, and it was Lill Warran they picked up dead. This item naturally suggests the next.
> *Nobody knows the person or persons who turned Lill Warran twice out of her grave.* Most people of the region are rather smugly pleased at the report that Lill Warran wasn't allowed rest in consecrated churchyard soil, and Pos Parrell, griefstricken, has buried her in his yard, where he intends that she will have peace. But, de Grandin, you will already have guessed the truth they have failed even to imagine: if Lill Warran was indeed a werewolf—and the black section of the grimoire undoubtedly told her how to be one at will—if, I say, Lill Warran was a werewolf. . . .

Thunstone sat up in the chair, the pen in his fingers. Somebody, or something, moved stealthily in the darkness outside.

There was a tapping whisper at the screen Pos Parrell had nailed over the window. Thunstone grimly forbore to glance. He made himself yawn, a broad hand covering his mouth—the reflex gesture, he meditated as he yawned, born of generations past who feared lest the soul might be snatched through the open mouth by a demon. Slowly he capped his pen, and laid it upon the unfinished letter to de Grandin. He rose, stretched and tossed aside his leather jacket. He stopped and pretended to untie his shoes, but did not take them off. Finally, cupping his palm around the top of the lamp chimney, he blew out the light. He moved to where Parrell had spread the pallet of quilts and lay down upon them. He began to breathe deeply and regularly. One hand, relaxed in its seeming, rested within an inch of the sword cane.

The climax of the adventure was upon him, he knew very well; but in the moments to follow he must possess himself with calm, must appear to be asleep in a manner to deceive the most skeptical observer.

Thus determined, he resolutely relaxed, from the toe-joints up. He let his big jaw go slack, his big hands curl open. He continued to breathe deeply and regularly, like a sleeper. Hardest of all was the task of conquering the swift race of heart and pulse, but John Thunstone had learned how to do that, too, because of necessity many times before. So completely did he contrive to pretend slumber that his mind went dreamy and vague around the edges. He seemed to float a little free of the pallet, to feel awareness at not too great a distance of the gates of dreamland.

But his ears were tuned to search out sounds. And outside in the dark the unknown creature continued its stealthy round.

It paused—just in front of the door, as John Thunstone judged. It knew that the root of John the Conqueror lay there, an obstacle; but not an obstacle that completely baffled. Such a herb, to turn back what Thunstone felt sure was besieging the dark cabin, would need to be wolfbane or garlic: or, for what grew naturally in these parts of the world, French lilac. John the Conqueror—Big John or Little John, as woodland gatherers defined the two varieties—was only "used to win," and might not assure victory. All it could do, certainly, was slow up the advance of the besieger.

Under his breath, very soft and very low, John Thunstone began to mutter a saying taught him by a white magician in a far-away city, half a prayer and half a spell against evil enemies:

"Two wicked eyes have overshadowed us, but two holy eyes are fixed upon us; the eyes of Saint Dunstan, who smote and shamed

the devil. Beware, wicked one; beware twice, wicked one; beware
thrice . . ."

In the next room, Thunstone could hear sounds. They were
sounds of dull, careful pecking. They came from the direction in
which, as he had seen, was set the closed casement window of Pos
Parrell's sleeping chamber.

With the utter silence he knew how to keep, Thunstone rolled
from his pallet, lying for a moment face down on the floor. He drew
up one knee and both hands, and rose to his full height. In one hand
he brought along the sword cane.

The pecking sound persisted as he slid one foot along the
rough planks of the floor, praying that no creak would sound. He
managed a step, another, a third. He was at the door leading to the
next room.

His free hand groped for a knob. There was none, only a latch
string. Thunstone pulled, and the door sagged silently open.

He looked into a room, the dimness of which was washed by
light from the moon outside. In the window, silhouetted against the
four panes, showed the outline of head and shoulders. A tinkling
whisper, and one of the panes fell inward, to shatter musically on
the boards below. Something had picked away the putty. A dark
arm crept in, weaving like a snake, to fumble at the catch. A
moment later the window was open, and something thrust itself in,
made the passage and landed on the floor.

The moonlight gave him a better look at the shape as it rose
from all fours and faced toward the cot where Pos Parrell lay, silent
and slack as though he were drugged.

John Thunstone knew that face from the picture in the room
where he had slept. It had the slanted, lustrous eyes, the cloud of
hair—not clubbed, but hanging in a great thunder cloud on either
side of the face. And the wide, full mouth did not smile, but quiv-
ered as by some overwhelming pulse.

"Pos," whispered the mouth of Lill Warran.

She wore a white robelike garment, such as is put on dead
women in that country. Its wide, winglike sleeves swaddled her
arms, but it fell free of the smooth, pale shoulders, the fine upper
slope of the bosom. Now as in life, Lill Warran was a forbiddingly
beautiful creature. She seemed to sway, to float toward Parrell.

"You love me," she breathed at him.

The sleeper stirred for the first time. He turned toward her, a hand moved sleepily, almost as though it beckoned her. Lill Warran winnowed to the very bedside.

"Stop where you are!" called John Thunstone, and strode into the room, and toward the bed.

She paused, a hand on the blanket that covered Parrell. Her face turned toward Thunstone, the moonlight playing upon it. Her mocking smile possessed her lips.

"You were wise enough to guess most of me," she said. "Are you going to be fool enough to try to stop what is bound to happen?"

"You won't touch him," said Thunstone.

She chuckled. "Don't be afraid to shout. You cannot waken Pos Parrell tonight—not while I stand here. He loves me. He always loved me. The others loved and then hated. But he loves me—though he thinks I am dead—"

She sounded archaic, she sounded measured and stilted, as though she quoted ill-rehearsed lines from some old play. That was in order, Thunstone knew.

"He loves you, that's certain," agreed Thunstone. "That means you recognize his helplessness. You think that his love makes him your easy prey. You didn't reckon with me."

"Who are you?"

"My name is John Thunstone."

Lill Warran glared, her lips writhed back. She, seemed as though she would spit.

"I've heard that name. John Thunstone! Shall I not dispose of you, right now and at once, you fool?"

SHE TOOK A STEP away from the bed. Her hands lifted, the winglike sleeves slipped back from them. She crooked her fingers, talon fashion, and Thunstone saw the length and sharpness of her nails.

Lill Warran laughed.

"Fools have their own reward. Destruction!"

Thunstone stood with feet apart. The cane lay across his body, its handle in his right fist, the fingers of his left hand clasping around the lower shank that made a sheath.

"You have a stick," said Lill Warran. "Do you think you can beat me away, like a dog?"

"I do."

"You cannot even move, John Thunstone!" Her hands weaved in the air, like the hands of a hypnotist. "You're a toy for me! I remember hearing a poem once: 'A fool there was—' " She paused, laughing.

"Remember the title of that poem?" he said, almost sweetly, and she screamed, like the largest and loudest of bats, and leaped.

In that instant, Thunstone cleared the long silver rapier from its hiding, and, as swiftly as she, extended his arm like a fencer in riposte.

Upon the needle-pointed blade, Lill Warran skewered herself. He felt the point slip easily, smoothly, into the flesh of her bosom. It grated on a bone somewhere, then slid past and through. Lill Warran's body slammed to the very hilt, and for a moment she was no more than arm's length from him. Her eyes grew round, her mouth opened wide, but only a whisper of breath came from it.

Then she fell backward, slack as an empty garment, and as Thunstone cleared his blade she thudded on the floor and lay with her arms flung out to right and left, as though crucified.

From his hip pocket Thunstone fished a handkerchief and wiped way the blood that ran from point to base of the silver weapon forged centuries before by Saint Dunstan, patron of those who face and fight creatures of evil.

To his lips came the prayer engraved upon the blade, and he repeated it aloud: "*Sic pereant omnes inimici tui, Domine* . . . So perish all thine enemies, O God."

"Huh?" sleepily said Pos Parrell, and sat up on his cot. He strained his eyes in the dimness. "What you say, Mister? What's happened?"

Thunstone moved toward the bureau, sheathing his silver blade. He struck a match, lifted the chimney from the lamp on the bureau and lighted it. The room filled with the warm glow from the wick.

Parrell sprang out of bed. "Hey, look. The window's open—it's broke in one pane. Who done that?"

"Somebody from outside," said Thunstone, standing still to watch.

Parrell turned and stared at what was on the floor. "It's Lill!" he bawled in a quivering voice. "Sink their rotten souls to hell, they come dug her up again and throwed her in here!"

"I don't think so," said Thunstone, and lifted the lamp. "Take a good look."

Moving, he shed light down upon the quiet form of Lill Warran. Parrell knelt beside her, his trembling hands touching the dark stain on her bosom.

"Blood!" he gulped. "That's fresh blood. Her wound was bleeding, right now. She wasn't dead down there in the grave!"

"No," agreed Thunstone quietly. "She wasn't dead down there in the grave. But she's dead now."

Parrell examined her carefully, miserably. "Yes, sir. She's dead now. She won't rise up no more."

"No more," agreed Thunstone again. "And she got out of her grave by her own strength. Nobody dug her up, dead or alive."

Parrell stared from where he knelt. Wonder and puzzlement touched his grief-lined, sharp-snouted face.

"Come out and see," invited Thunstone, and lifted the lamp from where it stood on the bureau. He walked through the front room and out of the door. Parrell tramped at his heels.

The night was quiet, with so little breeze that the flame of the lamp barely flickered. Straight to the graveside Thunstone led Parrell, stopped there and held the lamp high over the freshly opened hole.

"Look, Parrell," Thunstone bade him. "That grave was opened from inside, not outside."

Parrell stooped and stared. One hand crept up and wiped the low, slanting brow.

"You're right, I guess," said Parrell slowly. "It looks like what a fox does when he breaks through at the end of his digging—the dirt's flung outward from below, only bigger'n a fox's hole." Parrell straightened up. His face was like sick tallow in the light of the lamp. "Then its true, though it looks right pure down impossible. She was in there, alive, and she got out tonight."

"She got out the other two nights," said Thunstone. "I don't think I can explain to you exactly why, but night time was the time of her strength. And each time she came here to you—walked or crept all the way. Each time, again, she could move no more when it was dawn."

"Lill came to me!"

"You loved her, didn't you? That's why she came to you."

PARRELL TURNED TOWARD THE house. "And she must have loved me," he whispered, "to come to me out of the grave. Tonight, she didn't have so far to go. If she'd stayed alive—"

Thunstone started back to the house. "Don't think about that, Parrell. She's certainly dead now, and what she would have done if she'd stayed alive isn't for us to think about."

Parrell made no reply until they had once more entered the front door and walked through to where Lill Warran lay as they had left her. In the light of the lamp Thunstone carried her face was clearly defined.

It was a calm face, a face at peace and a little sorrowful. Yes, a sweet face. Lill Warran may not have looked like that in life, or in life-in-death, but now she was completely dead, she was of a gentle, sleeping beauty. Thunstone could see how Parrell, or any other man, might love a face like that.

"And she came to me, she loved me," breathed Parrell again.

"Yes, she loved you," nodded Thunstone. "In her own way she did love you. Let's take her back to her grave."

Between them they carried her out and to the hole. At its bottom was the simple coffin of pine planks, its lid thrown outward and upward from its burst fastenings. Thunstone and Parrell put the body into the coffin, straightened its slack limbs and lowered the lid. Parrell brought a spade and a shovel, and they filled and smoothed the grave.

"I'm going to say my little verse again," said Parrell. Standing with head bowed, he mumbled the lines:

"The raven crow is a coal, coal black.
The jay is a purple blue,
If ever I forget my own fair love,
Let my heart melt away like dew."

He looked up at Thunstone, tears streaming down his face. "Now she'll rest in peace."

"That's right. She'll rest in peace. She won't rise again."

"Listen, you mind going back to the house? I'll just watch here till morning. You don't think that'll hurt, do you?"

Thunstone smiled.

"No, it won't hurt. It will be perfectly all right. Because nothing whatever will disturb you."

"Or her," added Parrell.

"Or her," nodded Thunstone. "She won't be disturbed. Just keep remembering her as somebody who loved you, and whose rest will never be interrupted again."

Back in the house, Thunstone brought the lamp to the table

where he had interrupted his letter to de Grandin. He took his pen and began writing again:

> I was interrupted by events that brought this adventure to a good end. And maybe I'll wait until I see you before I tell you that part of it.
> But to finish my earlier remarks:
> If Lill Warran was a werewolf, and killed in her werewolf shape, it follows as a commonplace that she became a vampire after death. You can read as much in Montague Summers, as well as the work of your countryman, Cyprien Robert.
> And as a vampire, she would and did return, in a vampire's travesty of affection, to the one living person whose heart still turned to her.
> Because I half suspected all this from the moment I got wind of the story of Lill Warran, I brought with me the silver blade forged for just such battles by Saint Dunstan, and it was my weapon of victory.

He finished and folded the letter. Outside, the moon brightened the quiet night, in which it seemed no evil thing could possibly stir.

Midnight Sun

Brian Hodge

When Shepherd went off the air in Vancouver, it didn't neces-sarily seem a harbinger of worse things on the wind. Puz-zling, cause for concern, yes. But isolation at the roof of the world wove a quilt of insulation from what the rest of the world endured. Real life was something lived far beyond the Arctic Circle; they got it filtered through shortwave radio and made sense of it as best they could.

"Equipment malfunction?" Crandall put forth. "Not like Shep-herd could get replacement parts right away." Crandall sat before his shelves of shortwave gear, fingers intimate with every switch, dial, knob. Static squalled over the radio room's speakers, white noise, an audio blizzard of soulfreezing capabilities.

"Maybe," said Trask. He looked to Katy, Crandall's wife, if common-law vows exchanged under the northern lights consti-tuted a binding commitment in the eyes of God. Katy stood behind her husband, massaging his hunched shoulders. Tension was rampant. At her own workstation behind the radio setup, her VDT glowed green, the cursor pulsing and patient after the day's log-in date.

"Shepherd's last broadcast, did he give any buzzwords that he thought they might be onto him?" Trask asked her.

Katy shook her head. Her hair was blond, short, a self-cut bob. Disconcertingly perky. "No." She worked her tongue in one cheek,

contemplative. "A power outage, maybe? Like in Boston last winter?
It was three days before they got on the air again."

Trask nodded, remembering. *Radio Free Earth,* he thought. *Ain't it just the pits.*

"Want me to keep trying?" Crandall said.

"Ten more minutes. After that, try it on the hour. Don't want to
drain off the batteries for nothing."

Katy took her seat again, rolled it beside Crandall as he continued to conjure shortwave wizardry. "When do we write him off?"

Trask frowned. This was always the most unpleasant of tasks,
the absolute worst: passing judgment on something thousands of
miles away when he had no earthly idea what had transpired.

"Give it a week. If he's not on the air in a week, I doubt he will
be again." Coldhearted, it surely was.

Blame it on the climate.

TRASK UNDERSTOOD MILITARY FETISHISM, as it had come to a
hydra-headed, overbudgeted peak in the generations-past days before
the vampires proved a more formidable foe than communism had
ever dreamt of being. The military and the shadowed realms of justice—the troops and the spooks—had all fostered a love for initials.
Personnel were interchangeable, only the departmental initials dif-
fered. The triletter alphabet soup of the FBI, CIA, CID, DEA. More
complex beasts such as NATO and DARPA and SACNORAD.

Here in the frozen wastes they had no official name—nothing
run by mortals had been official for decades—but just the same,
Trask liked to think of their station as NARHO. Some silly acronym,
a nod to the past, hopelessly late twentieth-century militaristic.
Therein lay the comfort. Time was, the U.S. Army kicked ass.

NARHO. A distillation of North American Resistance Historical Outpost. The resistance movement's response to the
Gestapo-cum-KKK tactics of the suckheads. *Suckheads . . .* Every
armed conflict bred a fresh crop of perjoratives for the enemy.

The vampires' tactics, however, made sense when you
regarded them with a strategically analytical eye. Mankind's entire
history showed innumerable instances where an invader trying to
quell resistance would have had an easier time trying to hack Ama-
zonian underbrush to bare earth. Rebels grew annoyingly
entrenched, from Persians fighting Turkish invaders, to American
colonists revolting against British rule, to Afghan nomads standing

firm against the Soviets. And for every rebel who was ragtag and ill equipped, it seemed his passions boiled all the more ferocious. Such was the lot the suckheads were discovering in hot spots the world over.

How much easier, so they reasoned, might it be to crush a foe who was illiterate, and with no personal sense of historical perspective? For under their rule, a mortal who could not read and possessed no identity as part of that grand tradition known as humanity . . . he might as well be bred for slavery, or for slaughter.

The suckheads had not accomplished it during the previous generation, nor this one, nor might they even in the next. But if there was anything they had on their side, it was time.

Thus had been born NARHO. A skeleton staff of eight, a co-op effort with the sole purpose of establishing periodic radio contact with a number of resistance "reporters" as far away as reception could be maintained, who passed along the news of humanity fighting the good fight, and their oppressors. Compiled in one central, remote location, by computer and duplicated in typewriter hard copy. In hopes that one sunny day, mortal children could sit in a classroom with an underpaid teacher and whine about assigned chapters from their history text. Treading the bookbound footprints of those who had gone before. NARHO. If there was any assignment in the entire resistance requiring more faith, Trask didn't know what it could be. Because what they envisioned as the fruition of their ideals would, in all likelihood, occur beyond their lifetimes.

But, as D. Elton Trueblood had said, one has learned the meaning of humanity when he plants shade trees under which he knows full well he will never sit.

The Arctic Circle made an unlikely ground for the planting of such acorns, but the location had not been chosen idly. Canada's Ellesmere Island was 82,000 square miles of frozen desolation. Treeless, covered with mountains and glacial ice caps, foliated only by shrubs and ferns and mosses, and cursed with temperatures that even in summer rarely nudged above freezing. Robert Peary had used the white bluffs along its northern shore as base camp in 1909, when he made his successful run for the North Pole, a scant 413 miles away.

Altogether remote and unforgiving. That alone secured them against the vampires, prevented accidental discovery. Another factor was the polar day: over four months of nothing but sunlight each year, an automatic bane to vampire death squads. Only when the polar night fell each winter did the staff of NARHO vacate for four months to a secondary station south, near Hudson Bay. The rest of the year, home was a forgotten weather station near Ellesmere's northern end, halfway up one of the less craggy hillsides. Fortified, gun ports where once were windows, outer walls blended into surrounding environs by being packed with layers of ice and snow. Their helicopter was stashed beneath a white tarp in the northside valley. The only thing to give them away was the spire of radio antennas, and ranks of solar panels soaking up sunlight to keep them going. Against all odds.

* * *

TRASK COULDN'T SLEEP THAT night, a common malady, a side effect of the mantle of command. He allowed himself a half hour of turning with the frequency of a rotisserie, then decided his lungs craved fresh air. Sometimes the installation grew as stale as a locker room. He rose, suited up for outside. Early summer, and the polar day was still young. Long johns and a light parka nurtured ample warmth.

Weatherwise, Ellesmere was rarely more severe than winters he had endured much farther south. Humidity was routinely low, which helped considerably, and little actual precipitation fell. Several of the others among the current staff concurred. Crandall had come from Minnesota. Their chopper pilot, Markham, whose main job was shuttling them to Hudson Bay and back and flying the occasional Air Cav cowboy supply run, had come from Maine. To them, this was no big deal.

Trask found a clear boulder along the path up the summit, and here he sat. A mountain monarch surveying a kingdom whose serfs and vassals were the occasional caribou and musk oxen, bears and wolverines. Glacial ice stretched before him like a crystal milk sea; above, the sun was a dull red ball rolling west-to-east across the northern horizon. Witching hour sunlight. The world looked eerily blue and white. His hands thick-fingered with gloves, he opened an ancient, well-tended paperback, and began to read.

Ellie found him a half hour later. He first heard panting breath and scrabbling feet, and knew she had brought one of the sled dogs to sniff him out. Moments later, a husky was upon him, tail swaying like a furry metronome.

"Hi, Daddy," Ellie said.

"Baby." Trask patted the rock beside him. She settled, let the husky nuzzle nearby crevices in vain search for hidden tidbits. Their breath fogged, and he looked skyward. "What cheer. Another sunny day."

She laughed, the laugh of overstatement and the same thing seen too many days in a row. "I miss rain, Daddy. I think I miss that most of all. Rain." She clomped dangling boots together; powdered snow sifted. "I got bored on sentry." She cocked her head to look at the book in his hands. "What are you reading?"

He held it up. "Dick Gregory." It brought a smile from them both. Ellie had been born in a time when bedtime fairy tales and fables of happy comforts seemed like cruel lies. Even when her mother still lived, family life in the resistance was all she had ever known, for twenty-five years. He had instead read to her tales of her own heritage, of such forebears as Martin Luther King and George Washington Carver, Sojourner Truth and Harriet Tubman, Nelson Mandela and Steven Biko. Prophets of another age, long dead. So she would know, above all, where she had come from.

Smiling, Ellie looked very much like the brown child who had peered up at him from beneath mounds of tucked-in covers. A child who now toted an assault rifle with a silver crucifix epoxied to the stock when traveling outside, better safe than bled for food.

"Tell me my favorite story from that one." She glanced at the book as one might an old friend. "It's been years."

"Once upon a time," he said, smiling gently, "Dick Gregory was in a restaurant in the American south. He ordered a fried chicken, and when it came, he picked up his knife and fork, and some rednecks came over to his table. They just couldn't stand to see a black man without wanting to give him some hell. So they told him, 'Boy, whatever you do to that chicken, we're gonna do to *you*.'" Trask paused, well-worn dramatic effect. "Dick Gregory didn't say a word. Just picked up that chicken . . . and kissed it."

As they shared the lonely vigil of sentry together, Trask reflected back on those darker days, known to him only as words on a printed page. In his experience, there was no such thing as racism, not anymore. He was intimate with what it felt like to be despised and hunted as a virtue of species, but the color of his skin was another matter altogether. It had taken the threat of worldwide extinction to bury racial distinctions. A warm-blooded black man didn't look so bad next to a hungry suckhead, after all. Wasn't it just the human way? Not that he'd have it any other.

DAYS LATER. SIXTY MILES to the south, a landscape trapped in timeless winter raced beneath a low-altitude tandem pair of Chinook CH-47 transport helicopters. Military antiques, but well maintained. The ruling powers saw no need to build anew. The world was already a vast stockpile with far more resources than could ever be depleted. Each mammoth copter was born aloft by twin six-blade rotors, and the downwash was a furious cyclone. The passing gales scoured up clouds of crystalline snow, swept earth and rock and ice clean.

In the lead copter, leaning quiet and still against a steel bulkhead, Field Marshall Ammon gazed out a portal at the flash-cut land. So did most of the other troops, every last one wearing polarized sunglasses to reduce painful glare on sensitive eyes.

Vampires in daylight. None of them had quite gotten used to the idea.

Below, movement, white on white. Ammon homed in with those sensitive eyes, tracking. An Arctic fox went streaking over a hillock in terrified retreat from airborne assault, these strange birds of wind and steel. Ammon watched it, impassive, his face gaunt and his nose as regal as the prow of a royal flagship.

"You have to give the mortals their due," Ammon said to the officer beside him. "The kind of dedication it takes for them to survive in this environment, with their limited resources . . . "

"With all due respect, sir, I think this entire mission M.O. is one giant pain in the ass." Lieutenant Omega strained to be heard over the turbines driving the rotors. "We should have brought along a pair of Apache gunships. Pinpoint their location, and level it with a few Hellfires. No problems."

Ammon nodded wearily. "Your objections were duly noted before we left Montreal. I'll thank you *not* to repeat them again."

"Yes *sir*." Omega was too cloyingly enthusiastic to be plying anything but sarcasm. He smiled broadly; ghastly. His teeth and fangs were a dingy gray. Decades ago, while wiping out a resistance faction in the New Mexico desert, Omega had gotten separated from his unit. Too distant from shelter to travel on foot during nightfall before dawn's ravages, he'd been forced to live for nearly two months in an abandoned mine. All he had had for sustenance was the blood of rats. The bout with malnutrition still showed in his teeth.

Resourcefulness aside, Ammon thought him a disgrace to the uniform, an ill-mannered lout. And *Omega*, what an asinine name. As had many of the vampires, particularly in the military, he had renamed himself to christen his new life. Omega had chosen the name because he fancied himself the last being a mortal ever wanted to see.

As soon as Field Marshall Ammon had volunteered to the General of the Northeast Command to oversee this mission, and was subsequently informed as to the identity of his second-in-command, he had known a clash over directives was inevitable.

Directive One: Destroy all communication capabilities of the resistance faction on Ellesmere Island.

Directive Two: Confiscate all resistance documents on premises.

Directive Three: When at all possible, execute live capture of partisans and transport them back for public justice.

And lastly, the very wrinkle in technology which allowed them to show their faces to the sun in the first place . . .

Directive Four: Ascertain field effectiveness of Project Daybreak flesh treatment Lot #66J-B9.

Directive Four would take care of itself. Regarding the others, Ammon knew that Omega would prefer to act with all the subtlety of a sledgehammer. The lieutenant's sense of aesthetics had died along with his humanity. Assuming it had lived to begin with.

Ellesmere had been betrayed by one of its confidants. The use of mortals in the Secret Police had been yielding mixed results, but Vancouver was the current feather in the program's cap. A mortal agent, some lovely human female, had infiltrated the confidence of a partisan with a hidden ham radio. The partisan—code named Shepherd, real name now immaterial—was taken into custody, to disappear forevermore. With the Secret Police, little was left.

They had devised a technique to sustain brutal interrogation indefinitely, until every last droplet of information was wrung out. In their labs, the microbe in the salivary glands which, when transmitted by a bite, activated the change to vampirism had been isolated, then genetically engineered with recombinant DNA. It could be injected in varying potencies to uncooperative mortals. The scientifically altered changeover was excruciating, inflicting the victim with all the weaknesses of the vampire and none of the strengths. Of particular effectiveness in interrogation was to strap the screaming changeling beneath an ultraviolet sunlamp.

Shepherd had sold out his own local group *and* the one on Ellesmere before the inquisitors had dissolved him into gibbering stew meat.

"Twenty minutes to landing zone, sir." The copilot's voice was a tiny buzz in the left earpiece of Ammon's headset.

Ammon acknowledged, his eyes roving across the cabin. One of the troops, seated on his tiny apportioned sector of bench, had opened a small bottle of gray plastic. He tipped it back, swigged, cleansed a trickle of crimson from the pale corner of his mouth. He grimaced, leaned in toward the storm trooper beside him.

"Be glad when we get back to fresh food!" Ammon heard him shout over the turbines. "I hate these C rations!"

Soldiers were, after all, soldiers. Dead or not.

THE DOGS WERE THE first to know. A woefully inadequate alarm system in an underequipped installation, given wartime conditions. Resources for anything more sophisticated had simply not been there.

Halfway through what the clock called night, Trask was awakened by a ferocious baying of agitated sled dogs. He swung up to sit on his bed, already wearing long johns and woolen socks. He fumbled on a crate-size footlocker serving as a table and brought back a walkie-talkie, then whipped up the aerial and smacked the taste of sleep from his mouth.

"LaPeres. What is it?" The night's sentry did not answer. "*LaPeres?*"

Only the static of an empty frequency pulsed. Trask scowled. Not good, not good at all. The man was up on a rock outcropping just above the outpost, had a view of miles worth of panoramic vistas. And the dogs wouldn't make this sort of racket for no good reason. Huskies and malamutes were normally very quiet breeds.

Still stiff legged, Trask hobbled to the sole bedroom window, flipped aside the heavy tarp used half for insulation and half to thwart sunlight. Window space had been reduced, for security reasons, to a rectangle eighteen inches by twelve. Like a nineteenth-century photographer draping a camera shroud over head and shoulders, Trask put his face to the window and squinted at the glare.

His heart stuttered, then jockeyed up to the root of his tongue.

The French Canadian sentry—whose mission specialty was as their cook—hung impaled on a metal pole on the downward slope before the station. How they had crept up on him Trask couldn't say; but admittedly, a few years of duty up here, without incident, had abraded once-sharp instinctual awareness to dull nubs. Whatever. Someone had gotten close enough to excise him from active duty, silently, with what appeared to be a precision arrow. Crossbow, maybe.

But daylight, we got daylight up here . . .

Trask focused on LaPeres'sthroat. Torn and ravaged, while the arrow had struck him through the upper rib cage. The most telling sign of all was that the snow beneath his body was completely unbedewed by blood. He had been drained.

But it's daylight!

Nothing else to see out here. Yet. Trask went sprinting toward his bedroom door, flung it open, and charged into the narrow corridor. The walls were a claustrophobic institutional gray, faded by decades. He heard one or two others already stirring, no doubt raised by the dogs. Even so, he jammed a fist against an alarm pad anchored into the wall. Glass crunched, circuits connected. The alarm horns scattered throughout the station blurted an electronic choke, then revved in with resounding whoops. A cyclical, air-raid Armageddon that sculpted gooseflesh and chilled spinal fluid.

In moments, the remaining six staffers came pouring from their rooms, struggling against various stages of sleep. Their eyes, however, were burdened with a common denominator of dawning fear.

"What is it, what's going on?" This from Katy Crandall. Behind her, her husband was high-stepping into a pair of pants.

"They've found us." The three words he had dreaded most.

Clamor. Uproar. Trask noticed that Ellie was already toting her assault rifle into the hallway. He always wondered if she slept with the thing. For a fleeting, sinking moment he hated himself, the world, cosmic pranksters or whoever had seen fit to hurl it all into this state of existence. An assault rifle. What kind of thing was that for his daughter to be sharing her nights with? He had read of better days long past, and fathers who had dreaded the arrival of suitors with questionable motives regarding the daughters. Of how no man could trust another, younger one when his daughter's potential defloration was cinched behind the kid's zipper. Trask would have traded everything he still owned—

humanity and dignity and ethics were all that remained—to experience one anxious night of normal worry at her expense, a date
that would last into the netherhours and send him climbing walls,
snacking on fingernails. Then it was all gone, brutally shoved into moot status by real
responsibilities. Trask led them into the Common Room. More win-
dows, greater space to maneuver. They used the place for Ping-Pong,
for lounging. A gym mat softened calisthenics. A bookcase hulked
floor-to-ceiling in one corner, and beside it, a gun cabinet.

The entire station was suddenly rocked by a near-simultane-
ous pair of explosions rumbling from above, from the side. Floors
trembled, ceilings wavered, minute cracks disgorged dust. After
another moment there came a metallic grinding as the radio
tower crashed down over their heads. Crandall looked like a child
who had just watched the tide slush his sand castle into shapeless
hummocks.

"There were two blasts." This from Olafson, the blond Nordic
fellow serving as the unit medic. "What else did they get?"

"The panels! They blew the solar panels!" Sarah Reichert was
the electronics engineer who had wired the system together, and
she looked no less devastated than Crandall.

Trask seized her by the shoulders. "How much charge we got
stored up in the batteries?"

Sarah's dark eyes fluttered, rapid mental calculations. "If we stay
buttoned up tight . . . maybe two days. *If* we're lucky."

"It's a little too late to talk about luck *now*. " Ellie glanced back
over her shoulder from one of the windows, then resumed her
watch. So far she had taken LaPeres in stride. Then again, with the
things she had already seen . . . "Uh oh," she then said, and her
voice shrank, tiny, humbled.

Bedlam, Arctic style, madness on ice. The alarm horns, the con-
tinual frenzy of the sled dogs, a babble of voices. And something
new. Growing. The whirling beat of ominous wings.

"Choppers," said Markham, their pilot. "*Big* mothers."

The rest crowded to the windows overlooking the southern
slope and valley. A pair of olive drab transport copters—immense
machines, the dray horses of vertical lift-off—had churned in from
the south. They hovered for a moment, fine-tuning their positions
like circling dogs seeking the perfect spot in which to lie, then settled in swirling clouds of icy snow, some three hundred yards distant.

Rear cargo doors dropped down into ramps, and white-suited troops spilled out in formation. Maybe sixty in all. Armed. Dangerous. And wearing, of all things, sunglasses.

Trask heard himself groan. It was the sound of dreams dying. The sound a man makes who has seen the black smudges on the X-rays where his lungs were to have shown.

"What are they?" Katy asked. "Are they vampires? They can't be."

"Look at LaPeres, though," said Olafson. "He's dry as a bone."

"It can't be, *they* can't be!"' Katy wailed. "We've got sunlight!"

"I'll find out." Ellie's calm was like a windless ocean. She relinquished her assault rifle at the gun cabinet for a pair of bolt-action Remingtons with sniperscopes. Long-range, precision work. She opened the window, and warmth seeped out, cold wormed in. While the white-clad troops took up positions at the base of the hill, Ellie bolted a round into the chamber of one, then eased its muzzle out the window. Took aim, eye to scope. And fired.

Trask was watching through binoculars snatched from another cabinet. He saw one of the soldiers flop backward to land on his rump. A moment later, the soldier picked himself up and dusted himself off. Sound carried well in this relatively silent world, and Trask soon heard the arrogance of hooting and laughter.

"Bait the trap . . . " Ellie muttered, and fired again.

Target popped a second time. He staggered, neither fell nor bled.

" . . . and wax me a suckhead," Ellie concluded while switching rifles.

The targeted soldier had become the subject of general amuse-. ment rather than concern. This was folly. Lead bullets were jokes to them, and the soldier as much as called this out. Trask could read his lips through the binoculars, his gestures, then faintly heard his taunts after a three-second distance delay.

With her second rifle, Ellie fired. Once was all it took. The soldier poleaxed backward as his chest was skewered a third time, and high-intensity anguish was morbidly evident. A pair of very surprised comrades dragged him away while Ellie sent a few more rounds winging down. Dropped two more into convulsive spasms.

"What's with those bullets?" Crandall asked.

"Hollow points." Ellie drew the rifle inside and shut the window, now that the vampires were scurrying for better cover. "I drilled into them in the workshop and injected the hollows with garlic oil, then waxed them back over. They mushroom on impact."

It was momentary jubilation at best, swatting one or two mosquitos out of a hungry swarm. Because a minute later, they heard a third explosion, farther distant, and realized that their own Huey helicopter had just been fragmented in the north valley.

Trask figured that Ellie's marksmanship might have slowed an uphill assault by a few minutes while the suckheads regrouped, assessed the danger of doctored bullets. Time enough, at least, for him to shut down the maddening alarm and order everyone to their rooms long enough to suit up. Mere long johns and sleep clothes were not going to hack it. After they were dressed, weapons were dispensed, ammunition divvied. A puny cache to what they saw below.

"How the hell are they managing to walk around in daylight without wilting?" Crandall asked while fumbling with a Steyr AUG.

Sarah was peering over the lip of the window. "They're pretty heavily suited up. Look at those winter fatigues."

"I think that's just so they'll blend into the snow," Trask said. "Look at their heads. Okay, helmets, but their faces are bare." He looked across the room to Katy. "What's the last word we got on those vampire/human hybrids they were experimenting with? They ever come up with anything this dependable?"

"Not that we ever heard about. The hybrids were too screwed up, most of them were suicidal. Biological schizophrenia." Katy hunched her shoulders. "But projects like that are highly classified. Intelligence might have crapped out on us there."

Markham lugged over one of the larger machine guns, an M-60, and readied it beside the window. "Got a belt of tracers loaded in this, let's see if I can set one or two of those birds on fire."

"Go for one," Trask told him. "If some miracle pulls us through this alive, we'll need some way off this island, quick."

"Will do."

Markham and Ellie brought the window back down. More warm air was swapped for cold, and their pilot maneuvered half the M-60 out.

Voices from below weren't the only noise delayed by distance. Gunshots were likewise. Trask heard a faint zipping noise, barely a whisper, and the next thing he knew, most of Markham's skull had trajected up onto the ceiling with a ripe melon burst. The splotch dripped while the body remained upright. A moment of surrealism, and then the heavy rifle shot rolled uphill to their ears. At last, Markham's body unhinged onto the floor. Olafson scrambled over, but the cause was lost at a glance. The back of Markham's head yawned into a crater.

"Retaliation is only fair, don't you think? One of yours for three of mine?" It was the voice of doom, given the amplification. A cultured, sonorous voice used to giving orders and having them followed. Trask peered out, trying to locate its source. Unlikely, though, that a commanding officer would be standing in the open.

"This is Field Marshall Ammon, of the Northeast Command. I'll credit you with enough intelligence to realize that your installation is now shut down. Permanently."

"Ammon, Field Marshall." Trask snapped his fingers at Katy. "Ring a bell?"

She nodded, blond bangs brushing her eyes. "I think so."

"Get on the computer, see what you can dig up on him. I want to know who this is we're dealing with. Stay on there and read it to me over this." Trask tossed her his walkie-talkie while running to a cabinet for another. "Go, go."

Katy scrambled into one of the intersecting hallways. Boot steps clattered, faded.

Outside, Ammon continued. "There's little certainty for mortals these days, but *you* can be certain of one thing: Your group *will* be leaving Ellesmere Island with us. And soon. Whether as casualties or as prisoners, that is your decision. I leave that to you."

Ammon's voice thundered over glacial plains, rebounded from icy hillsides, severe as a winter storm. It brought howling fears which had long been held, usually without effort, at arm's length and beyond. Existence in the Arctic had toughened them up in many respects, but in others, the inherent safety factors had let them grow soft. They had all but forgotten what it was like to live in constant fear of boots stomping down atop their backs, of fangs at their throats. Actual confrontation was as demoralizing as a plague.

"I found him." Katy's voice crackled triumphant over the new walkie-talkie. "He's on a disc that Markham brought back from a supply pickup a couple years ago."

"Let's hear it."

Katy made a humming noise, as if scanning the screen first. "Field Marshall Ammon . . . age indeterminate, suspected officer in the United States Army, maybe Marines, which would make him over a hundred years old. Let's see, service history, up through twenty-eight years ago he was assigned to the Southeast Command, covering most of the eastern half of the U.S. Commendations out the ying-yang. Was officer in charge of the military response to the Baltimore uprising. Flushed out partisan strongholds in Appalachia, the Smoky Mountains, and in a complex of Kentucky coal mines. Served as field adviser to the Vampiric Chiefs of Staff in Washington. Minimal loss of partisan life in most of the conflicts where he was the officer in command. Meaning—"

"Meaning we got a suckhead who likes to take us alive so they can use us later," Trask finished. "Screw that."

"Maybe so . . . But at any rate, you get the idea reading this that there are those who'd rather be taken prisoner by him than most any of the others. Says here by all reports, POWs aren't slaughtered by the troops. He won't allow that."

"So he's a soft touch." Ellie frowned from across the room. "Tell that to LaPeres."

"To continue," Katy said. "Transferred to the Northeast Command twenty-eight years ago, stationed in Montreal ever since. Military adviser to Project Daybreak, it says . . . whatever that is. No reliable intelligence confirmation as to what that is."

Trask shut his eyes. "Ten to one that has something to do with why these suckheads are walking around in sunlight." He sighed. "Anything else?"

"Just service stats, same old stuff. You've heard enough. Except . . . Let me scroll back a minute to the beginning, this was interesting." Trask heard the staccato pecking of a single key. "Yeah. Here. His name, Ammon. A-M-M-O-N. Whatever his human name was is unknown, but somebody tapped into the origin of this one. Ammon was a god revered by the ancient Egyptians for military victories. *And* originally the patron of Thebes. Hooo, this guy picked an obscure one, didn't he?"

"Thanks, Katy," Trask whispered. "Might as well get back here."

He took quick stock of the others in the room. Controlled panic rode the crest of the moment. Someone had draped a rag over what remained of Markham's head, though the cloth had stained through. Out of sight, out of mind was not apt to work in this room.

"I must say I'm impressed. You people have done your homework."

The walkie-talkie had come alive again in his hand, with the same voice that had roared from loudspeakers below. Same voice, different tone. Softer, gentler, were that possible. Yet more than a trifle unnerving to hear it coming from within. Secondary invasion, a psychological triumph. Someone must have been scanning frequencies for Ammon, helped him lock onto crosstalk.

"The channel is secured. From this end, at least," came the field marshall's voice. "I'm the only one who can hear you now. Answer. Please. Whom do I have the honor of addressing?"

Trask looked up, sought faces. Ellie appeared wary; Crandall shrugged. Why not? What was the old standard? Right . . . Name, rank, serial number.

He thumbed the transmit key. "This is Richard Trask, operations commander of the North American Resistance Historical Outpost."

"Now we're even. We both have names." Ammon paused a moment, during which Trask could hear a raggedly drawn breath. "Commander Trask. What I'm about to ask of you is highly irregular. I . . . was wondering if it was possible for the two of us to meet. Face-to-face."

"I can hear you just fine," Trask said. "Whatever you've got to say, you can do it over the air."

"Take some time to think it over. The base of these hills is as close to a no-man's-land as we're going to find around here." A static pause, moments of contemplation. "I understand your reluctance, but it could make all the difference in the way you leave."

"Don't trust him, Dad," said Ellie.

"Don't worry, babe."

Ammon continued with the relentless persuasiveness of a politician. "If I'd wanted to wipe you out, all it would have taken were a few Stinger missiles. Or greater charges when we blew your tower and your solar panels. We've had the opportunity all along."

"No dice, Ammon. I've got no reason to leave here and put my trust in you."

"A show of good faith, would that do it?" Not easily dissuaded, this one. Trask was having a tough time figuring him. If only Ammon didn't sound so utterly *sincere.* "Very well. I could be court-martialed and staked for telling you this. About us, and sunlight? Project Daybreak, you were right. My kind has come to the conclusion that human allies are not enough to guard our sleep during daylight hours. So we've adapted something from your world, advanced your technology in sunscreen applications, of all things. Designed for our particular skin. Project Daybreak. And *we* are the field test. Only so much can be learned in a laboratory. This location is ideal. Low humidity, no precipitation to worry about washoff. So, there you have it. I've just broken four regulations."

"Sunscreen," Olafson muttered, and slumped against a wall. Hysterical laughter welled sadly up from inside him. "We're sitting here with our butts in the wringer because of Hawaiian Tropic From Hell?"

Trask found it a terrible irony, seeds of their own destruction sown decades ago, nurtured in leisure time and the need to prevent tender hide from burning on the beach. It was laughably tragic.

"Are you still with me, Trask? Keep in mind that you've got quite a sharpshooter up there. *I'll* be in the cross hairs too."

He felt a queer moment of paternal pride. *That's my girl.*

Conflicting trains of thought went careening, vying for supremacy. Ammon was indeed setting himself up for target practice if this was mere subterfuge. On the other hand, this was precisely the shifty tactics Ammon might have applied in the other standoffs he had encountered. Anyone could order an artillery barrage or mount a kamikaze charge; it took genuine finesse to outwait and psychologically maneuver an opponent into surrender. Speculating trickery, though, there seemed little to be gained by killing Trask, certainly counterproductive to enticing the rest of NARHO to cooperate.

Yet here was the kicker. Didn't Trask, as commander, have a responsibility to investigate every way out of such a situation?

Time to put it to a vote.

Not that five against could actually overrule what he had already decided anyway.

WITHIN THE CRAMPED CONFINES of his command post in the Chinook, Ammon clipped the hand mike to its bracket on the radio. Listened to the hiss of static, then switched the unit off. Relief; he had fostered an almost bittersweet longing to meet this man, this Richard Trask, face-to-face. Through the portal, Ammon watched the nearby troops. They milled about, desultory, taking care to exploit the Chinooks and hillocks and rocks as shields from sniper fire. Better wrap things up quickly. Subjecting them to prolonged inactivity seemed less than prudent. They were, of course, night fighters, and as such, they were without peer as a simple virtue of species. Depth of night vision surpassed even that of cats. And they were reptilian, in a sense, emitting no true body temperature of their own, instead assuming that of their environment, within reason. Therefore, they were invisible even to infrared night vision sensors.

Night fighters. Leave them standing too long with nothing much to do, beneath a polar sun which would not set for months, and even the most disciplined among them was bound to grow edgy. Compounded by the unease most surely felt, consciously or beneath the surface, over being guinea pigs for Project Daybreak.

The three casualties notwithstanding, it had so far gone splendidly. After initially touching down some twenty miles south, a forward team had been dispatched with radio sweepers to pinpoint the installation. That accomplished, the sentry was then excised and the targeted objects were wired to blow. The Chinooks and remaining troops were radioed to advance, and when they were ten miles distant, explosions sent the radio tower and solar unit and partisan helicopter blasting into fragments.

Anticlimactic, then, a face-to-face meeting. The storm troopers, particularly Lieutenant Omega, were not apt to like it. They were pumped and primed for heavier sport.

Philistines, one and all.

Some things transcended duty, dictates of species, territorial imperative. There existed, without doubt, absolutes in the grand scheme of things, precepts and responsibilities mandated as a simple matter of being a sentient creation, regardless of genetic encoding and whom you called comrades of a like kind. And Ammon knew that if he could prevent one more travesty in the name of furthering the master race, it was well-worth tampering with the goodwill of his underlings. He was not in charge to be loved.

As he rose, snugging the faded officer's dress uniform hat atop his head, Field Marshall Ammon tried to recall his own days lived as a mortal. Generations gone, they were glimpsed as smoke through a translucent window: insubstantial, deceiving . . . elusive. He could recall little of mortal emotions and compulsions beyond a sense of incompleteness, petty scrabblings for crumbs of success and recognition. It seemed, in retrospect, quite pointless. Yet there was surely more, there had to have been; he was merely unable to conjure it. Perhaps that was the doing of the vampirism microbe itself, biochemical propaganda leeched into the brain so that its dominion would not be challenged.

Ammon strode back down the ramp descending from the Chinook's tail. The chilly breeze wafting past his face was not unpleasant. He sent a private to fetch Omega; when the lieutenant arrived, his haggard face was wary with anticipation of screwball orders to come.

"I'm going to be meeting face-to-face with their commander in a few minutes, at the base of the hillside. There is to be no shooting. No aggression on our part whatsoever, unless in response to direct aggression from them. Is that clear?"

Omega reached up beneath his helmet to scratch at the mat of his hair. Gray eyes frowned behind polarized lenses, and a tic of indignation yanked the corner of his heavy mouth.

"You're taking a hell of a risk, sir."

"The risks are mutual, Lieutenant. I'm just trying to bring about a peaceful solution here."

Omega stamped idly at the ground with one boot tip and impatiently rapped a gloved hand against the stock of his M-16. Finally, "Sir? More and more I'm having to question just who it is your loyalties are with."

Ammon scanned up the hillside, white and gray against rich blue sky. The rectangular windows etched into the outpost's coating of ice and snow. Last bastion of rationality? Ammon's face was as hard as marble.

"No shooting, Lieutenant, pass the order. And when we return to Montreal, consider yourself on demerit report for insubordination."

He left Omega's grudging *Yes sir* hanging frozen in the air behind him. And boots crunching across crusts of ice, he moved for the frontline, beyond, for no-man's-land.

THEY MET AT THE base of the summit, each forsaking the safety of cohorts and shelter. Trask felt, in an odd way, that the advantage was his. Superiority of numbers and armaments couldn't mean much to the field marshall when all were behind him, and his own neck was on the block as the next potential casualty. Beneath Trask's parka, a walkie-talkie rode clipped to his waistband, transmit button locked on. Every word spoken here would be broadcast into NARHO, and his trust in Ellie and her aim was bedrock.

"A black man!" was the first thing out of Ammon's mouth, not what Trask expected at all. The field marshall uttered a delighted little laugh. "Your pigmentation was a natural evolution to help your ancestors cope with the equatorial sun." Another chuckle. "I hope you appreciate the irony here."

"I appreciate nothing about this whole situation." Bile gave weight to his words. "You got me down here, now what do you want?"

Ammon stood ramrod straight, the knee-length tails of his woolen coat fluttering in the breeze. He cut quite the imposing figure here at the roof of the world. "First, I'd like us to drop the vocal hostilities. I'm not here to spar."

Trask fell silent, as Ammon seemed to fold himself into brooding rumination. His eyes were shielded, yet Trask knew they gazed off into distances too vast to be fathomed. By mortals, at least.

"I . . . volunteered for this assignment," Ammon said.

"Am I supposed to be flattered?"

Ammon raised a flat hand, *halt*. "Hear me out." The hand lowered. "You've always been a reading man, haven't you?"

Trask slowly nodded. This line of questioning was nothing like he had anticipated. "Whenever I've been able to."

"That's what I thought. So was I, a long time ago. When I was . . . like you. I had a library in my home that covered walls. *Walls*, Trask. It gave me pleasure like nothing else." A tiny smile twisted up one corner of Ammon's stiff-lipped mouth. "Ever read Johann Wolfgang von Goethe? The German poet?"

Trask shook his head. "Him I missed."

"Goethe said, 'Sin writes histories; goodness is silent.' " Again, the peculiar smile. "Believe it or not, I admire what you're doing here. Genuinely. It's quite possibly the most altruistic thing I've seen in the entire war between our kinds."

Trask could only stare. A charitable assessment from his hunter and supposed executioner. Go figure.

Ammon sighed. "I never tire of the blood, because that is what I am, and I make no apologies for that. But I am *so* tired of all the killing . . . "

OMEGA WATCHED THE CHUMMY little exchange from some one hundred yards, and felt rage seething within. To rip, to tear. To exterminate. It's what warriors did. And what separated the merely competent from the true leaders but willingness to seize the initiative?

He cradled in his hands a staple of ordnance from the days of the United States Green Machine. An M-79 grenade launcher, a single-shot, break-breech weapon accurate enough to fire an explosive or smoke canister through a window at more than 150 yards. Its fat, stubby barrel whispered promises of blood and glory.

And when he placed it in the hands of the young private before him, he *knew* the soldier felt the power. Unholy and cleansing and unerringly *right*. The kid's residual doubts would be easy to erase.

"Everybody's eyes are on those two." Omega cocked his head toward the summit. "If you just fade back, flank your way around left and come up behind those rocks and shrubs, what, seventy-five yards off . . . no one'll ever know you were there. No one'll ever know it was you."

Eyes widened behind the soldier's lenses. "But, sir . . . Field Marshall Ammon . . . he's a—a legend."

"Even legends have later turned out to be collaborators with the enemy, son. Better to retire him now than let him disgrace his command." Omega sniffed, a nice touch of sentiment. "Casualties happen in war all the time. It's the way old warriors are *supposed* to die. He'll receive full honors . . .

"And you'll receive yours. I'll see to that."

Aha, ambition. The vital hook had been sunk.

Omega smiled, a fearsome sight given those gray teeth. "I can tell, you have one hell of a future under *my* command . . . "

The soldier clasped the weapon. Firm, resolute. Determined.

A reborn master of misdirection.

IF THIS WASN'T ONE for the atlas of oddities, Trask didn't know what else could be. Absolutely unprecedented. A high-ranking vampire actually confessing doubts of his own kind to a labeled enemy. Trask listened, spellbound, wondering just how enthralled the rest were uphill, crowded around the other walkie-talkie.

"When I was mortal, ninety-some years ago," said Ammon, "I considered myself something of a philosopher. And the greatest injustice of life and the achievements of man was that the world's great thinkers took decades to perfect their visions. Their science. Their art. Whatever. Decades, Trask. Except . . . by the time their minds had been honed into brilliance . . . it was nearly time for their bodies to die. And those minds had to die right along with them."

Ammon shifted his stance, regretfully shook his head. "And then *we* were given the chance for true immortality. Sixty, seventy years go by, and one of us is still warming up. Before us lies eternity. Can you imagine the possibilities for achievement inherent in all that?"

"Oh yeah, I can imagine," Trask said. "But all that potential looks like it's just gone to waste, now, doesn't it?"

Ammon's affirmative nod was heartbreakingly sincere. "A soldier true to his creed never wants to fight. He simply has the know-how and realizes he must. Glory was a Hollywood fallacy, if you recall what Hollywood was. But I honestly held the hope that wars would become a thing of the past."

"Must've been a rude awakening."

"Between your kind and mine? I expected that." Ammon's fists clenched before him. "But between ourselves? It's a betrayal of everything inside us. Internecine war has decimated vampire populations in Eastern Europe, around the Mediterranean, and in Central America."

Sparks of hope began to flicker within Trask. Maybe there was a way out of this situation yet.

"But do you know," Ammon said slowly, "the one thing that sickens me most . . . is the book burnings. I've seen them light up the night skies from Atlanta to Winnipeg. We're burning up the one true way mortals learned to give their minds a lifetime of their own."

Trask felt touched, soul deep. Here was proof that the core of humanity was not necessarily eradicated by the change in species.

Ammon proceeded. "We embrace your technologies, when they suit us . . . but we routinely reject your philosophies out of hand. And this I cannot understand. I have to wonder if it's not done out of fear." He smiled bitterly. "Mortals were once insatiable about learning all they could of their antecedents, about dinosaurs, even. For all that had come before, you wanted to know the truth. And ourselves? Physically, we've advanced as far beyond you as you are beyond Neanderthal. But we're afraid of what your minds actually thought . . . Because once, our minds *were* yours."

"And in comparison," said Trask, catching his final drift.

"And in comparison, I think most of us fear that we don't stack up. We've done no better. Maybe we've even done worse." Ammon smiled wistfully. "Adversity brings out such a nobility in your kind. And I'm ashamed to admit . . . *I don't see it in mine.*"

Trask had to ponder life beyond the Arctic. Real life, on the real frontlines. How bad it must truly be. If Ammon could overlook the shameful foibles of humanity—the racism, the religious fanaticism, the endless civil wars, and all the rest comprising man's darker past—if he could overlook all that, see that as preferable, even, then today's world below must be a horrendous place indeed.

"Albert Einstein. Steven Hawking. Dickens. Shakespeare. Bruno Bettelheim. Margaret Mead. Ray Bradbury. Buckminster Fuller. Erich Fromm." Ammon sounded off the names as if tolling a funereal bell. "All those and more, I've watched them turned to ash. Hating every moment. *And* the so-called official stance on recorded history. They say what importance does history hold for *us*, when we remember it all firsthand? But they forget: You can't reinvent the past."

Trask almost felt as if he were watching this in the third person. Detachment was the only path when you realized you were grudgingly coming to respect the one assigned to hunt you down.

"You're talking treason, you know," Trask said.

"It's not treason to want your kind to live up to its potential. World War Two, Erwin Rommel. He was a patriot *and* respected by his enemies. Was he a traitor to Germany because he was appalled at what he saw Adolph Hitler doing to it? I think not."

They fell silent, poised at that precarious brink of war and peace. With the odds tilted alarmingly toward mismatch. Were it to lead to a firefight, the outcome was a foregone conclusion. Only how long it took NARHO to crumble remained flexible.

"So where does that leave us, here and now?" said Trask.

Ammon took a moment to look behind him, back at the huge helicopters and his vampiric AlpenKorps, poised and ready to strike. "I can guarantee you only two things: If you dig in and resist, you will be killed, I can't prevent that. But if you surrender and come with me, I can guarantee you safe passage to Montreal."

"Die here or die there, what's the difference? I'd rather get into it here."

Ammon shook his head tersely. "I'm not without influence. And there are those I know of who are . . . sympathetic to your kind. I can't guarantee you anything after we get to Montreal, except hope. There's a chance to get you relocated, somewhere else, free . . . "

Trask's eyes narrowed. "Officially? Or unofficially?"

"It would have to be engineered behind the scenes. And a scapegoat would have to be found to blame for the mistake of, well, misdirecting you. But it could happen."

"*Why?* Why would you take that risk for us?"

For the first time, Ammon's composure seemed to thaw from the stem professional into what might be coined amiable. He grinned, and Trask noticed he seemed careful not to exhibit his fangs. "I always wanted to make it into *somebody's* history book. I find it a more intriguing method of achieving immortality, anyway."

Trask stood still, eyes boring into the ice at his feet. Back off a moment, absorb this all. Out of every conceivable ultimatum he had readied his ears to hear, *Trust me* was at the bottom of the list. Well, worse, actually; it hadn't even made the list.

He glanced up. "Your dossier said you were a crafty bastard. I've still got no reason to trust you."

Ammon nodded, perfectly frank. "What do you have to gain by not?"

Crossroads. But when crapshooting for life and hope, one place was as good as another to die, he supposed. The gamble was worth it.

"This won't be entirely my decision. I'll have to clear this with everyone. And I won't force anyone who's dead set against it."

"I understand. I'll wait for your word at the radio."

"I'd shake your hand," Trask said, "but it probably wouldn't look right."

"Probably not." Ammon drew himself up to full height, nonetheless, and of all the surprises to just keep coming, he snapped a salute along the scuffed bill of his hat.

Trask returned it, spun on his heel to move back up the slope.

Sound performed screwy pirouettes on the glaciers. It was swallowed by snow, it caromed off ice. Trask's ears registered something, somewhere, a hybrid between a crack and a thump. Heart plummeted from hopeful bouyance to gut-level despair, without the certainty of just what it had been. There was no need for precise identification. He turned. *This is how it ends, then, this—*

A half-dozen yards away, Ammon exploded. He first twitched, as if struck by a heavy blow, then erupted from within into organic pulp, solid and liquid parting company to hurl in unidentifiable masses across the ground. The blast wrapped itself around Trask in concussive embrace, slickened him with residue from his onetime enemy, and hurled him to the ice. Breath was knocked from him, ribs shoved out of alignment, flesh and muscles alike made raw. A jagged claw of ice tore at his cheek, and as he wallowed, ears muffled and numb from the blast, he could nevertheless hear a call to arms from behind the vampires' lines.

"They've killed the field marshall . . . move in!"

The responding roar of assent was the most frightening sound *en masse* that he had ever heard. Still reeling, Trask heard the gunfire directed his way. Felt his parka and body punctured five times, six; he lost track. A blizzard of goose down whirled from his parka, and he was spun onto his back. Leaking, breath bubbling merrily in his lungs.

Over the din, he heard it, a lone, lost wail from above. Called from an open window. *"Daddy . . . !"* So much pain, so dreadfully much.

He lay still as all around him the vampire army surged forward in a maelstrom of automatic weapons, and the launching of shoulder-fired missiles that arced uphill to make rubble of the outpost. The hammer blows of demon gods. Heavy boot steps thundered in his ears. With a corpse-eye view of a battlefield, he saw little more than vast sky and towering soldiers in onrushing flash cuts. And soon, there was smoke.

So this was how it was to end, an impatient enemy triggered by treachery and sacrifice. Ammon had been right. *They're as bad as we ever were, at our very worst.*

Trask played possum, unfocusing his eyes to divorce from them any semblance of life and sentience. And when the army was fighting its way uphill with the fury of plundering Huns, he ratcheted his head around to gaze their way. They were paying him no mind. Back to feed later, no doubt, but for now he was ignored.

He then looked to the bulk of the mess that had been Field Marshall Ammon. Sundered flesh and shattered bone within the shreds of a uniform, steaming under daylight into ashen decay. It was understandable. Couldn't very well have coated his insides with sunscreen.

But the sun, and the flesh . . .

He groped beneath his parka, wrenched the walkie-talkie to his mouth. "Ellie . . . baby . . . ?" Each word was a rasp, effort beyond Herculean. He released the transmit key from its lock-on.

"Daddy? *Daddy?*" It crackled over the tiny speaker along with the roar of gunfire. "I love you, Daddy, I—"

"You listen to me, El." He released the key long enough to retch blood and phlegm from his mouth. Did not want her hearing *that.* "Whole building's wired to blow. Remember when Sarah rigged it?"

A daughter's tears. "Yes . . . "

"Blow it, honey. Don't let them take you. I've seen what they do . . . " Another wracking cough. "But if you got time . . . switch the charges to thermites. Heat that whole hill up like hell, baby."

"I don't understand. Why?" A frantic rattle of gunfire, and in her background, someone shrieked. Repeatedly.

"Remember what you told me you missed most?"

A moment's recollection. Everlasting. "The rain."

"Do it," Trask whispered. "Only you'll know when the time's right to push that button. . . . "

He went limp. To speak was as draining as a sluice gate. But he could listen, the speaker beside his ear. Ellie had apparently taken her unit along, transmitter locked as she worked running and frenzied. He heard everything, could only imagine the sights to match the sounds. Gunfire aplenty, and muffled explosions as the vampires tried to blast their way past steel reinforced doors. He heard the voices of his comrades as tears were shed, as frantic good-byes were made, as actions were taken to make death count for something, however minute. Ultimate meaning grew very important.

The machinations of death could be cruel beyond measure. But death itself was not without its mercies. It blotted, it soothed. It teased and caressed, that coldest of lovers. Arctic air found its way into his body through the perforations, but he could no longer feel its sting.

Trask's mind floated, still lucid, now tranquil. Sorrow over the life he had imposed upon his daughter began to dwindle. He had not chosen the life all mortals were forced to lead. No. He had, instead, guided her toward that noblest of endeavors. Truth. Ellie had done her heritage and her humanity proud. No regrets, no.

"Daddy . . . you think . . . " Ellie was panting, breath hoarse and ragged in her throat. Pained. She had been shot, he knew, and was gamely trying to keep him from knowing. Behind her, the battle raged, and he squeezed his eyes shut. " . . . you think maybe someday . . . somebody'll dig this place out . . . and know who we were . . . what we did?"

Transmit. "I know they will."

"Katy . . . she's copied our discs onto blanks . . . wired 'em onto the dogs' collars . . . give us one more chance to get the word out."

A moment later, a muffled blast—from inside—tore out the side exit at the kennel. White polar suits went bowling away, and moments later, a horde of baying fur came streaking out the blown doorway. Sled dogs, eight in all. He could see some sort of small dark packet affixed to the collar of each.

Other vampires opened fire, shooting at anything that moved. Dog after dog was hit, yelping as they pitched downward, or tumbled down icy slopes with footing lost. But three made it. *Three.* Trask watched them, fleet-footed and sure, muscles in perfect synchronization as they strained at limits, beyond limits, untold generations of breeding having molded them into machines born only to run.

"Go," Trask whispered, and they vanished over the peaks, triumphant, padded feet kicking up sprays of snow in their wake. "Go . . . " Perhaps, someday, they might be found. Or make their own way south, over frozen straits and channels next winter, back to the mainland. Cargo intact. *Maybe.*

Please God, let it be so. Deathbed prayers were always the most fervent. Then, faith had been the essence of their mission all along.

"Daddy?" Ellie, devoid of her own regrets. Only pain remained.

"I . . . I'm holding hands with Sarah . . . I think . . . she just died." .

"You know what to do, El."

"Daddy?" Fathomless wells of sorrow. *"They're here."*

Beyond regrets or not, Trask couldn't help the one last, great sob that wrenched free. No man could hear his daughter announce the arrival of her violators without feeling the end of the world.

"Love you, Ellie," he choked.

"Love you too, Daddy."

"Love—"

And the mountainside disappeared into smoke and fire.

When the first thermite heat wave reached him, tropical in its kiss, Trask smiled, because it was good. Then came the avalanche of glacial debris. He felt at one with generations of forebears, whose struggles against slave traders trying to impose mandates of illiteracy and domination and erasure of Afro-history had made him feel so close to the struggles of today. The oppressor was always doomed to failure. He could die happy. Buried. A frozen legacy, an iceman for some centuries-distant excavator to free, and ponder.

Tons of snow and ice packed above and around the outpost were liquified, vaporized, a low-slung cloud of moisture that quickly condensed and rained back down. Upturned, cold, pale faces watched it course down. Many were already mortally wounded from the blasts, or from the fires. Others had lost their lenses, and staggered blindly about.

But one and all endured the cleansing rinse, faces coming clean, washed bare, exposed. And flesh began to smolder and peel. A dance of death in appeasement to the whims of a mountain king. No shelter, and nothing but daylight for miles, and miles, and miles.

Some truths are always painfully self-evident.

DAYLIGHT REMAINED FOR MONTHS.

But as all cycles must end, the sun finally sank beneath the horizon. Night reintroduced itself to the ice-capped Ellesmere once again, and darkness fell upon the ruins of invader and partisan alike. Over the months, there had been precious little intrusion by wind to scatter the dregs, and here they mingled, cold and brittle and utterly alone . . .

Husks of sun-dried flesh, like parchment, and thousands upon thousands of sheets of paper, most incomplete and ashen along the edges. But miraculously legible, in many cases.

Ellesmere's population of Arctic hares had ebbed considerably as of late. Among the scorched litter, fresh footprints, padded paws of those who had come seeking nourishment where such was all too sparse. And finding none, the paw prints led away, east, toward Greenland, toward the unknown, toward frozen shores.

Revelations in Black

Carl Jacobi

It was a dreary, forlorn establishment way down on Harbor Street. An old sign announced the legend: "Giovanni Larla—Antiques," and a dingy window revealed a display half masked in dust.

Even as I crossed the threshold that cheerless September afternoon, driven from the sidewalk by a gust of rain and perhaps a fascination for all antiques, the gloominess fell upon me like a material pall. Inside were half darkness, piled boxes, and a monstrous tapestry, frayed with the warp showing in worn places. An Italian Renaissance wine cabinet shrank despondently in its corner and seemed to frown at me as I passed.

"Good afternoon, *Signor*. There is something you wish to buy? A picture, a ring, a vase perhaps?"

I peered at the squat, pudgy bulk of the Italian proprietor there in the shadows and hesitated.

"Just looking around," I said, turning my eyes to the jumble about me. "Nothing in particular . . . "

The man's oily face moved in smile as though he had heard the remark a thousand times before. He sighed, stood there in thought a moment, the rain drumming and swishing against the outer pane. Then very deliberately he stepped to the shelves and glanced up and down them considering. I moved to his side, letting my eyes sweep across the stacked array of ancient oddities. At length he drew forth an object which I perceived to be a painted chalice.

"An authentic sixteenth-century Tandart," he murmured. "A work of art, *Signor.*"

I shook my head. "No pottery," I said. "Books perhaps, but no pottery."

He frowned slowly. "I have books too," he replied, "rare books which nobody sells but me, Giovanni Larla. But you must look at my other treasures too."

There was, I found, no hurrying the man. A quarter of an hour passed, during which I had to see a Glycon cameo brooch, a carved chair of some indeterminate style and period, and a muddle of yellowed statuettes, small oils and one or two dreary Portland vases. Several times I glanced at my watch impatiently, wondering how I might break away from this Italian and his gloomy shop. Already the fascination of its dust and shadows had begun to wear off, and I was anxious to reach the street.

But when he had conducted me well toward the rear of the shop, something caught my fancy. I drew then from the shelf the first book of horror. If I had but known the terrible events that were to follow, if I could only have had a foresight into the future that September day, I swear I would have avoided the book like a leprous thing, would have shunned that wretched antique store and the very street it stood on like places accursed. A thousand times I have wished my eyes had never rested on that cover in black. What writhings of the soul, what terrors, what unrest, what madness would have been spared me!

But never dreaming the hideous secret of its pages I fondled it casually and remarked:

"An unusual book. What is it?"

Larla glanced up and scowled.

"That is not for sale," he said quietly. "I don't know how it got on these shelves. It was my poor brother's."

The volume in my hand was indeed unusual in appearance. Measuring but four inches across and five inches in length and bound in black velvet with each outside corner protected with a triangle of ivory, it was the most beautiful piece of bookbinding I had ever seen. In the center of the cover was mounted a tiny piece of ivory intricately cut in the shape of a skull. But it was the title of the book that excited my interest. Embroidered in gold braid, the title read:

"*Five Unicorns and a Pearl.*"

I looked at Larla. "How much?" I asked and reached for my wallet.

He shook his head. "No, it is not for sale. It is . . . it is the last work of my brother. He wrote it just before he died in the institution."

"The institution?" I queried.

Larla made no reply but stood staring at the book, his mind obviously drifting away in deep thought. A moment of silence dragged by. There was a strange gleam in his eyes when finally he spoke. And I thought I saw his fingers tremble slightly.

"My brother, Alessandro, was a fine man before he wrote that book," he said slowly. "He wrote beautifully, *Signor*, and he was strong and healthy. For hours I could sit while he read to me his poems. He was a dreamer, Alessandro; he loved everything beautiful, and the two of us were very happy.

"All . . . until that terrible night. Then he . . . but no . . . a year has passed now. It is best to forget." He passed his hand before his eyes and drew in his breath sharply.

"What happened?" I asked sympathetically, his words arousing my curiosity.

"Happened, *Signor*? I do not really know. It was all so confusing. He became suddenly ill, ill without reason. The flush of sunny Italy, which was always on his cheek, faded, and he grew white and drawn. His strength left him day by day. Doctors prescribed, gave medicines, but nothing helped. He grew steadily weaker until . . . until that night."

I looked at him curiously, impressed by his perturbation.

"And then—?" I urged.

Hands opening and closing, Larla seemed to sway unsteadily; his liquid eyes opened wide to the brows, and his voice was strained and tense as he continued:

"And then . . . oh, if I could but forget! It was horrible. Poor Alessandro came home screaming, sobbing, tearing his hair. He was . . . he was stark raving mad!

"They took him to the institution for the insane and said he needed a complete rest, that he had suffered from some terrific mental shock. He . . . died three weeks later with the crucifix on his lips."

For a moment I stood there in silence, staring out at the falling rain. Then I said:

"He wrote this book while confined to the institution?"

Larla nodded absently.

"Three books," he replied. "Two others exactly like the one you have in your hand. The bindings he made, of course, when he was quite well. It was his original intention, I believe, to pen in them by hand the verses of Marini. He was very clever at such work. But the wanderings of his mind which filled the pages now, I have never read. Nor do I intend to. I want to keep with me the memory of him when he was happy. This book has come on these shelves by mistake. I shall put it with his other possessions."

My desire to read the few pages bound in velvet increased a thousandfold when I found they were unobtainable. I have always had an interest in abnormal psychology and have gone through a number of books on the subject. Here was the work of a man confined in the asylum for the insane. Here was the unexpurgated writing of an educated brain gone mad. And unless my intuition failed me, here was a suggestion of some deep mystery. My mind was made up. I must have it.

I turned to Larla and chose my words carefully.

"I can well appreciate your wish to keep the book," I said, "and since you refuse to sell, may I ask if you would consider lending it to me for just one night? If I promised to return it in the morning?"

The Italian hesitated. He toyed undecidedly with a heavy gold watch chain.

"No. I am sorry . . . "

"Ten dollars and back tomorrow unharmed."

Larla studied his shoe.

"Very well, *Signor*, I will trust you. But please, I ask you, please be sure and return it."

That night in the quiet of my apartment I opened the book. Immediately my attention was drawn to three lines scrawled in a feminine hand across the inside of the front cover, lines written in a faded red solution that looked more like blood than ink. They read:

"*Revelations meant to destroy but only binding without the stake. Read, fool, and enter my field, for we are chained to the spot. Oh wo unto Larla.*"

I mused over these undecipherable sentences for some time without solving their meaning. At last, shrugging my shoulders, I turned to the first page and began the last work of Alessandro Larla, the strangest story I had ever in my years of browsing through old books, come upon.

"On the evening of the fifteenth of October I turned my steps into the cold and walked until I was tired. The roar of the present was in the distance when I came to twenty-six bluejays silently contemplating the ruins. Passing in the midst of them I wandered by the skeleton trees and seated myself where I could watch the leering fish. A child worshiped. Glass threw the moon at me. Grass sang a litany at my feet. And the pointed shadow moved slowly to the left.

"I walked along the silver gravel until I came to five unicorns galloping beside water of the past. Here I found a pearl, a magnificent pearl, a pearl beautiful but black. Like a flower it carried a rich perfume, and once I thought the odor was but a mask, but why should such a perfect creation need a mask?

"I sat between the leering fish and the five galloping unicorns, and I fell madly in love with the pearl. The past lost itself in drabness and—"

I laid the book down and sat watching the smoke-curls from my pipe eddy ceilingward. There was much more, but I could make no sense to any of it. All was in that strange style and completely incomprehensible. And yet it seemed the story was more than the mere wanderings of a madman. Behind it all seemed to lie a narrative cloaked in symbolism.

Something about the few sentences—just what I cannot say— had cast an immediate spell of depression over me. The vague lines weighed upon my mind, hung before my eyes like a design, and I felt myself slowly seized by a deep feeling of uneasiness.

The air of the room grew heavy and close. The open casement and the out-of-doors seemed to beckon to me. I walked to the window, thrust the curtain aside, stood there, smoking furiously. Let me say that regular habits have long been a part of my makeup. I am not addicted to nocturnal strolls or late meanderings before seeking my bed; yet now, curiously enough, with the pages of the book still in my mind I suddenly experienced an indefinable urge to leave my apartment and walk the darkened streets.

I paced the room nervously, irritated that the sensation did not pass. The clock on the mantel pushed its ticks slowly through the quiet. And at length with a shrug I threw my pipe to the table, reached for my hat and coat and made for the door.

Ridiculous as it may sound, upon reaching the street I found that urge had increased to a distinct attraction. I felt that under no circumstances must I turn any direction but northward, and although this way led into a district quite unknown to me, I was in a moment pacing forward, choosing streets deliberately and heading without knowing why toward the outskirts of the city. It was a brilliant moonlit night in September. Summer had passed and already there was the smell of frosted vegetation in the air. The great chimes in Capitol tower were sounding midnight, and the buildings and shops and later the private houses were dark and silent as I passed.

Try as I would to erase from my memory the queer book which I had just read, the mystery of its pages hammered at me, arousing my curiosity, dampening my spirits. "Five Unicorns and a Pearl!" What did it all mean?

More and more I realized as I went on that a power other than my own will was leading my steps. It was absurd, and I tried to resist, to turn back. Yet once when I did momentarily come to a halt that attraction swept upon me as inexorably as the desire for a narcotic.

It was far out on Easterly Street that I came upon a high stone wall flanking the sidewalk. Over its ornamented top I could see the shadows of a dark building set well back in the grounds. A wrought-iron gate in the wall opened upon a view of wild desertion and neglect. Swathed in the light of the moon, an old courtyard strewn with fountains, stone benches and statues lay tangled in rank weeds and undergrowth. The windows of the building, which evidently had once been a private dwelling, were boarded up, all except those on a little tower or cupola rising to a point in the front. And here the glass caught the blue-gray light and refracted it into the shadows.

Before that gate my feet stopped like dead things. The psychic power which had been leading me had now become a reality. Directly from the courtyard it emanated, drawing me toward it with an intensity that smothered all reluctance.

Strangely enough, the gate was unlocked; and feeling like a man in a trance I swung the creaking hinges and entered, making my way along a grass-grown path to one of the benches. It seemed that once inside the court the distant sounds of the city died away, leaving a hollow silence broken only by the wind rustling through the tall dead weeds. Rearing up before me, the building with its dark wings, cupola and facade oddly resembled a colossal hound, crouched and ready to spring.

There were several fountains, weatherbeaten and ornamented with curious figures, to which at the time I paid only casual attention. Farther on, half hidden by the underbrush, was the lifesize statue of a little child kneeling in position of prayer. Erosion on the soft stone had disfigured the face, and in the half-light the carved features presented an expression strangely grotesque and repelling. How long I sat there in the quiet, I don't know. The surroundings under the moonlight blended harmoniously with my mood. But more than that I seemed physically unable to rouse myself and pass on.

It was with a suddenness that brought me electrified to my feet that I became aware of the real significance of the objects about me. Held motionless, I stood there running my eyes wildly from place to place, refusing to believe. Surely I must be dreaming. In the name of all that was unusual this . . . this absolutely couldn't be. And yet—

It was the fountain at my side that had caught my attention first. Across the top of the water basin were *five stone unicorns*, all identically carved, each seeming to follow the other in galloping procession. Looking farther, prompted now by a madly rising recollection, I saw that the cupola, towering high above the house, eclipsed the rays of the moon and threw *a long pointed shadow* across the ground *at my left*. The other fountain some distance away was ornamented with the figure of a stone fish, *a fish* whose empty eye-sockets *were leering* straight in my direction. And the climax of it all—the wall! At intervals of every three feet on the top of the street expanse were mounted crude carven stone shapes of birds. And counting them I saw that *those birds were twenty-six bluejays*.

Unquestionably—startling and impossible as it seemed—I was in the same setting as described in Larla's book! It was a staggering revelation, and my mind reeled at the thought of it. How strange, how odd that I should be drawn to a portion of the city I had never before frequented and thrown into the midst of a narrative written almost a year before!

I saw now that Alessandro Larla, writing as a patient in the institution for the insane, had seized isolated details but neglected to explain them. Here was a problem for the psychologist, the mad, the symbolic, the incredible story of the dead Italian. I was bewildered, confused, and I pondered for an answer.

As if to soothe my perturbation there stole into the court then a faint odor of perfume. Pleasantly it touched my nostrils, seemed to blend with the moonlight. I breathed it in deeply as I stood there by the curious fountain. But slowly that odor became more noticeable, grew stronger, a sickish sweet smell that began to creep down my lungs like smoke. And absently I recognized it. Heliotrope! The honeyed aroma blanketed the garden, thickened the air, seemed to fall upon me like a drug.

And then came my second surprise of the evening. Looking about to discover the source of the irritating fragrance I saw opposite me, seated on another stone bench, a woman. She was dressed entirely in black, and her face was hidden by a veil. She seemed unaware of my presence. Her head was slightly bowed, and her whole position suggested a person deep in contemplation.

I noticed also the thing that crouched by her side. It was a dog, a tremendous brute with a head strangely out of proportion and eyes as large as the ends of big spoons. For several moments I stood staring at the two of them. Although the air was quite chilly, the woman wore no over-jacket, only the black dress relieved solely by the whiteness of her throat.

With a sigh of regret at having my pleasant solitude thus disturbed I moved across the court until I stood at her side. Still she showed no recognition of my presence, and clearing my throat I said hesitatingly:

"I suppose you are the owner here. I . . . I really didn't know the place was occupied, and the gate . . . well, the gate was unlocked. I'm sorry I trespassed."

She made no reply to that, and the dog merely gazed at me in dumb silence. No graceful words of polite departure came to my lips, and I moved hesitatingly toward the gate.

"Please don't go," she said suddenly, looking up. "I'm lonely. Oh, if you but knew how lonely I am!" She moved to one side on the bench and motioned that I sit beside her. The dog continued to examine me with its big eyes.

Whether it was the nearness of that odor of heliotrope, the suddenness of it all, or perhaps the moonlight, I did not know, but at her words a thrill of pleasure ran through me, and I accepted the proffered seat.

There followed an interval of silence, during which I puzzled my brain for a means to start conversation. But abruptly she turned to the beast and said in German:

"Fort mit dir, Johann!"

The dog rose obediently to its feet and stole slowly off into the shadows. I watched it for a moment until it disappeared in the direction of the house. Then the woman said to me in English which was slightly stilted and marked with an accent:

"It has been ages since I have spoken to anyone. . . . We are strangers. I do not know you, and you do not know me. Yet . . . strangers sometimes find in each other a bond of interest. Supposing . . . supposing we forget customs and formality of introduction? Shall we?"

For some reason I felt my pulse quicken as she said that. "Please do," I replied. "A spot like this is enough introduction in itself. Tell me, do you live here?"

She made no answer for a moment, and I began to fear I had taken her suggestion too quickly. Then she began slowly:

"My name is Perle von Mauren, and I am really a stranger to your country, though I have been here now more than a year. My home is in Austria near what is now the Czechoslovakian frontier. You see, it was to find my only brother that I came to the United States. During the war he was a lieutenant under General Mackensen, but in 1916, in April I believe it was, he . . . he was reported missing.

"War is a cruel thing. It took our money; it took our castle on the Danube, and then—my brother. Those following years were horrible. We lived always in doubt, hoping against hope that lie was still living.

"Then after the armistice a fellow officer claimed to have served next to him on grave-digging detail at a French prison camp near Monpré. And later came a thin rumor that he was in the United States. I gathered together as much money as I could and came here in search of him."

Her voice dwindled off, and she sat in silence staring at the brown weeds. When she resumed, her voice was low and wavering.

"I . . . found him . . . but would to God I hadn't! He . . . he was no longer living."

I stared at her. "Dead?" I asked.

The veil trembled as though moved by a shudder, as though her thoughts had exhumed some terrible event of the past. Unconscious of my interruption she went on:

"Tonight I came here—I don't know why—merely because the gate was unlocked, and there was a place of quiet within. Now have I bored you with my confidences and personal history?"

"Not at all," I replied. "I came here by chance myself. Probably the beauty of the place attracted me. I dabble in amateur photography occasionally and react strongly to unusual scenes. Tonight I went for a midnight stroll to relieve my mind from the bad effect of a book I was reading."

She made a strange reply to that, a reply away from our line of thought and which seemed an interjection that escaped her involuntarily.

"Books," she said, "are powerful things. They can fetter one more than the walls of a prison."

She caught my puzzled stare at the remark and added hastily: "It is odd that we should meet here."

For a moment I didn't answer. I was thinking of her heliotrope perfume, which for a woman of her apparent culture was applied in far too great a quantity to manifest good taste. The impression stole upon me that the perfume cloaked some secret, that if it were removed I should find . . . but what? It was ridiculous, and I tried to cast the feeling aside.

The hours passed, and still we sat there talking, enjoying each other's companionship. She did not remove her veil, and though I was burning with a desire to see her features, I had not dared ask her to. A strange nervousness had slowly seized me. The woman was a charming conversationalist, but there was about her an indefinable something which produced in me a distinct feeling of unease.

It was, I should judge, but a few moments before the first streaks of dawn when it happened. As I look back now, even with mundane objects and thoughts on every side, it is not difficult to realize the dire significance, the absolute baseness of that vision. But at the time my brain was too much in a whirl to understand.

A thin shadow moving across the garden attracted my gaze once again into the night about me. I looked up over the spire of the deserted house and stared as if struck by a blow. For a moment I thought I had seen a curious cloud formation racing low directly above me, a cloud black and impenetrable with two winglike ends strangely in the shape of a monstrous flying bat.

I blinked my eyes hard and looked again.

"That cloud!" I exclaimed, "that strange cloud! . . . Did you see—"

I stopped and stared dumbly.

The bench at my side was empty. The woman had disappeared.

During the next day I went about my professional duties in the law office with only half interest, and my business partner looked at me queerly several times when he came upon me mumbling to myself. The incidents of the evening before were rushing through my mind in grand turmoil. Questions unanswerable hammered at me. That I should have come upon the very details described by mad Larla in his strange book: the leering fish, the praying child, the twenty-six bluejays, the pointed shadow of the cupola—it was unexplainable; it was weird.

"Five Unicorns and a Pearl." The unicorns were the stone statues ornamenting the old fountain, yes—but the pearl? With a start I suddenly recalled the name of the woman in black: *Perle* von Mauren. The revelation climaxed my train of thought. What did it all mean?

Dinner had little attraction for me that evening. Earlier I had gone to the antique-dealer and begged him to loan me the sequel, the second volume of his brother Alessandro. When he had refused, objected because I had not yet returned the first book, my nerves had suddenly jumped on edge. I felt like a narcotic fiend faced with the realization that he could not procure the desired drug. In desperation, yet hardly knowing why, I offered the man money, more money, until at length I had come away, my powers of persuasion and my pocketbook successful.

The second volume was identical in outward respects to its predecessor except that it bore no title. But if I was expecting more disclosures in symbolism I was doomed to disappointment. Vague as "Five Unicorns and a Pearl" had been, the text of the sequel was even more wandering and was obviously only the ramblings of a mad brain. By watching the sentences closely I did gather that Alessandro Larla had made a second trip to his court of the twenty-six bluejays and met there again his "pearl."

There was a paragraph toward the end that puzzled me. It read: *"Can it possibly be? I pray that it is not. And yet I have seen it and heard it snarl. Oh, the loathsome creature! I will not, I will not believe it."*

I closed the book with a snap and tried to divert my attention elsewhere by polishing the lens of my newest portable camera. But again, as before, that same urge stole upon me, that same desire to visit the garden. I confess that I had watched the intervening hours until I would meet the woman in black again; for strangely enough in spite of her abrupt exit before, I never doubted but that she would be there waiting for me. I wanted her to lift the veil. I wanted to talk with her. I wanted to throw myself once again into the narrative of Larla's book.

Yet the whole thing seemed preposterous, and I fought the sensation with every ounce of willpower I could call to mind. Then it suddenly occurred to me what a remarkable picture she would make, sitting there on the stone bench, clothed in black, with a classic background of the old courtyard. If I could but catch the scene on a photographic plate? . . .

I halted my polishing and mused a moment. With a new electric flash-lamp, that handy invention which has supplanted the old mussy flash-powder, I could illuminate the garden and snap the picture with ease. And if the result were satisfactory it would make a worthy contribution to the International Camera Contest at Geneva next month.

The idea appealed to me, and gathering together the necessary equipment I drew on an ulster (for it was a wet, chilly night) and slipped out of my rooms and headed northward. Mad, unseeing fool that I was! If only I had stopped then and there, returned the book to the antique-dealer and closed the incident! But the strange magnetic attraction had gripped me in earnest, and I rushed headlong into the horror.

A FALL RAIN WAS drumming the pavement, and the streets were deserted. Off to the east, however, the heavy blanket of clouds glowed with a soft radiance where the moon was trying to break through, and a strong wind from the south gave promise of clearing the skies before long. With my coat collar turned well up at the throat I passed once again into the older section of the town and down forgotten Easterly Street. I found the gate to the grounds unlocked as before, and the garden a dripping place masked in shadow.

The woman was not there. Still the hour was early, and I did not for a moment doubt that she would appear later. Gripped now with the enthusiasm of my plan, I set the camera carefully on the stone fountain, training the lens as well as I could on the bench where we had sat the previous evening. The flash lamp with its battery handle I laid within easy reach.

Scarcely had I finished my arrangements when the crunch of gravel on the path caused me to turn. She was approaching the stone bench, heavily veiled as before and with the same sweeping black dress.

"You have come again," she said as I took my place beside her.

"Yes," I replied, "I could not stay away."

Our conversation that night gradually centered about her dead brother, although I thought several times that the woman tried to avoid the subject. He had been, it seemed, the black sheep of the family, had led more or less of a dissolute life and had been expelled from the University of Vienna not only because of his lack of respect for the pedagogues of the various sciences but also because of his queer unorthodox papers on philosophy. His sufferings in the war prison camp must have been intense. With a kind of grim delight she dwelt on his horrible experiences in the grave-digging detail which had been related to her by the fellow officer. But of the manner in which he had met his death she would say absolutely nothing.

Stronger than on the night before was the sweet smell of heliotrope. And again as the fumes crept nauseatingly down my lungs there came the same sense of nervousness, that same feeling that the perfume was hiding something I should know. The desire to see beneath the veil had become maddening by this time, but still I lacked the boldness to ask her to lift it.

Toward midnight the heavens cleared and the moon in splendid contrast shone high in the sky. The time had come for my picture.

"Sit where you are," I said. "I'll be back in a moment."

Stepping quickly to the fountain I grasped the flash-lamp, held it aloft for an instant and placed my finger on the shutter lever of the camera. The woman remained motionless on the bench, evidently puzzled as to the meaning of my movements. The range was perfect. A click, and a dazzling white light enveloped the courtyard about us. For a brief second she was outlined there against the old wall. Then the blue moonlight returned, and I was smiling in satisfaction.

"It ought to make a beautiful picture," I said.

She leaped to her feet.

"Fool!" she cried hoarsely. "Blundering fool! What have you done?"

Even though the veil was there to hide her face I got the instant impression that her eyes were glaring at me, smoldering with hatred. I gazed at her curiously a she stood erect, head thrown back, body apparently taut as wire, and a slow shudder crept down my spine. Then without warning she gathered up her dress and ran down the path toward the deserted house. A moment later she had disappeared somewhere in the shadows of the giant bushes.

I stood there by the fountain, staring after her in a daze. Suddenly, off in the umbra of the house's facade there rose a low animal snarl.

And then before I could move, a huge gray shape came hurtling through the long weeds, bounding in great leaps straight toward me. It was the woman's dog, which I had seen with her the night before. But no longer was it a beast passive and silent. Its face was contorted in diabolic fury, and its jaws were dripping slaver. Even in that moment of terror as I stood frozen before it, the sight of those white nostrils and those black hyalescent eyes emblazoned itself on my mind, never to be forgotten.

Then with a lunge it was upon me. I had only time to thrust the flash-lamp upward in half protection and throw my weight to the side. My arm jumped in recoil. The bulb exploded, and I could feel those teeth clamp down hard on the handle. Backward I fell, a scream gurgling to my lips, a terrific heaviness surging upon my body.

I struck out frantically, beat my fists into that growling face. My fingers groped blindly for its throat, sank deep into the hairy flesh. I could feel its very breath mingling with my own now, but desperately I hung on.

The pressure of my hands told. The dog coughed and fell back. And seizing that instant I struggled to my feet, jumped forward and planted a terrific kick straight into the brute's middle.

"Fort mit dir, Johann!" I cried, remembering the woman's German command.

It leaped back and, fangs bared, glared at me motionless for a moment. Then abruptly it turned and slunk off through the weeds.

Weak and trembling, I drew myself together, picked tip my camera and passed through the gate toward home.

Three days passed. Those endless hours I spent confined to my apartment suffering the tortures of the damned.

On the day following the night of my terrible experience with the dog I realized I was in no condition to go to work. I drank two cups of strong black coffee and then forced myself to sit quietly in a chair, hoping to soothe my nerves. But the sight of the camera there on the table excited me to action. Five minutes later I was in the dark room arranged as my studio, developing the picture I had taken the night before. I worked feverishly, urged on by the thought of what an unusual contribution it would make for the amateur contest next month at Geneva, should the result be successful.

An exclamation burst from my lips as I stared at the still-wet print. There was the old garden clear and sharp with the bushes, the statue of the child, the fountain and the wall in the background, but the bench—the stone bench was empty. There was no sign, not even a blur of the woman in black.

My brain in a whirl, I rushed the negative through a saturated solution of mercuric chloride in water, then treated it with ferrous oxalate. But even after this intensifying process the second print was like the first, focused in every detail, the bench standing in the foreground in sharp relief, but no trace of the woman.

I stared incredulously. She had been in plain view when I snapped the shutter. Of that I was positive. And my camera was in perfect condition. What then was wrong? Not until I had looked at the print hard in the daylight would I believe my eyes. No explanation offered itself, none at all; and at length, confused unto weakness, I returned to my bed and fell into a heavy sleep.

Straight through the day I slept. Hours later I seemed to wake from a vague nightmare, and had not strength to rise from my pillow. A great physical faintness had overwhelmed me. My arms, my legs, lay like dead things. My heart was fluttering weakly. All was quiet, so still that the clock on my bureau ticked distinctly each passing second. The curtain billowed in the night breeze, though I was positive I had closed the casement when I entered the room.

And then suddenly I threw back my head and screamed from the bottomest depths of my soul! For slowly, slowly creeping down my lungs was that detestable odor of heliotrope!

Morning, and I found all was not a dream. My head was ringing, my hands trembling, and I was so weak I could hardly stand. The doctor I called in looked grave as he felt my pulse.

"You are on the verge of a complete collapse," he said. "If you do not allow yourself a rest it may permanently affect your mind. Take things easy for a while. And if you don't mind, I'll cauterize those two little cuts on your neck. They're rather raw wounds. What caused them?"

I moved my fingers to my throat and drew them away again tipped with blood.

"I . . . I don't know," I faltered.

He busied himself with his medicines, and a few minutes later reached for his hat.

"I advise that you don't leave your bed for a week at least," he said. "I'll give you a thorough examination then and see if there are any signs of anemia." But as he went out the door I thought I saw a puzzled look on his face.

Those subsequent hours allowed my thoughts to run wild once more. I vowed I would forget it all, go back to my work and never look upon the books again. But I knew I could not. The woman in black persisted in my mind, and each minute away from her became a torture. But more than that, if there had been a decided urge to continue my reading in the second book, the desire to see the third book, the last of the trilogy, was slowly increasing to an obsession. It gripped me, etched itself deep into my thoughts.

At length I could stand it no longer, and on the morning of the third day I took a cab to the antique store and tried to persuade Larla to give me the third volume of his brother. But the Italian was firm. I had already taken two books, neither of which I had returned. Until I brought them back he would not listen. Vainly I tried to explain that one was of no value without the sequel and that I wanted to read the entire narrative as a unit. He merely shrugged his shoulders and toyed with his watch chain.

Cold perspiration broke out on my forehead as I heard my desire disregarded. Like the blows of a bludgeon the thought beat upon me that I must have that book. I argued. I pleaded. But to no avail.

At length when Larla had turned the other way I gave in to desperation, seized the third book as I saw it lying on the shelf, slid it into my pocket, and walked guiltily out. I make no apologies for my action. In the light of what developed later it may be considered a temptation inspired, for my will at the time was a conquered thing blanketed by that strange lure.

Back in my apartment I dropped into a chair and hastened to open the velvet cover. Here was the last chronicling of that strange series of events which had so completely become a part of my life during the past five days. Larla's volume three. Would all be explained in its pages? If so, what secret would be revealed?

With the light from a reading-lamp glaring full over my shoulder I opened the book, thumbed through it slowly, marveling again at the exquisite hand-printing. It seemed then as I sat there that an almost palpable cloud of intense quiet settled over me, a mental miasma muffling the distant sounds of the street. I was vaguely aware of an atmosphere, heavy and dense, in which objects other than the book lost their focus and became blurred in proportion.

For a moment I hesitated. Something psychic, something indefinable seemed to forbid me to read farther. Conscience, curiosity, that queer urge told me to go on. Slowly, like a man in a hypnotic trance wavering between two wills, I began to turn the pages, one at a time, from back to front.

Symbolism again. Vague wanderings with no sane meaning.

But suddenly my fingers stopped! My eyes had caught sight of the last paragraph on the last page, the final pennings of Alessandro Larla. I stared downward as a terrific shock ripped through me from head to foot. I read, re-read, and read again those words, those blasphemous words. I brought the book closer. I traced each word in the lamplight, slowly, carefully, letter for letter. I opened and closed my eyes. Then the horror of it burst like bomb within me.

"*What shall I do? She has drained my blood and rotted my soul. My pearl is black, black as all evil. The curse be upon her brother, for it is he who made her thus. I pray the truth in these pages will destroy them forever.*

"*But my brain is hammering itself apart. Heaven help me, Perle von Mauren and her brother, Johann, are vampires!*"

With a scream I leaped to my feet.

"Vampires!" I shrieked. "Vampires! Oh, my God!"

I clutched at the edge of the table and stood there swaying, the realization of it surging upon me like the blast of a furnace. Vampires! Those horrible creatures with a lust for human blood, fiends of hell, taking the shape of men, of bats, of dogs. I saw it all now, and my brain reeled at the horror of it.

Oh, why had I been such a fool? Why had I not looked beneath the surface, taken away the veil, gone farther than the perfume? That damnable heliotrope was a mask, a mask hiding all the unspeakable foulness of the grave.

My emotions burst out of control then. With a cry I swept the water glass, the books, the vase from the table, smote my fist down upon the flat surface again and again until a thousand little pains were stabbing my flesh.

"Vampires!" I screamed. "No, no—oh God, it isn't true!"

But I knew that it was. The events of the past days rose before me in all their horror now, and I could see the black significance of every detail.

The brother, Johann—some time since the war he had become a vampire. When the woman sought him out years later he had forced this terrible existence upon her too. Yes, that was it.

With the garden as their lair the two of them had entangled poor Alessandro Larla in their serpentine coils a year before. He had loved the woman, had worshiped her madly. And then he had found the truth, the awful truth that had sent him stumbling home, stark, raving mad.

Mad, yes, but not mad enough to keep him from writing the facts in his three velvet-bound books for the world to see. He had hoped the disclosures would dispatch the woman and her brother forever. But it was not enough.

Following my thoughts, I whipped the first book from the table stand and opened the front cover. There again I saw those scrawled lines which had meant nothing to me before.

"Revelations meant to destroy but only binding without the stake. Read, fool, and enter my field, for we are chained to the spot. Oh, wo unto Larla!"

Perle von Mauren had written that. Fool that I was, unseeing fool! The books had not put an end to the evil life of her or her brother. No, only one thing could do that. Yet the exposures had not been written in vain. They were recorded for mortal posterity to see.

Those books bound the two vampires, Perle von Mauren and her brother, Johann, to the old garden, kept them from roaming the night streets in search of victims. Only him who had once passed through the gate could they pursue and attack.

It was the old metaphysical law: evil shrinking in the face of truth.

Yet if the books had bound their power in chains they had also opened a new avenue for their attacks. Once immersed in the pages of the trilogy, the reader fell helplessly into their clutches. Those printed lines had become the outer reaches of their web. They were an entrapping net within which the power of the vampires always crouched.

That was why my life had blended so strangely with the story of Larla. The moment I had cast my eyes on the opening paragraph I had fallen into their coils to do with as they had done with Larla a year before. I had been lured, drawn relentlessly into the tentacles of the woman in black. Once I was past the garden gate the binding spell of the books was gone, and they were free to pursue me and to—

A giddy sensation rose within me. Now I saw why the scientific doctor had been puzzled. Now I saw the reason for my physical weakness. Oh, the foulness of it! She had been—feasting on my blood!

With a sobbing cry I flung the book to a far corner, turned and began madly pacing up and down the room. Cold perspiration oozed from every pore. My heart pounded like a runner's. My brain ran wild.

Was I to end as Larla had ended, another victim of this loathsome being's power? Was she to gorge herself further on my life and live on?

Were others to be preyed upon and go down into the pits of despair? No, and again no! If Larla had been ignorant of the one and only way in which to dispose of such a creature, I was not. I had not vacationed in south Europe without learning something of these ancient evils. Frantically I looked about the room, took in the objects about me. A chair, a table, a taboret, one of my cameras with its long tripod. I stared at the latter as in my terror-stricken mind a plan leaped into action. With a lunge I was across the floor, had seized one of the wooden legs of the tripod in my hands. I snapped it across my knee. Then, grasping the two broken pieces, both now with sharp splintered ends, I rushed hatless out of the door to the street.

A moment later I was racing northward in a cab bound for Easterly Street.

"Hurry!" I cried to the driver as I glanced at the westering sun. "Faster, do you hear?"

We shot along the crossstreets, into the old suburbs and toward the outskirts of town. Every traffic halt found me fuming at the delay. But at length we drew up before the wall of the garden.

Tossing the driver a bill, I swung the wrought-iron gate open and with the wooden pieces of the tripod still under my arm, rushed in. The courtyard was a place of reality in the daylight, but the moldering masonry and tangled weeds were steeped in silence as before.

Straight for the house I made, climbing the rotten steps to the front entrance. The door was boarded up and locked. Smothering an impulse to scream, I retraced my steps at a run and began to circle the south wall of the building. It was this direction I had seen the woman take when she had fled after I had tried to snap her picture. The twenty-six bluejays on the wall leered at me like a flock of harpies.

Well toward the rear of the building I reached a small half-open door leading to the cellar. For a moment I hesitated there, sick with the dread of what I knew lay before me. Then, clenching hard the two wooden tripod stakes, I entered.

Inside, cloaked in gloom, a narrow corridor stretched before me. The floor was littered with rubble and fallen masonry, the ceiling interlaced with a thousand cobwebs.

I stumbled forward, my eyes quickly accustoming themselves to the half-light from the almost opaque windows. A maddening urge to leave it all and flee back to the sunlight was welling up within me now. I fought it back. Failure would mean a continuation of the horrors—a lingering death—would leave the gate open for others.

At the end of the corridor a second door barred my passage. I thrust it open—and stood swaying there on the sill staring inward. A great loathing crept over me, a stifling sense of utter repulsion. Hot blood rushed to my head. The air seemed to move upward in palpable swirls.

Beyond was a small room, barely ten feet square, with a low-raftered ceiling. And by the light of the open door I saw side by side in the center of the floor—two white wood coffins.

How long I stood there leaning weakly against the stone wall I don't know. There was a silence so profound the beating of my heart pulsed through the passage like the blows of a mallet. And there was a slow penetrating odor drifting from out of that chamber that entered my nostrils and claimed instant recognition. Heliotrope! But heliotrope defiled by the rotting smell of an ancient grave.

Then suddenly with a determination born of despair I leaped forward, rushed to the nearest coffin, seized its cover and ripped it open.

Would to heaven I could forget the sight that met my eyes. There lay Perle von Mauren, the woman in black—unveiled.

That face—how can I describe it? It was divinely beautiful, the hair black as sable, the cheeks a classic white. But the lips—oh God! those lips! I grew suddenly sick as I looked upon them. They were scarlet, crimson . . . and sticky with human blood.

I moved like an automaton then. With a low sob I reached for one of the tripod stakes, seized a flagstone from the floor and with the pointed end of the wood resting directly over the woman's heart, struck a crashing blow. The stake jumped downward. A sickening crunch—and a violent contortion shook the coffin. Up to my face rushed a warm, nauseating breath of rot and decay.

I wheeled and hurled open the lid of her brother's coffin. With only a flashing glance at the young, masculine, Teutonic face, I raised the other stake high in the air and brought it stabbing down with all the strength in my right arm. Red blood suddenly began to form a thick pool on the floor.

For an instant I stood rooted to the spot, the utter obscenity of it all searing its way into my brain like a hot sword. Even in that moment of stark horror I realized that not even the most subtle erasures of Time would be able to remove that blasphemous sight from my inner eye.

It was a scene so abysmally corrupt I pray heaven my dreams will never find it and re-envision its unholy tableau. There before me, focused in the shaft of light that filtered through the open door like the miasma from a fever swamp, lay the two white caskets.

And within them now, staring up at me from eyeless sockets—two gray and moldering skeletons, each with its hideous leering head of death.

The rest is but a vague dream. I seem to remember rushing madly outside, along the path to the gate and down the street, down Easterly, away from that accursed garden of the jays.

At length, utterly exhausted, I reached my apartment, burst open the door, and staggered in. Those mundane surroundings that confronted me were like balm to my burning eyes. But as if in mocking irony there centered into my gaze three objects lying where I had left them, the three volumes of Larla.

I moved across to them, picked them up and stared down vacantly upon their black sides. These were the hellish works that had caused it all. These were the pages that were responsible. . . .

With a low cry I turned to the grate on the other side of the room and flung the three of them onto the still glowing coals.

There was an instant hiss, and a line of yellow flame streaked upward and began eating into the velvet. I watched the fire grow higher . . . higher . . . and diminish slowly.

And as the last glowing spark died into a blackened ash there swept over me a mighty feeling of quiet and relief.

NELLIE FOSTER

August Derleth

Mrs. Kraft came hurriedly from the house, closed the white gate behind her, and half ran across the dusty street. With one hand she held her long skirts clear of the walk; with the other she pressed a white handkerchief tightly to her lips. Her dark eyes were fixed on the green and white house at the end of the block, almost hidden in the shade of overhanging elms of great age.

The gate stood open, and Mrs. Kraft stepped quickly onto the lawn, forgetting to close the gate behind her. She avoided the low veranda, going around the side of the house, and entered the kitchen through the open door at the back.

Mrs. Perkins was leafing through her recipe book when the shadow of Mrs. Kraft momentarily darkened her door. She looked up and said, "How do, Mrs. Kraft? You're out early this morning." She smiled.

Mrs. Kraft did not smile. She stood quite still, her handkerchief still pressed tightly against her mouth, nodding curtly to acknowledge her neighbor's greeting.

Mrs. Perkins looked at her oddly. "What is it, Mrs. Kraft?" she asked a little nervously.

Mrs. Kraft took the handkerchief away from her mouth, clenching it tightly in her hand, and said, "It happened again last night."

Mrs. Perkins put her recipe book aside suddenly. "How do you know?" she asked breathlessly. Her eyes were unnaturally wide.

"How do you know, Mrs. Kraft?"

Her visitor opened her hand jerkily. "It was my niece this time. She saw the woman, too. I didn't want Andrew to let the child go out last night, but she would have her way. She wanted to go to her Aunt Emmy's."

"Beyond the cemetery," breathed Mrs. Perkins. "But she came back before dark, surely?"

Mrs. Kraft shook her head. "No. At dusk, just before the street lights went on. The woman was there, standing in the road. The child was afraid, even when the woman took her hand and walked along with her."

"What did she do? Oh, I hope nothing serious happened!"

"The same as before. The woman kissed the child, and the little one went to sleep. This morning she is so weak, she couldn't get up. Loss of blood, the doctor said."

Mrs. Perkins clasped her hands helplessly in her lap. "What can we do, Mrs. Kraft? Nobody would believe us if we said what this must be."

Mrs. Kraft made an impatient movement with her head. Then she leaned forward, her dark eyes shining, speaking in a low voice. "The child knew the woman."

Mrs. Perkins started. "It wasn't . . . wasn't—"

Mrs. Kraft nodded. "Nellie Foster—not yet a month dead!"

Mrs. Perkins wove her fingers together nervously. She had gone pale, and her uneasiness was more pronounced than her visitor's.

"My niece is the third child, Mrs. Perkins. We must do something, or it will continue—and the children may die."

Mrs. Perkins said nothing. Her visitor went on.

"I'm going to do something, if you won't," she said. "Tonight I'm going to watch at the cemetery. There won't be another child to be taken like that."

"I don't know what I can do," murmured Mrs. Perkins quietly. "I get so nervous. If I saw Nellie Foster, I'd probably scream."

Mrs. Kraft shook her head firmly. "That would never do," she admitted.

"Did you go to the minister?" asked Mrs. Perkins.

Mrs. Kraft pressed her lips tightly together before she spoke. Then she said,

"He said there were no such things. He said only ignorant people believed in vampires."

Mrs. Perkins shook her head in disapproval. "He asked me how Nellie Foster could have become one, and I told him about the cat jumping over her coffin. He smiled, and wouldn't believe me." Mrs. Kraft stood up, nodding her head. "And I know it's Nellie Foster, because I was out to the cemetery this morning, and there were three little holes in the grave—like finger holes, going way down deep."

"What are you going to do?"

"I don't know yet. But I'll watch, and I won't let her get out of the cemetery."

"Maybe the men could do something," suggested Mrs. Perkins hopefully.

"It would be worse than telling the minister, to go to them. They'd laugh. If he wouldn't believe it, they wouldn't," said Mrs. Kraft scornfully. "It will be left for someone else to do."

"I wish I could help," said Mrs. Perkins.

Mrs. Kraft looked at her reflectively, her eyes hardening. "You can, if you want."

Mrs. Perkins nodded eagerly.

"If I'm to go to the cemetery, I've got to be protected."

The other woman nodded. Mrs. Kraft pursed her lips firmly. "I need something," she went on, "and I'd like to use that blessed crucifix your son brought from Belgium, the one Cardinal Mercier gave him, a very old one, he said it was."

For a moment Mrs. Perkins wavered. Her lips faltered a little. Then, quailing before the stern eyes of Mrs. Kraft, she moved noiselessly to get the crucifix.

Mrs. Kraft attached it to a black ribbon around her neck, and tucked it out of sight in the bosom of her black dress. Then she rose to go.

"I'll tell you what happened in the morning, Mrs. Perkins. And if I don't come"—Mrs. Kraft faltered—"then something's wrong. And if I'm not here before noon, you'd best go to the cemetery, perhaps, and look around a bit."

Mrs. Perkins quavered, "You don't think she'd go for you, Mrs. Kraft?"

"They don't only go for children, Mrs. Perkins. I've read about them. If they can't die, they have to have blood—and we've blood, too."

Nodding her head sagely, Mrs. Kraft went from the house, her lips still pursed, her hand still tightly clenching her handkerchief.

Mrs. Kraft sat on the back porch with Mrs. Perkins a little after sunrise the next morning. The dew was not yet gone; it hung heavily on the hollyhocks and the delphinium. The early sunlight threw long shadows across the garden.

Mrs. Kraft was talking. "I got there just after sunset and hid behind the oak tree near old Mr. Prince's grave, and watched for Nellie Foster. When the moon came up, I saw something on her grave, something gray. It was like a part of someone lying there, and it was moving. It was misty, and I couldn't see it well. Then I saw a hand, and then another, and after that a face," Mrs. Kraft coughed a little; Mrs. Perkins shuddered.

"And then?" prompted Mrs. Perkins. She leaned forward, fascinated.

"It was Nellie Foster," Mrs. Kraft went on in a low voice. "She was crawling out of her grave. I could see her plainly then in the moonlight. It was Nellie, all right. I'd know her anywhere. She pulled herself out—it was like a mist coming out of those holes in the grave, those little holes."

"What did you do?"

"I think I was scared. I didn't move. When the mist stopped coming there was Nellie standing on the grave. Then I ran toward her, holding the cross in my hand. Before I could reach her, she was gone."

Mrs. Kraft's face twisted suddenly in pain. "This morning they found the little Walters girl, like the others. I should have watched beside the grave. I should have stopped Nellie. I shouldn't have let her get out. It's my fault that the little Walters girl was attacked. My fault. I could have stopped Nellie. I could have watched there all night. I should have gone forward before she got out of the grave."

She rose suddenly, disturbed. "I'm going now, Mrs. Perkins. Let me keep the cross a little longer. I'll need it tonight."

Mrs. Perkins nodded, and her visitor was gone, her black-clothed figure walking quickly across the road. Mrs. Perkins watched her go, wondering about Nellie Foster, hoping that soon something might be done to stop her coming from her grave. There was her own little Flory to think about. What if some day Nellie Foster should see her, and then they would find little Flory? Mrs. Perkins shuddered. "Oh Lord, give me the power to do something," she thought. "Let me help." Then she thought, "And Nellie Foster

was always such a nice girl! It's hard to believe." She went into the
house, shaking her head.

She had intended to go over to see Mrs. Kraft just after dinner,
to talk about doing something, but a sudden storm struck the town,
and for six hours it raged, pouring rain, darkening the village. For
six hours only lightning flashes brightened the darkness. Then, at
seven o'clock, the sky cleared abruptly, and the setting sun came out
to finish the July day in a blaze of rainbow glory.

Mrs. Perkins finished washing the supper dishes, saw her Flory go
out to play until dark, and finally started for Mrs. Kraft's. Going out to
the sidewalk, she saw an elderly man coming quickly down the street.
Mr. Shurz, she thought. Seems in a hurry, too. She pondered this.
Something on his mind, likely. She purposely slowed her pace.

At the gate she met him. He would have gone past had he not
spied her suddenly. Then he stopped breathlessly. "Miz' Perkins,
have y'heard the news?"

Mrs. Perkins shook her head. "Lightning strike somewhere?" she
asked.

"If only 'twere that, Miz' Perkins, Ma'am. The old man shook his
head dolefully. "The like of this we've never had in this town before,
'slong as I can remember. This afternoon during the storm, someone
got into the cemetery and dug open Nellie Foster's grave!"

Mrs. Perkins leaned over the gate, her hands tightly clenched
on the pointed staves. "What?" she whispered hoarsely. "What's that
you say, Mr. Shurz?"

" 'Tis just as I say, Miz' Perkins. Some one dug into Nellie
Foster's grave, in all that storm, too, and opened the coffin, Miz'
Perkins, Ma'am, *and druv a stake clean through her body!*"

"A stake . . . through her body!" She shook her head. "Just what
Mrs. Kraft said should be done," she murmured to herself.

Mr. Shurz did not hear her. He nodded vehemently. "Clean
through, Miz' Perkins, Ma'am. And a powerful lot of blood there
were, too; 'twas a surprize to Doctor Barnes. A strange, unnatural
thing, the doctor said."

"But surely the coffin was covered again?"

"Partly, only partly, Miz' Perkins. Seems the man got scared away."

"Oh . . . it was a man, then?"

Mr. Shurz looked at her, smiling vacuously. " 'Course 'twas a
man, Miz' Perkins."

"He was seen, then?"

Mr. Shurz shook his head. "Oh, no, he wasn't seen. No, ma'am, he wasn't seen. Too slick for that, he was."

Mrs. Perkins felt her heart pounding in her breast. She felt suddenly that she was stifling. She opened the gate and stepped on to the sidewalk at Mr. Shurz's side, walking along with him. She did not hear what he was saying.

Mrs. Kraft was out on her lawn. She was pale, dishevelled. Mrs. Perkins was thinking: I hope he won't notice anything; I hope he won't notice anything. Mr. Shurz stopped with Mrs. Perkins. Mrs. Perkins could barely bring herself to say, "How do, Mrs. Kraft?"

Then, as Mr. Shurz was repeating his story to Mrs. Kraft, Mrs. Perkins's eyes fell on the stain of red clay on Mrs. Kraft's hands, a stain at first difficult to wash away. She wanted to look away from Mrs. Kraft's rough hands, but she could not. Then she noticed that Mr. Shurz had seen the stain, too.

"Bin diggin' in red clay, have you Miz' Kraft?" He laughed hollowly. "Looks mighty like that clay they dug away off Nellie Foster's coffin, now." He wagged his head.

Mrs. Perkins felt faint. She heard him talking, rambling on. Deep down in her she wanted to say something, anything, to change the subject, but she could not. Then she heard Mrs. Kraft speaking.

"I've been digging in the garden, Mr. Shurz," she smiled politely, despite her white drawn face. "This stain is mighty hard to get off your hands."

Mrs. Perkins heard herself saying, "That's right. I warned Mrs. Kraft not to touch the red clay when we were digging up her sweet william right after the storm, but she wouldn't listen." She was thinking, "Oh Lord, don't let him look into the garden; don't let him see how black the ground is there."

Mr. Shurz grinned broadly and shrugged his shoulders. " 'Tis a good time to dig a garden, after rain. Well, I must be off. We'll be catching him who meddled with Nellie Foster!"

The women, standing one on each side of the fence, watched the old man go down the street. Mrs. Perkins was afraid to look at Mrs. Kraft. Then she heard her neighbor cough lightly, and turned.

Mrs. Kraft was holding out the crucifix. "I don't think I'll need it any more, Mrs. Perkins," she was saying.

SPECIAL

Richard Laymon

The outlaw women, wailing and shrieking, fled from the encampment. All but one, who stayed to fight.

She stood by the campfire, a sleek arm reaching up to pull an arrow from the quiver on her back. She stood alone as the men began to fall beneath the quick fangs of the dozen raiding vampires.

"She's mine!" Jim shouted.

None of his fellow Guardians gave him argument. Maybe they wanted no part of her. They raced into the darkness of the woods to chase down the others.

Jim rushed the woman.

You get her and you get her.

She looked innocent, fierce, glorious. Calmly nocking the arrow. Her thick hair was golden in the firelight. Her legs gleamed beneath the short leather skirt that hung low on her hips. Her vest spread open as she drew back her bowstring, sliding away from the tawny mound of her right breast.

Jim had never seen such a woman.

Get her!

She glanced at him. Without an instant of hesitation, she pivoted away and loosed her arrow.

Jim snapped his head sideways. The shaft flew at Strang's back. Hit him with a thunk. The vampire hurled the flapping body of an outlaw from his arms and whirled around, his black eyes fixing on the woman, blood spewing from his wide mouth as he bellowed, "Mine!"

Jim lurched to a halt.

Eyes narrowed, lips a tight line, the woman reached up for another arrow as Strang staggered toward her. Jim was near enough to hear breath hissing through her nostrils. He gazed at her, fascinated, as she fit the arrow onto the bowstring. Her eyes were on Strang. She pulled the string back to her jaw. Her naked breast rose and fell as she panted for air.

She didn't let the arrow fly.

Strang took one more stumbling stride, foamy blood gushing from his mouth, arms outstretched as if to reach beyond the campfire and grab her head. Then he pitched forward. His face crushed the flaming heap of wood, sending up a flurry of sparks. His hair began to blaze.

The woman met Jim's eyes.

Get her and you get her.

He'd never wanted any woman so much.

"Run!" he whispered. "Save yourself."

"Eat shit and die," she muttered, and released her arrow. It whizzed past his arm.

Going for her, Jim couldn't believe that she had missed. But he heard the arrow punch into someone, heard the roar of a wounded vampire, and knew that she'd found her target. For the second time, she had chosen to take down a vampire rather than protect herself from him. And she hadn't run when he'd given her the chance. What kind of woman *is* this?

With his left hand, he knocked the bow aside. With his right, he swung at her face. His fist clubbed her cheek. Her head snapped sideways, mouth dropping open, spit spraying out. The punch spun her. The bow flew from her hand. Her legs tangled and she went down. She pushed at the ground, got to her hands and knees, and scurried away from Jim.

Let her go?

He hurried after her, staring at her legs. Shadows and firelight fluttered on them. Sweat glistened. The skirt was so short it barely covered her rump and groin.

You get her and you get her.

She thrust herself up.

I'm gonna let her go, Jim thought. They'll kill me, and they'll probably get her anyway, but . . .

Instead of making a break for the woods, she whirled around, jerked a knife from the sheath at her hip, and threw herself at Jim. The blade ripped the front of his shirt. Before she could bring it back across, he caught her wrist. He yanked her arm up high and drove a fist into her belly. Her breath exploded out. The blow picked her up. The power of it would've hurled her backward and slammed her to the ground, but Jim kept his grip on her wrist. She dangled in front of him, writhing and wheezing. Her sweaty face was twisted with agony.

One side of her vest hung open.

She might've had a chance.

I got her, I get her.

Jim cupped her warm, moist breast, felt its nipple pushing against his palm.

Her fist crashed into his nose. He saw it coming, but had no time to block it. Pain exploded behind his eyes. But he kept his grip, stretched her high by the trapped arm, and punched her belly until he could no longer hold her up.

Blinking tears from his eyes, sniffing up blood, he let her go. She dropped to her knees in front of him and slumped forward, her face hitting the ground between his feet. Crouching, he pulled a pair of handcuffs from his belt. Blood splashed the back of her vest as he picked up her limp arms, pulled them behind her, and snapped the cuffs around her wrists.

"THAT ONE PUT UP a hell of a scrap," Roger said.

Jim, sitting on the ground beside the crumpled body of the woman, looked up at the grinning vampire. "She was pretty tough," he said. He sniffed and swallowed some more blood. "Sorry I couldn't stop her quicker."

Roger patted him on the head. "Think nothing of it. Strang was always a pain in the ass, anyway, and Winthrop was such an atrocious brown-noser. I'm better off without them. I'd say, taken all 'round, that we've had a banner night."

Roger crouched in front of the woman, clutched the hair on top of her head, and lifted her to her knees. Her eyes were shut. By the limp way she hung there, Jim guessed she must still be unconscious.

"A looker," Roger said. "Well worth a broken nose, if you ask me." He chuckled. "Of course, it's not *my* nose. But if I were you, I'd

be a pretty damn happy fellow about now." He eased her down
gently and walked off to join the other vampires.

While they waited for all the Guardians to return with the
female prisoners, they searched the bodies of the outlaws, took
whatever possessions they found interesting, and stripped the
corpses. They tossed the clothing into the campfire, not one of
them bothering to remove Strang from the flames.

Joking and laughing quite a bit, they hacked the bodies to pieces.
The banter died away as they began to suck the remaining blood from
severed heads, stumps of necks and arms and legs, from various limbs
and organs. Jim turned his eyes away. He looked at the woman. She
was lucky to be out cold. She couldn't see the horrible carnage. She
couldn't hear the grunts and sighs of pleasure, the sloppy wet sounds,
the occasional belch from the vampires relishing their feast. Nor could
she hear the women who'd been captured and brought in by the other
Guardians. They were weeping, pleading, screaming, vomiting.

When he finally looked away from her, he saw that all the
Guardians had returned. Each had a prisoner. Bart and Harry both
had two. Most of the women looked as if they'd been beaten. Most
had been stripped of their clothes.

They looked to Jim like a sorry bunch.

Not one stood proud and defiant.

I got the best of the lot, he thought.

Roger rose to his feet, tossed a head into the fire, and rubbed
the back of his hand across his mouth. "Well, folks," he said, "how's
about heading on back to the old homestead?"

Jim picked up the woman. Carrying her on his shoulder, he
joined the procession through the woods. Other Guardians compli-
mented him on his catch. Some made lewd suggestions about her. A
few peeked under her skirt. Several offered to trade, and grumbled
when Jim refused.

At last, they found their way to the road. They hiked up its
moonlit center until they came to the bus. Biff and Steve, Guardians
who'd stayed behind to protect it from outlaws and vampire gangs,
waved greetings from its roof.

On the side of the black bus, in huge gold letters that glim-
mered with moonlight, was painted: ROGER'S ROWDY RAIDERS.

The vampires, Guardians, and prisoners climbed aboard.

Roger drove.

An hour later, they passed through the gates of his fortified estate.

THE NEXT DAY, JIM slept late. When he woke up, he lay in bed for a long time, thinking about the woman. Remembering her courage and beauty, the way her breast had felt in his hand, her weight and warmth and smoothness while she hung over his shoulder on the way to the bus.

He hoped she was all right. She'd seemed to be unconscious during the entire trip. Of course, she might've been pretending. Jim, sitting beside her, had savored the way she looked in the darkness and felt quick rushes of excitement each time a break in the trees permitted moonlight to wash across her.

The other Guardians were all busy ravishing their prisoners during the bus ride. Some had poked fun at him, asked if he'd gone queer like Biff and Steve, offered to pay him for a chance to screw Sleeping Beauty.

He wasn't sure why he had left her alone during the trip. In the past, he'd never hesitated to enjoy his prisoners.

But this woman was different. Special. Proud and strong. She deserved better than to be molested while out cold and in the presence of others.

Jim would have her soon. In privacy. She would be alert, brave, and fierce.

Soon.

But not today.

For today, the new arrivals would be in the care of Doc and his crew. They would be deloused and showered, then examined. Those judged incapable of bearing children would go to the Doner Ward. Each Doner had a two-fold job: to give a pint of blood daily for the estate's stockroom, and to provide sexual services not only for the Guardian who captured her but also for any others, so inclined, once he'd finished.

The other prisoners would find themselves in the Specialty Suite.

It wasn't a suite, just a barracklike room similar to the Doner Ward. But those assigned to it did receive special treatment. They weren't milked for blood. They were fed well.

And each Special could only be used by the Guardian who had captured her.

Mine will be a Special, Jim thought. She's gotta be. She *will* be. She's young and strong.

She'll be mine. All mine.

At least till Delivery Day.

He felt a cold, spreading heaviness.

That's a long time from now, he told himself. Don't think about it.

Moaning, he climbed out of bed.

He was standing guard in the north tower at ten the next morning when the two-way radio squawked and Doc's voice came through the speaker. "Harmon, you're up. Specialty Suite, Honors Room Three. Bennington's on his way to relieve you."

Jim thumbed the speak button on his mike. "Roger," he said.

Heart pounding, he waited for Bennington. He'd found out last night that his prisoner, named Diane, had been designated a Special. He'd hoped this would be the day, but he hadn't counted on it; Doc only gave the okay if the timing was right. In Doc's opinion, it was only right during about two weeks of each woman's monthly cycle.

Jim couldn't believe his luck.

Finally, Bennington arrived. Jim climbed down from the tower and made his way across the courtyard toward the Specialty Suite. He had a hard time breathing. His legs felt weak and shaky.

He'd been in Honor Rooms before. With many different outlaw women. But he'd never felt like this: excited, horribly excited, but also nervous. Petrified.

Honors Room Three had a single large bed with red satin sheets. The plush carpet was red. So were the curtains that draped the barred windows, and the shades of the twin lamps on either side of the bed.

Jim sat down on a soft, upholstered armchair. And waited. Trembling.

Calm down, he told himself. This is crazy. She's just a woman.

Yeah, sure.

Hearing footfalls from the corridor, he leapt to his feet. He turned to the door. Watched it open.

Diane stumbled in, shoved from behind by Morgan and Donner, Doc's burly assistants. She glared at Jim.

"Key," Jim said.

Morgan shook his head. "I wouldn't, if I were you."

"I brought her in, didn't I?"

"She'll bust more than your nose, you give her half a chance."

Jim held out his hand. Morgan, shrugging, tossed him the key to the shackles. Then the two men left the room. The door bumped shut, locking automatically.

And he was alone with Diane.

From the looks of her, she'd struggled on the way to the Honors Room. Her thick hair was mussed, golden wisps hanging down her face. Her blue satin robe had fallen off one shoulder. Its cloth belt was loose, allowing a narrow gap from her waist to the hem at her knees. She was naked beneath the robe.

Jim slipped a finger under the belt. He pulled until its half-knot came apart. Then he spread the robe and slipped it down her arms until it was stopped by the wrist shackles.

Guilt subdued his excitement when he saw the livid smudges on her belly. "I'm sorry about that," he murmured.

"Do what you're going to do," she said. Though she was trying to sound tough, he heard a slight tremor in her voice.

"I'll take these shackles off," he said. "But if you fight me, I'll be forced to hurt you again. I don't want to do that."

"Then don't take them off."

"It'll be easier on you without them."

"Easier *for* you.

"Do you know why you're here?"

"It seems pretty obvious."

"It's not that obvious," Jim said, warning himself to speak with care. The room was bugged. A Guardian in the Security Center would be eavesdropping, and Roger himself was fond of listening to the Honors Room tapes. "This isn't . . . just so I can have fun and games with you. The thing is . . . I've got to make you pregnant."

Her eyes narrowed. She caught her lower lip between her teeth. She said nothing.

"What that means," Jim went on, "is that we'll be seeing each other every day. At least during your fertile times. Every day until you conceive. Do you understand?"

"Why do they want me pregnant?" she asked.

"They need more humans. For guards and staff and things. As it is, there aren't enough of us."

She gazed into his eyes. He couldn't tell whether or not she believed the lie.

"If you don't become pregnant, they'll put you in with the Doners. It's much better for you here. The Doners . . . all the Guardians can have them whenever they want."

"So, it's either you or the whole gang, huh?"

"That's right."

"Okay."

"Okay?"

She nodded.

Jim began taking off his clothes, excited but uncomfortably aware of the scorn in her eyes.

"You must be a terrible coward," she said.

He felt heat spread over his skin.

"You don't seem evil. So you must be a coward. To serve such beasts."

"Roger treats us very well," he said.

"If you were a man, you'd kill him and all his kind. Or die trying."

"I have a good life here."

"The life of a dog."

Naked, he crouched in front of Diane. His face was inches from her tuft of golden down. Aching with a hot confusion of lust and shame, he lowered his eyes to the short length of chain stretched taut between her feet. "I'm no coward," he said, and removed the steel cuffs.

As the shackles fell to the carpet, she pumped a knee into his forehead. Not a powerful blow, but enough to knock him off balance. His rump hit the floor. He caught himself with both hands while Diane dropped backward, curling, jamming her thighs tight against her chest. Before he could get up, she somehow slipped the hand shackles and trapped robe under her buttocks and up the backs of her legs. They cleared her feet. Her hands were suddenly in front of her, cuffs and chain hidden under the draping robe.

As her heels thudded the floor, Jim rushed her. She spread her legs wide, raised her knees, and stretched her arms out straight overhead. The robe was a glossy curtain molded to her face and breasts.

Jim dove, slamming down on her. She grunted. Clamped her legs around him. He reached for her arms. They were too quick for him. The covered chain swept past his eyes. Went tight around his throat. Squeezed.

Choking, he found her wrists. They were crossed behind his head. He tugged at them. Parted them. Felt the chain loosen. Forced them down until the chain pressed into Diane's throat.

Her face had come uncovered. Her eyes bulged. Her lips peeled back. She twisted and bucked and squirmed.

When he entered her, tears shimmered in her eyes.

THE NEXT DAY, JIM let Morgan and Donner chain her to the bed frame before leaving.

She didn't say a word. She didn't struggle. She lay motionless and glared at Jim as he took her.

When he was done but still buried in her tight heat, he whispered, "I'm sorry." He hoped the microphone didn't pick it up.

For an instant, the look of hatred in her eyes changed to something else. Curiosity? Hope?

"What are you sorry about, Jim?"

"Sorry?"

"You apologized. What did you apologize for?"

"To who?"

"YOU'VE GONE SOFT ON her," Roger said. "Can't say I blame you. She's quite a looker. Feisty too. But she's obviously messing you up. I'm afraid someone else'll have to take over. We'll work a trade with Phil. You can do his gal, and he'll do yours. It'll be better for everyone."

"Yes, sir."

Phil's gal was named Betsy. She was a brunette. She was pretty. She was stacked. She was not just compliant, but enthusiastic. She said that she'd hated being an outlaw, living in the wilds, often hungry and always afraid. This, she said, was like paradise.

Jim had her once a day.

Each time, he closed his eyes and made believe she was Diane.

HE LONGED FOR HER. He dreamed about her. But she was confined to the Specialty Suite, available only to Phil, so he would probably never have a chance to see her again. It ate at him. He began to hope she would fail to conceive. In that case, she would eventually be sent to the Doner Ward.

A terrible fate for someone with her spirit. But at least Jim would be able to see her, go to her, touch her, have her. And she would be spared the final horror which awaited the Specials. Doc had judged her to be fertile, however, so Jim knew there was little chance of ever seeing her again.

Jim was in the Mess Hall a week after being reassigned to Betsy, trying to eat lunch though he had no appetite, when the alarm suddenly blared. The PA boomed, "Guardian down, Honor Room One! Make it snappy, men!"

Jim and six others ran from the Mess Hall. Sprinting across the courtyard, he took over the lead. He found Donner waiting in the corridor. The man, gray and shaky, pointed at the closed door of Honor Room One.

Jim threw the door open.

Instead of a bed, this room was equipped with a network of steel bars from which the Special could be suspended, stretched, and spread in a variety of positions.

Diane hung by her wrists from a high bar. There were no restraints on her feet. She was swinging and twisting at the ends of her chains as she kicked at Morgan. Her face wore a fierce grimace. Her hair clung to her face. Her skin, apparently oiled by Phil, gleamed and poured sweat. The shackles had cut into her wrists, and blood streamed down her arms and sides.

Phil lay motionless on the floor beneath her wild, kicking body. His head was turned. Too much.

She'd broken his neck?

How could she?

Even as Jim wondered, he saw Morgan lurch forward and grab one of her darting ankles. Diane shot her other leg high. With a cry of pain, she twisted her body and hooked her foot behind Morgan's head. The big man stumbled toward her, gasping with alarm. He lost his hold on her ankle. That leg flew up. In an instant, he was on his knees, his head trapped between her thighs.

Morgan's dilemma seemed to snap the audience of Guardians out of their stunned fascination.

Jim joined the others in their rush to the rescue.

He grabbed one leg. Bart grabbed the other. They forced her thighs apart, freeing Morgan. The man slumped on top of Phil's body, made a quick little whimpery sound, and scurried backward.

"Take Phil out of here," said Rooney, the head Guardian.

The body was dragged from under Diane and taken from the room.

"What'll we do with her?" Jim asked

"Let her hang," Rooney said. "We'll wait for tonight and let Roger take care of her."

They released her legs and backed up quickly.

She dangled, swaying back and forth, her eyes fixed on Jim.
He paused in the doorway. He knew he would never see her
again.

HE WAS WRONG.

He saw her a month later when he relieved Biff and began his new
duty of monitoring video screens in the Security Center. Diane was on
one of the dozen small screens. Alone. In the Punishment Room.

Jim couldn't believe his eyes. He'd been certain that Roger had
killed her—probably torturing her, allowing the other vampires
small samples of her blood before draining her himself. Jim had seen
that done, once, to a Doner who tried to escape. Diane's crime had
been much worse. She'd murdered a Guardian.

Instead of taking her life, however, Roger had merely sent her
to the Punishment Room. Which amounted to little more than solitary confinement.

Incredible. Wonderful.

NIGHT AFTER NIGHT, ALONE in the Security Center, Jim watched her.

He watched her sleep on the concrete floor, a sheet wrapped
around her naked body. He watched her sit motionless, crosslegged,
gazing at the walls. He watched her squat on a metal bucket to
relieve herself. Sometimes, she gave herself sponge baths.

Frequently, she exercised. For hours at a time, she would
stretch, run in place, kick and leap, do sit-ups and push-ups and
handstands. Jim loved to watch her quick, graceful motions, the
flow of her sleek muscles, the way her hair danced and how her
breasts jiggled and swayed. He loved the sheen of sweat that made
her body glisten.

He could never see enough of her.

Every day, he waited eagerly for the hour when he could relieve
Biff and be alone with Diane.

When he had to go on night raids, he was miserable. But he did
his duty. He rounded up outlaw women. Some became Specials, and
he visited them in Honor Rooms, but when he was with them he
always tried to pretend they were Diane.

Then one night, watching her exercise, he noticed that her
belly didn't look quite flat.

"No," he murmured.

THROUGHOUT THE WINTER, HE watched her grow. Every night, she seemed larger. Her breasts swelled and her belly became a bulging mound.

He often wondered whose child she was bearing. It might be his. It might be Phil's.

He worried, always, about Delivery Day.

DURING HIS FREE TIME, he began making solitary treks into the woods surrounding the estate.

He took his submachine gun and machete.

He often came back with game, which he delivered afterward to Jones in the kitchen. The grinning chef was always delighted to receive the fresh meat. He was glad to have Jim's company while he prepared it for the Guardians' evening meal.

SPRING CAME. ONE MORNING at six, just as Bart entered the Security Center to relieve Jim of his watch, Diane flinched awake grimacing. She drew her knees up. She clutched her huge belly through the sheet.

"What gives?" Bart asked.

Jim shook his head.

Bart studied the monitor. "She's starting contractions. I'd better ring up Doc."

Bart made the call. Then he took over Jim's seat in front of the video screens.

"I think I'll stick around," Jim said.

Bart chuckled. "Help yourself."

He stayed. He watched the monitor. Soon, Doc and Morgan and Donner entered the cell. They flung the sheet aside. Morgan and Donner forced Diane's legs apart. Doc inspected her. Then they lifted her onto a gurney and strapped her down. They rolled the gurney out of the cell.

"I'll pick 'em up in the Prep Room," Bart muttered. "That's what you want to see, right?" He leered over his shoulder.

Jim forced a smile. "You got it."

Bart fingered some buttons. The deserted Punishment Room vanished from the screen, and the Prep Room appeared.

Doc and his assistants rolled the gurney in.

He soaked a pad with chloroform and pressed it against Diane's nose and mouth until she passed out. Then the straps were unfastened. After being sprayed with water, she was rubbed with white foam. All three men went at her with razors.

"Wouldn't mind that job," Bart said.

Jim watched the razors sweep paths through the foam, cutting away not only Diane's thick golden hair, but also the fine down. The passage of the blades left her skin shiny and pink. After a while, she was turned over so the rest of her body could be lathered and shaved.

Then the men rinsed her and dried her with towels.

They carried her from the gurney to the wheeled, oak serving table. The table, a rectangle large enough to seat only six, was bordered by brass gutters for catching the runoff. At the corners of one end—Roger's end—were brass stirrups.

Feeling sick, Jim watched the men lift Diane's limp body onto the table. They bent her legs. They strapped her feet into the stirrups. They slid her forward to put her within easy reach of Roger. Then they cinched a belt across her chest, just beneath her breasts. They stretched her arms overhead and strapped her wrists to the table.

"That's about it for now," Bart said. "If you drop by around seven tonight, that's about when they'll be basting her. She'll be awake then too. That's about the time the panic really hits them. It's usually quite a sight to behold."

"I've seen," Jim muttered, and left the room.

HE RETURNED TO THE barracks and tried to sleep. It was no use. Finally, he got up and armed himself. Steve let him out the front gate. He wandered the woods for hours. With his submachine gun, he bagged three squirrels.

In the late afternoon, he ducked into the hiding place he'd found in a clump of bushes. He lashed together the twenty wooden spears which he'd fashioned during the past weeks. He pocketed the small pouch containing the nightcap mushrooms which he had gathered and ground to fine powder.

He carried the spears to the edge of the forest. Leaving them propped against a tree, he stepped into the open. He smiled and waved his squirrels at the north tower. The gate opened, and he entered the estate.

He took the squirrels to Jones in the kitchen. And helped the cheerful chef prepare stew for the Guardians' supper.

JUST AFTER SUNSET, JIM went to the Security Center and knocked.

"Yo." Biff's voice.

"It's Jim. I want to see the basting."

"You're a little early," Biff said. Moments later, he opened the door. He exhaled sharply and folded over as Jim rammed a knife into his stomach.

DIANE WAS AWAKE, SWEATY and grunting, struggling against the restraints, gritting her teeth and flinching rigid each time a contraction hit her.

Jim stared at the screen. Without hair and eyebrows, she looked so *odd*. Freakish. Even her figure, misshapen by the distended belly and swollen breasts, seemed alien. But her eyes were pure Diane. In spite of her pain and terror, they were proud, unyielding.

Doc entered the Prep Room, examined her for a few moments, then went away.

Jim checked the other screens.

In the Doner Ward, the women had been locked down for the Guardians' evening mealtime. Some slept. Others chatted with friends in neighboring beds. Jim made a quick count.

In the Specialty Suite, Morgan and Donner were just returning a woman from an Honors Room. They led her to one of the ten empty beds, shoved her down on it, and shackled her feet to the metal frame. Jim counted heads.

Thirty-two Doners. Only sixteen Specials. Generally, however, the Doners were older women who'd been weakened by the daily loss of blood and by regular mistreatment at the hands of the Guardians. The Specials were fewer in number, but younger and stronger. Though some appeared to be in late stages of their pregnancies, most were not very far along, and many of the newer ones had probably not even conceived yet.

It'll be the Specials, Jim decided.

He watched Morgan and Donner leave the suite.

In the mess hall, Guardians began to eat their stew.

In the floodlit courtyard, Steven and Bennington climbed stairs to the north and west towers, carrying pots of dinner to the men on watch duty. When they finished there, they should be heading for the other two towers.

Morgan and Donner entered the mess hall. They sat down, and Jones brought them pots of stew.

Doc entered the Prep Room. He set a bowl of shimmering red fluid onto the table beside Diane's hip. He dipped in a brush. He began to paint her body. The blood coated her like paint.

In the mess hall, Baxter groaned and staggered away from the table, clutching his belly.

In the Banquet Room, there was no camera. But Jim knew that Roger and his pals would be there, waiting and eager. The absence of the usual table would've already tipped them off that tonight would be special. Even now, Roger was probably picking five to sit with him at the serving table. The unfortunate four would only get to watch and dine on their usual fare of Doner blood.

In the mess hall, Guardians were stumbling about, falling down, rolling on the floor.

In the Prep Room, Doc set aside the brush and bowl. He rolled the serving table toward the door. Diane shook her crimson, hairless head from side to side and writhed against the restraints.

Jim rushed out of the Security Center.

"ALL HELL'S BROKEN LOOSE!" he shouted as he raced up the stairs to the north tower. "Don't touch your food! Jones poisoned it!"

"Oh shit!" Harris blurted, and spat out a mouthful.

"Did you swallow any?" Jim asked, rushing toward him.

"Not much, but . . . "

Jim jerked the knife from the back of his belt and slashed Harris'sthroat. He punched a button on the control panel.

By the time he reached the front gate, it was open. He ran out, dashed across the clear area beyond the wall, and grabbed the bundle of spears.

The gate remained open for him. Apparently, the poison had taken care of the Guardian on the west tower.

Rushing across the courtyard, he saw two Guardians squirming on the ground.

At the outer door of the Specialty Suite, Jim snatched the master key off its nail. He threw the door open and rushed in.

"All right, ladies! Listen up! We're gonna kill some vampires!"

BLASTS POUNDING HIS EARS, Jim blew apart the lock. He threw his gun aside, kicked the door, and charged into the Banquet Room.

Followed by sixteen naked Specials yelling and brandishing spears.

For just an instant, the vampires around the serving table continued to go about their business—greedily lapping the brown, dry blood from Diane's face and breasts and legs as Roger groped between her thighs. The four who watched, goblets in hand, were the first to respond.

Then, roaring, they all abandoned the table and attacked.

All except Roger.

Roger stood where he was. He met Jim's eyes. *"You dumb fuck!"* he shouted. "Take care of him, guys!"

The vampires tried. They all rushed Jim.

But were met, first, by Specials. Some went down with spears in their chests while others tossed the women away or slammed them to the floor or snapped their spines or ripped out their throats.

Jim rushed through the melee. He halted at the near end of the table as Roger cried out, "Is *this* why you're here?" His hands delved. Came up a moment later with a tiny, gleaming infant. "Not enough to share, I'm afraid." Grinning, he raised the child to his mouth. With a quick nip, he severed its umbilical cord.

One hand clutching the baby's feet, he raised it high and tilted back his head. His mouth opened wide. His other hand grasped the top of its head.

Ready to twist it off. Ready to enjoy his special, rare treat.

"No!" Diane shrieked.

Jim hurled his spear. Roger's hand darted down. He caught the shaft, stopping its flight even as the wooden point touched his chest. "Dickhead," he said. "You didn't really think . . . "

Jim launched himself at Diane. He flew over her body, smashed down on her, slid through the wide *V* of her spread legs and reached high and grabbed the spear and rammed it deep into Roger's chest.

The vampire bellowed. He staggered backward. Coughed. Blood exploded from his mouth, spraying Jim's face and arms. He dropped to his knees and looked up at the infant that he still held high. He lowered its head toward his wide, gushing mouth.

Jim flung himself off the end of the table and landed on the spear. As its shaft snapped under his weight, bloody vomit cascaded over his head. Pushing himself up, he saw the baby dangling over Roger's mouth. The vampire snapped futilely at its head. Jim scurried forward and grabbed the child as Roger let go and slumped against the floor.

AFTERWARD, THE DONERS WERE released.

They helped with the burials.

Eleven dead Specials were buried in the courtyard, their graves marked by crosses fashioned of spears.

Morgan, Donner, and the Guardians, who'd all succumbed to the poison, were buried beyond the south wall of the estate.

The corpses of Roger and his fellow vampires were taken into the woods to a clearing where two trails crossed. The heads were severed. The torsos were buried with the spears still in place. The heads were carried a mile away to another crossing in the trail. There, they were burned. The charred skulls were crushed, then buried.

After a vote by the women, Doc and three Guardians who'd missed the poisoned squirrels were put to death. Jones had also missed the meal. But the women seemed to like him. He was appointed chef. Jim was appointed leader.

He chose Diane to be his assistant.

The child was a girl. They named her Glory. She had Diane's eyes, and ears that stuck out in very much the same way as Jim's.

The small army lived in Roger's estate, and seemed happy.

Frequently, when the weather was good, a squad of well-armed volunteers would board the bus. Jim driving, they would follow roads deep into the woods. They would park the bus and wander about, searching. Sometimes they found vampires and took them down with a shower of arrows. Sometimes they found bands of outlaws and welcomed these strangers into their ranks.

ONE MORNING, WHEN A commotion in the courtyard drew Jim's attention, he looked down from the north tower and saw Diane gathered around the bus with half a dozen other women. Instead of their usual leather skirts and vests, they were dressed in rags.

Diane saw him watching, and waved. Her hair had grown, but it was still quite short. It shone like gold in the sunlight.

She looked innocent, glorious.

She and her friends were painting the bus pink.

GOD-LESS MEN

James Kisner

East Texas:

The people of Shannonbaugh, a dirtball little town on the outskirts of nowhere, had a problem.

Somebody was killing their young women in an unusual way—
draining them of their blood through holes in their necks.

Like in the movies. Like when vampires did it.

Sheriff Lucas McIntyre didn't buy that vampire bullshit, but he
did know one thing: people didn't keep running after they got hit
with two or maybe three .357 Magnum slugs.

Not regular people anyhow. But the guy Lucas saw running
away from the car with the dead young woman in it took the shots
he fired at him—Lucas saw him jerk with the impact—but didn't
stop for a second.

Lucas had tried to follow the trail of blood the guy left, but it
went only a few feet then suddenly disappeared. As if the guy himself had somehow disappeared.

It didn't make a damn bit of sense.

LUCAS HAD TO TELL the preacher, Reverend John Satchel, about the
dead woman personally. She was the preacher's daughter.

Reverend Satchel was in his late fifties, a medium-sized man
who generally wore a wide-brimmed black felt hat, a plaid shirt,

and jeans when he wasn't in the pulpit. His face was craggy and weatherbeaten, the face of a man who had seen too much—even before this tragedy.

Rumor was that before he replaced the late Reverend Paige, Satchel was involved with snake-handling cults and other renegade Christian sects. He'd neither confirm nor deny the rumors. But his visage bore the stamp of having seen hellfire up close and personal, like no other preacher.

His son had been in trouble with the law a couple of times, mostly because of drinking and driving, and his daughter had been his only solace in life. She was a good Christian girl who made her father proud—who would've made her mother proud, too, if Lona Satchel hadn't passed on ten years before.

Satchel turned from the dead girl on the table in the clinic, trembling and nodding his bald head.

"A God-less man did this," he muttered, wiping his brow with an orange bandanna. "God-less man took my Beth."

"This is number six," Lucas said quietly. "It's more than I can handle, Reverend. We need the Feds now, for sure. I should've called them in sooner—before this . . . "

"I know of a man," Satchel said, turning his bloodshot eyes in Lucas's direction, his bushy eyebrows dripping from the heat, "a man who is a specialist in these matters."

"What in hell you mean, Reverend?"

"A tracker. A *real* detective who's dealt with this kind of evil before. The *federals* will not take it seriously and they will not catch our man."

"But, Reverend, don't you think we should . . . ?"

Satchel stood firm, staring up in Lucas's eyes with a determination that scared the young man. "I know what's right, by God. I'm a preacher." He lowered his gravelly voice an octave. "And it takes a God-less man to catch another one."

"I don't understand."

"You shot him. He kept on going. You're not dealing with a normal man. Maybe not even a *mortal* man. Maybe some kind of monster. Whatever he or it is, is certainly not something of God."

Lucas realized Satchel was buying into the vampire theory, though he didn't come right out and say it. What kind of preacher would believe in vampires? And what was this heavy talk about "God-less" men?

Lucas tried to argue, but the preacher wouldn't budge. So the sheriff agreed to call in the specialist, the vampire hunter.

How could he deny Satchel when his daughter had been slain?

IT WAS ANOTHER HOT day that July when the diminutive, bronze-skinned man appeared in Lucas's small office, but the man didn't remove his straw hat or wipe his brow, despite the lack of air conditioning. He wasn't even sweating.

Lucas, thirty-five, with thinning blond hair and azure blue eyes, remained behind his desk, staring up at the short Indian with ill-concealed disdain. His own shirt was soaked, and the fan buzzing in the corner offered little respite from the humidity.

"You don't look like a detective, Cochise," he said. He leaned back in his chair a bit to give his guest a look at his lanky, tall body and the gun at his side. He always greeted strangers in more a physical than a verbal way, figuring it was best to intimidate anyone who might cause trouble before they even thought about it.

"I'm not a detective. I just get paid for what I do, White Eyes." The man evidently wasn't impressed by Lucas's body language. "And my name is not 'Cochise.' "

Lucas relaxed a little. He'd had dealings with Indians before and knew some of them were hard-headed and easily offended. This one, though small, had an air of confidence about him, a no-bullshit stance that Lucas had to admire.

"Sit down, Mr. . . . ?"

"Sundance. Joe Sundance."

"Right, Sundance." He watched as Sundance sat down rather stiffly in the folding chair at the corner of his desk. The Indian wore a denim shirt and jeans, with snakeskin boots. He made eye contact with Lucas without flinching, another admirable trait in the sheriff's book of reckoning.

"What's your problem?" Sundance asked.

Lucas looked away, out the window at the cracked pavement running through the center of town. Across the street he saw a rich local climbing into a red Cadillac after leaving the hardware store. A kid rode past on a small bicycle. Then a big red dog ambled by in the opposite direction, his nose to the ground, following some odd scent. Lucas suddenly felt foolish; Shannonbaugh was a small, *normal* town. Weird things just did not happen here. Six girls didn't get killed savagely. By a monster.

Yet he had invited a man who was known as a vampire hunter to come help him. As if that were normal police procedure. He hadn't anticipated how ridiculous and foolish he would feel when the time came to deal with the man.

Sundance waited patiently.

Damn him, Lucas thought, wishing he'd go away. Finally, he said, "Well, we've had a slew of killings lately, and the evidence points to something—well, maybe I don't know—something unusual." He wondered how Satchel even *knew* about people like this Sundance guy. Maybe the old man had handled more than snakes in his time.

"You don't believe in Changers, do you?"

Lucas was caught off guard both by the question and the Indian's unaffected manner of speaking. "What the hell do you mean?"

"Changers. Vampires."

"Oh. Hell, no, I don't. Why should I?"

"Because that is what is killing women here, and that is what will continue to kill them until it is stopped."

"I think it's just some sick bastard."

"Could be. Some people like to think they are Changers, just like some people like to think they are God, or trees."

"Why would anyone like to think he was a damn tree?"

"Why would anyone like to think he was a damn vampire?"

"I don't know."

"Me, neither." Sundance almost smiled, but his rugged face wasn't built for handling that expression. His long black hair was streaked with gray, and Lucas guessed he was fifty or so, though it was hard to tell with Indians. He might be a hundred.

"Let's cut through all the crap, Sundance," Lucas bristled. "I was against calling you here, but you're here now, so maybe you can help me. I don't have but one deputy and he's part-time and dumber than owl shit to boot. You're probably a good tracker if nothing else, so, whether this character is a vampire or not, you're hired."

"Fine with me. You don't have to believe if you don't want to."

"So what do you normally do first?"

"I want to see his latest victim—if you haven't buried her yet."

"No problem. She's in cold storage over at the clinic, which serves as funeral home and morgue in this town."

"Let's go. We need to do much before nightfall."

"Why's that?"

"He will strike again tonight. I feel it."

Lucas said nothing. He realized he was going to be weirded out by the Indian no matter what he said or did and decided, grudgingly, to accept it. He grabbed his hat, motioned to the door, and followed Sundance out into the hot sun.

SHE WAS ABOUT NINETEEN, and even with most of the blood gone from her body, it was evident Beth was attractive, especially with that long blonde hair. It was a damn shame the killer was picking out the best local specimens of womanhood to prey on.

Why couldn't he attack nasty fat old women with bitchy attitudes that not many people would miss?

Lucas considered asking Sundance that, but the little man was busy studying the holes on Beth's neck.

"Judging from the space between the holes, I'd say this Changer is an adult."

"I could've told you that. I shot the son of a bitch."

"I know. Preacher Satchel told me. I was stating the fact for the record."

Lucas started to ask "What record?" but decided against it.

"So what else?"

"If a chemist took some blood from the wounds, he would find a substance there such as vampire bats secrete when they feed on animals—something in their saliva that keeps the blood from coagulating."

"Should I get someone to examine it?"

"If you want. Makes no difference now. Woman is dead."

"But that'd prove something, wouldn't it?"

"Proves your killer is a Changer and not a madman who only *thinks* he's one. But woman still is dead, and so will the next one be. Do what you want. Now take me to where she was found."

About two miles outside of town was a Lover's Lane, on an old gravel road that led up to a ridge overlooking a forest, where the preacher's daughter had been found in her car.

"Now Beth was a good girl," Lucas told Sundance, "but she wasn't perfect. The preacher knew she went out occasionally, though I doubt she let anyone go all the way with her. So I figure she was making out with the guy, then he kills her. The damnedest thing about it is there are no signs of struggle. How in hell could he do that to her without her fighting back?"

"Magic eyes."

"Say what?"

"Hypnotism. Changers are like snakes who hypnotize birds. The woman submitted without fighting. As I suspect the other victims apparently did."

"That's right," Lucas admitted.

"Bad sign."

"Why?"

"A lunatic may think he's a vampire, but he usually has to kill, then drink. Only a true Changer has the magic eyes to drink while the victim lives."

"Maybe not. Maybe he . . . " Lucas had no "maybe" to apply now that he thought about it.

Sundance asked to see where the man had run to and Lucas showed him. There were still dark brown spots on the ground where the blood had leaked.

"And it stops here."

"Bad sign." Sundance was down on his haunches, dipping his finger in the browned dirt. He wet his finger so dirt would stick to it, then brought it up to his nose to sniff. "Bad sign."

"Now what?"

"Two possibilities, both bad. One is Changer has special blood that coagulates almost instantly. Ordinary bullets may make hole, but not for long. By now, he's probably healed."

"Bullshit."

"The universe is full of bullshit, Sheriff."

"What's the other possibility?"

"He took off like an eagle. Some Changers can become different animals, depending on the necessity of the moment."

"Now you *are* bullshitting me, Sherlock." Lucas removed his hat and wiped his forehead, marveling again at how the Indian didn't sweat.

"I don't make the rules," Sundance replied. "I only report the facts." A cool breeze came out of nowhere, and he shivered. "Tonight will be a good time for the Changer. It will rain. It will be hard to find him in time. He will not expect us."

"How the hell will we know where to look? He's killed in several different places."

"I have an idea where he will *come* from."

Lucas scratched his head in amazement. "How in blazes could you have an idea? We don't have a goddamn clue."

"There are no atheists in foxholes, Sheriff. Remember that when the time comes."

Lucas's mouth dropped open at the apparent non-sequitur. Was Sundance being inscrutable to irritate him, or did his words really mean something?

Or was it all a bunch of crap, a show for the gullible White Man resented by all Indians?

Lucas decided to wait and see. But if Sundance *was* jerking him around, he'd kick his ass from here to Houston.

AN HOUR BEFORE SUNSET, after a quick dinner at Belle's Cafe and Service Station, Joe Sundance and Sheriff Lucas McIntyre went together to gather what Sundance called his "trapping apparatus," which he kept in a cloth bag behind the bench seat in the ancient Chevy pickup truck he drove.

Sundance struggled to unwedge the heavy bag from its hiding place. When he finally pulled it loose and set it on the ground, Lucas saw it was three feet long, about a foot and a half high, and another foot or so deep. A beaded figure was sewn on one side of the bag—some kind of bird as far as Lucas could make it out—and on the other side was a representation of a crucifix, not in beads, but in embroidery.

Lucas had to ask, "You a Christian?"

"I am a God-fearing man."

"But are you a Christian?"

"No. I worship my Gods."

"Then why the cross on the suitcase?"

"You never see a vampire movie?"

"Now, Sundance, don't try to tell me that even half the horsecrap in a movie is . . ."

" . . . more than half is based on some legend which some people believe somewhere. In every part of the world there have been Changers, some say since the beginning of time. So every part of the world has a way of dealing with them. Myself, I am a pragmatist."

"A what?"

"A practical man. I don't have to believe in Jesus for Him—or in this case His symbol—to have power. I've got Holy Water, garlic, ten-inch spikes, a wooden stake and mallet, among other things in my bag, as well as a well-honed *kukri*—in short, my friend, all the necessities for killing Changers, vampires, or even mortal men."

"What the hell is a 'coo-kree'?"

Sundance almost smiled as a child might who wanted to show off his toys, then knelt, unzipped the bag, and pulled out a knife with a curved blade that was at least a foot long.

"This is a *kukri*, Sheriff. Ask a Vietnam vet. This weapon can behead a man with a single motion." Sundance demonstrated by slicing the air, and Lucas shuddered.

"Put that goddamn sickle away. I'm not going to let you go around chopping people's heads off."

"You may want me to when the time comes. Chop off Changer's head, destroy it, or stuff mouth with garlic, bury—Changer dead for good."

"You're a sick fuck," Lucas said solemnly. "I've half a mind to send you packing."

"Wait till after tonight, Sheriff. After I do my job."

Lucas watched Sundance drop the knife in the bag, then take out a small brass crucifix before zipping it shut. He tucked it in one of his shirt pockets and stood.

"All right, Sundance," Lucas said, "you get one chance."

"One is all I need." He cast his eyes to the sky. The temperature had dropped ten degrees and dark clouds were forming overhead. "Here comes the rain. And night soon, too." He hefted the bag over his shoulder by its strap. "Come, it's time to go after the Changer. He should be stirring soon."

"But where the hell are we going?"

Sundance got into the sheriff's car, tossing the bag in the back seat and closing the door on the passenger side. "You're driving."

Lucas got in and slammed his door shut. "Where, for God's sake?"

"The good preacher's house—drive there."

"Now, wait a minute . . . "

"We have no time for argument, Sheriff. Besides, what have you got to lose?"

"Just my badge."

"Better than losing your ass, Sheriff. Take it from one who knows."

Lucas grumbled, then started the engine as the first big drops of rain pelted the windshield. He switched on the wipers, put the car in drive, then drove slowly to the edge of town, while Sundance sat and watched quietly.

By the time they reached Satchel's home, the rain was a dense sheet before them, and the sky had darkened.

It was night at last, and Sundance finally showed some fear. The little man was sweating like a pig as Lucas turned off the engine. Lucas rested his hand casually on his .357, determined to be ready for something, even if he wasn't sure what it was.

They sat and watched and waited while the rain fell and it grew darker and darker.

THE REVEREND'S HOUSE WAS a small old frame structure, one story high, with a pointed roof. There was a porch out front on which sat a rusty swing glider, which the wind was causing to sway back and forth, making it emit tiny shrieks.

"Somebody ought to 'oil that thing," Lucas whispered.

Sundance said nothing. They were parked off the road on the edge of the woods that circled part of the town. They could see both the front and back door of the house. Sundance watched intently, barely breathing it seemed to Lucas, as if he were a cat and not a man.

After an hour of sitting in the rain, listening to the porch glider squeak and seeing nothing, Lucas spoke up.

"Why are we here?"

"You will see."

"You know, Reverend Satchel recommended you, though I don't know how the hell he would know about a guy like you."

"People who need me find me," Sundance said simply.

"What I'm getting at—well, if Satchel called you, why are we watching him?" Lucas cast an uneasy glance at Sundance. "Damn, you don't think *he's* the killer?"

"No, I don't."

"Then who . . . ?"

Sundance stared out into the rain. It seemed a couple of minutes before he answered.

"He has a son, doesn't he?"

Lucas didn't know what to say. Maybe Sundance was the lunatic in this situation. Maybe Satchel himself. Maybe Satchel was crazy enough to think his son would kill his own baby sister. Which would make Jeremy Satchel crazy, too.

Hell, maybe *he'd* be screwy before this was over.

LUCAS AWOKE WITH A start, then realized he had been jabbed in the ribs and yelped.

"What the hell?"

"He preys." Sundance pointed toward the back of the house where a figure draped in a dark plastic rain poncho was departing.

"That's Jeremy . . . "

" . . . the reverend's son," Sundance finished. "Follow him. Slowly. At a distance. But do not lose him."

Lucas started the car and edged out on the road. "Why doesn't he take the old man's Buick?"

"It would raise suspicion. He doesn't need it, anyhow. He is fleet of foot. See how he moves. Like a wraith. Like a low cloud."

Lucas watched and had to confirm what Sundance observed. Jeremy Satchel seemed almost to float along the shoulder of the road as he headed into town. "I'll be damned."

The rain had slackened somewhat, so visibility was much improved and they could follow Jeremy at a safe distance and still see him clearly enough not to lose him.

"You have any idea where he's going?"

Sundance shook his head. "This is your town, Sheriff. Who is close by?"

Lucas thought a moment. "Two possibilities. A couple of blocks down, Linda Stumpf. Twentyish. Works at the restaurant. What the hell time is it?"

"After midnight."

"She'd be home then on a weeknight."

"And the other?"

"A nurse. Thirty or so. Lives in the trailer park. The only single woman there."

"Which is closer?"

"About the same from here, depending on whether you go north or east."

"He turns east."

"Linda."

"Hurry, Sheriff. We need to get there ahead of him if we can."

"I can go in from the back."

"Do it!"

They parked in the alley behind a small duplex in one half of which Linda Stumpf lived. Sundance dragged the bag from the back seat and they approached cautiously.

The rain was coming down hard again by the time they reached the back door.

"I hope you're right," Lucas said, rapping on the door.

"A hungry man goes for the quickest meal. He has not fed since the preacher's daughter. He is no doubt famished and crazy with the great thirst that drives his kind."

"Quit that vampire talk for a while, Sundance. It's getting on my nerves. We have to *prove* Jeremy's the killer, you know. We can't just assume . . . "

The door opened and an attractive brunette woman with a full bosom, barely covered by a robe, greeted them.

"Why, Sheriff, what y'all doin' at my door this time of night?"

"Saving your life, I hope."

Linda blanched. "You mean . . . ?"

"We think he's picked you next."

"Come on in out of the rain, then, Lucas." She ushered the sheriff and Sundance into her kitchen. "Who's this?"

"Special deputy," Lucas said quickly. Then he glared at Sundance. "Well, hot shot, what now?"

"Turn out the light. Lady, go back in your bed."

"Whatever for? I was going to make some coffee for you and . . . "

"Do it," Lucas said. "No time to explain anything."

Linda nodded nervously and switched off the kitchen light. She led the sheriff and Sundance down a hall which was dimly lit by a night light in an outlet near the bedroom. "I leave that on in case I have to go tinkle in the middle of the night," Linda said. "Y'all know what I mean?"

"Hurry," Sundance whispered.

Linda hesitated at her bedroom door. "Are you coming in my bedroom, too?"

"Yes," Sundance said. "We'll hide by the bed."

"Can I trust this Indian?"

"Yeah, sure. He won't molest you. Just get in the bed and pretend you're asleep."

"I don't know if I can."

"Hurry. He comes!" Sundance pushed her toward the bed, which was barely illuminated by a street lamp shining in through the curtained windows, then pulled Lucas down with him as he dropped to the floor.

"How do you know . . . ?"

"Listen."

Lucas heard the sound of rain hitting something soft. "What is it?"

"The poncho. He may walk in silence like the night, but the rain cannot be hushed as it hits his cloak."

As the sheriff and Sundance huddled on the floor next to the bed, Linda drew the covers up around her neck.

"Keep your eyes shut," Sundance ordered. "He must not suspect."

The sound of wood resisting pressure squeaked in the room. There was a shadow at the window of a man trying to pull it open.

"That window won't open," Linda whispered. "Painted shut."

"Shush!"

"He'll give up," Lucas said.

"No," Sundance muttered. He unzipped the bag.

Lucas could hear him pulling something out.

The shadow stopped tugging on the window abruptly.

"Damn!" Lucas said.

"Oh, my God, I peed my pants!" Linda gasped.

"No time . . . " Sundance said.

Then there was an explosion of glass and splintered wood as the shadow hurled itself through the window, hit the floor with a roll, and sprang up on the bed, immediately pinning Linda's arms down.

She screamed.

Lucas stood up and drew his pistol.

The shadow hissed.

Sundance turned a bright flashlight on the shadow, revealing the snarling features of Jeremy Satchel, whose mouth was gaping open. Sharp fangs jutted from his teeth. His eyes were yellowish and blood-shot, his brown hair matted to his head from rain and sweat. He looked much older than his twenty-five years—*much*, much older.

"Stop, Jeremy!" Lucas yelled.

"He will not," Sundance said.

"Do something," Linda said, beginning to thrash under Jeremy.

Jeremy let go of one of her wrists and swung at Lucas. When he connected, the sheriff was jolted halfway across the room. Then Jeremy grabbed Linda's wrist again and started to press down on her, his lips quivering as he sought her neck.

He had apparently forgotten about Sundance.

Sundance had the small crucifix in his hand now. He thrust it under Jeremy's face.

Jeremy growled and swatted the offensive symbol away.

"So you do not believe in this God," Sundance said.

A *God-less man*, Lucas thought.

Jeremy paused to laugh. "If there is a God, why would he allow *things*—creatures—like me to exist?"

Lucas had recovered enough to throw on the overhead light. Somehow he had managed to hold on to his pistol, so he lifted it and aimed for Jeremy's shoulder.

"I'll stop him!" He pulled the trigger and part of Jeremy peeled off and splattered both Sundance and the girl. Linda screamed louder than ever when the blood hit her face. Jeremy shuddered but quickly regained his hold on the woman and resumed his attack.

Sundance tossed the crucifix on the floor, then ducked down to get something else from the bag.

"If you do not believe in one God," he said, rising with the curved knife in one hand and something wooden in the other, "other gods will find you. *My* Gods will do." He brandished a carved eagle in Jeremy's direction and the young man found himself unable to move. "This God condemns you! This God that *I* believe in!"

"No!" Jeremy squealed, obviously shocked by the eagle's effect on him—so much so that he let go of the woman to cover his face.

Sundance took advantage of Jeremy's reaction quickly. He wielded the knife and with a single swift motion neatly lopped off the vampire's head and the hands covering the face.

The beheaded body, gushing dark blood from the neck, pitched forward on Linda, who emitted sounds that might have caused earthquakes in less-sturdy surroundings.

Jeremy's head bounced across the floor, landing at Lucas's feet; the eyes seemed to be staring in amazement. The two severed hands flew into the corner.

Lucas's stomach heaved. He thought the eyes blinked. Reflexively, he shot the head, blowing a good third of it away.

"Good," Sundance said. "You have saved me having to destroy it." He pushed the body away from Linda, and tried to calm her. "It is over."

It was many hours before she calmed down, and many more hours before Lucas was able to explain what happened without choking on his own words.

Sundance remained inscrutable throughout it all.

THE NEXT DAY, SUNDANCE was waiting for Lucas in his office when he finally arrived, around noon.

Lucas's face was ashen and there were dark circles under his eyes. "It was the damnedest thing," he said quietly to Sundance as he sat behind his desk. "The reverend didn't get that upset. He even insisted I tell him every detail of what happened. The only thing he wanted was for me not to mention anything about the vampire part. As if I would."

"It is to be expected."

"He even seemed relieved."

"That, too, is to be expected."

"I don't get it," Lucas said. "None of it. Why *Jeremy?*"

"He didn't believe in God. Someone—some *thing*—another Changer, perhaps, took advantage of that to make him into one of their kind."

"But surely he didn't believe in the eagle thing you had."

"But *I* did, my friend. That is why there are no atheists in foxholes. Every soldier believes in a god, and the enemy that doesn't is easier to overcome."

"It's too simple."

"Not simple at all. I make it simple so I don't have to talk about it for three hours."

"But Satchel—he said you were a 'God-less' man."

Sundance nodded gravely. "To him, yes. To him there's but one God. No sweat. My faith is as strong as his. We both end up in paradise or . . . " He paused and his eyes almost twinkled. " . . . in hell."

"You're a strange bird, Sundance."

Sundance nodded imperceptibly, then started toward the door. "My work here is finished. My bill will go to the reverend—by his request. I am tired and the journey back home is long."

"Wait a minute. Since you know everything, maybe you can tell me why Satchel wasn't so upset today."

"Another simple thing. He summoned me. He *knew*."

"He *wanted* you to destroy his son?"

"It is always a loved one who calls to put them out of their misery. The preacher's son was suffering torments I hope neither you nor I will ever endure. And the preacher was suffering too, knowing his son had forsaken *his* God. He tried to live with it, the horror of his son, but when Jeremy killed his sister, Satchel could no longer protect him."

"So you suspected him from the beginning."

"Yes."

"Then why go through all the rigmarole of inspecting the body and staking out the place?"

"I had to be sure. It was possible the preacher was mistaken, too."

"Sounds reasonable and damned logical. I guess I underestimated you."

"People often do." Sundance pulled the door open.

Lucas stood. "I'll walk you out."

Outside, before Sundance got into his truck, he stopped and confronted Lucas.

"Tell me, Sheriff, do you believe in vampires now?"

Lucas's brow wrinkled as he considered all he had seen in the last twenty-four hours.

"I'm damned if I know," he said finally. "Cutting anybody's head off is going to stop them."

"Sounds reasonable," Sundance replied. He shook hands with Lucas and climbed up into the truck. "Good knowing you, Sheriff."

"What now, Chief?" Lucas asked.

"People who need me find me," he said, starting the engine. "You'd be surprised how much business I get."

STRAGELLA

Hugh B. Cave

Night black as pitch and filled with the wailing of a dead wind, sank like a shapeless specter into the oily waters of the Indian Ocean, leaving a great gray expanse of sullen sea, empty except for a solitary speck that rose and dropped in the long swell.

The forlorn thing was a ship's boat. For seven days and seven nights it had drifted through the waste, bearing its ghastly burden. Now, groping to his knees, one of the two survivors peered away into the East, where the first glare of a red sun filtered over the rim of the world.

Within arm's reach, in the bottom of the boat, lay a second figure, face down. All night long he had lain there. Even the torrential shower, descending in the dark hours and flooding the dory with life-giving water, had failed to move him.

The first man crawled forward. Scooping water out of the tarpaulin with a battered tin cup, he turned his companion over and forced the stuff through receded lips.

"Miggs!" The voice was a cracked whisper. "Miggs! Good God, you ain't dead, Miggs? I ain't left all alone out here—"

John Miggs opened his eyes feebly.

"What's—what's wrong?" he muttered.

"We got water, Miggs! Water!"

"You're dreamin' again, Yancy. It—it ain't water. It's nuthin' but sea—'

"It rained!" Yancy screeched. "Last night it rained. I stretched the tarpaulin. All night long I been lyin' face up, lettin' it rain in my mouth!"

Miggs touched the tin cup to his tongue and lapped its contents suspiciously. With a mumbled cry he gulped the water down. Then, gibbering like a monkey, he was crawling toward the tarpaulin.

Yancy flung him back, snarling.

"No you won't!" Yancy rasped. "We got to save it, see? We got to get out of here."

Miggs glowered at him from the opposite end of the dory. Yancy sprawled down beside the tarpaulin and stared once again over the abandoned sea, struggling to reason things out.

They were somewhere in the Bay of Bengal. A week ago they had been on board the *Cardigan*, a tiny tramp freighter carrying its handful of passengers from Maulmain to Georgetown. The *Cardigan* had foundered in the typhoon off the Mergui Archipelago. For twelve hours she had heaved and groaned through an inferno of swirling seas. Then she had gone under.

Yancy's memory of the succeeding events was a twisted, unreal parade of horrors. At first there had been five men in the little boat. Four days of terrific heat, no water, no food, had driven the little Persian priest mad, and he had jumped overboard. The other two had drunk salt water and died in agony. Now he and Miggs were alone.

The sun was incandescent in a white hot sky. The sea was calm, greasy, unbroken except for the slow, patient black fins that had been following the boat for days. But something else, during the night, had joined the sharks in their hellish pursuit. Sea snakes, hydrophiinae, wriggling out of nowhere, had come to haunt the dory, gliding in circles round and round, venomous, vivid, vindictive. And overhead were gulls wheeling, swooping in erratic arcs, cackling fiendishly and watching the two men with relentless eyes.

Yancy glanced up at them. Gulls and snakes could mean only one thing—land! He supposed they had come from the Andamans, the prison isles of India. It didn't much matter. They were here. Hideous, menacing harbingers of hope!

His shirt, filthy and ragged, hung open to the belt, revealing a lean chest tattooed with grotesque figures. A long time ago—too

long to remember—he had gone on a drunken binge in Goa. Jap
rum had done it. In company with two others of the *Cardigan's* crew
he had shambled into a tattooing establishment and ordered the
Jap, in a bloated voice, to "paint anything you damned well like,
professor. Anything at all!" And the Jap, being of a religious mind
and sentimental, had decorated Yancy's chest with a most beautiful
crucifix, large, ornate, and colorful.

It brought a grim smile to Yancy's lips as he peered down at it.
But presently his attention was centered on something else—something unnatural, bewildering, on the horizon. The thing was a
narrow bank of fog lying low on the water, as if a distorted cloud
had sunk out of the sky and was floating heavily, half submerged in
the sea. And the small boat was drifting toward it.

In a little while the fog bank hung dense on all sides. Yancy
groped to his feet, gazing about him. John Miggs muttered something beneath his breath and crossed himself.

The thing was shapeless, grayish-white, clammy. It reeked—
not with the dank smell of sea fog, but with the sickly, pungent
stench of a buried jungle or a subterranean mushroom cellar. The
sun seemed unable to penetrate it. Yancy could see the red ball
above him, a feeble, smothered eye of crimson fire, blotted by
swirling vapor.

"The gulls," mumbled Miggs. "They're gone."

"I know it. The sharks, too—and the snakes. We're all alone,
Miggs."

An eternity passed, while the dory drifted deeper and deeper
into the cone. And then there was something else—something that
came like a moaning voice out of the fog. The muted, irregular,
sing-song clangor of a ship's bell!

"Listen!" Miggs cackled. "You hear—"

But Yancy's trembling arm had come up abruptly, pointing ahead.

"By God, Miggs! Look!"

Miggs scrambled up, rocking the boat beneath him. His bony
fingers gripped Yancy's arm. They stood there, the two of them,
staring at the massive black shape that loomed up, like an ethereal
phantom of another world, a hundred feet before them.

"We're saved," Miggs said incoherently. "Thank God, Nels—"

Yancy called out shrilly. His voice rang through the fog with a
hoarse jangle, like the scream of a caged tiger. It choked into

silence. And there was no answer, no responsive outcry—nothing so much as a whisper.

The dory drifted closer. No sound came from the lips of the two men as they drew alongside. There was nothing—nothing but the intermittent tolling of that mysterious, muted bell.

Then they realized the truth—a truth that brought a moan from Miggs's lips. The thing was a derelict, frowning out of the water, inanimate, sullen, buried in its winding sheet of unearthly fog. Its stern was high, exposing a propeller red with rust and matted with clinging—weeds. Across the bow, nearly obliterated by age, appeared the words: *Golconda—Cardiff*.

"Yancy, it ain't no real ship! It ain't of this world—"

Yancy stooped with a snarl, and picked up the oar in the bottom of the dory. A rope dangled within reach, hanging like a black serpent over the scarred hull. With clumsy strokes he drove the small boat beneath it; then, reaching up, he seized the line and made the boat fast.

"You're—goin' aboard?" Miggs said fearfully.

Yancy hesitated, staring up with bleary eyes. He was afraid, without knowing why. The *Golconda* frightened him. The mist clung to her tenaciously. She rolled heavily, ponderously in the long swell, and the bell was still tolling softly somewhere within the lost vessel.

"Well, why not?" Yancy growled. "There may be food aboard. What's there to be afraid of?"

Miggs was silent. Grasping the ropes, Yancy clambered up them. His body swung like a gibbet-corpse against the side. Clutching the rail, he heaved himself over, then stood there, peering into the layers of thick fog, as Miggs climbed up and dropped down beside him.

"I—don't like it," Miggs whispered. "It ain't—"

Yancy groped forward. The deck planks creaked dismally under him. With Miggs clinging close, he led the way into the waist, then into the bow. The cold fog seemed to have accumulated here in a sluggish mass, as if some magnetic force had drawn it. Through it, with arms outheld in front of him, Yancy moved with shuffling steps, a blind man in a strange world.

Suddenly he stopped—stopped so abruptly that Miggs lurched headlong into him. Yancy's body stiffened. His eyes were wide, glaring at the deck before him. A hollow, unintelligible sound parted his lips.

Miggs cringed back with a livid screech, clawing at his shoulder. "What—what is it?" he said thickly.

At their feet were bones. Skeletons—lying there in the swirl of vapor. Yancy shuddered as he examined them. Dead things they were, dead and harmless, yet they were given new life by the motion of the mist. They seemed to crawl, to wriggle, to slither toward him and away from him.

He recognized some of them as portions of human frames. Others were weird, unshapely things. A tiger skull grinned up at him with jaws that seemed to widen hungrily. The vertebrae of a huge python lay in disjointed coils on the planks, twisted as if in agony. He discerned the skeletonic remains of tigers, tapirs, and jungle beasts of unknown identity. And human heads, many of them, scattered about like an assembly of mocking, dead-alive faces, leering at him, watching him with hellish anticipation. The place was a morgue—a charnel house!

Yancy fell back, stumbling. His terror had returned with triple intensity. He felt cold perspiration forming on his forehead, on his chest, trickling down the tattooed crucifix.

Frantically he swung about in his tracks and made for the welcome solitude of the stern deck, only to have Miggs clutch feverishly at his arm.

"I'm goin' to get out of here, Nels! That damned bell—these here things—"

Yancy flung the groping hands away. He tried to control his terror. This ship—this *Golconda*—was nothing but a tramp trader. She'd been carrying a cargo of jungle animals for some expedition. The beasts had got loose, gone amuck, in a storm. There was nothing fantastic about it!

In answer, came the intermittent clang of the hidden bell below decks and the soft lapping sound of the water swishing through the thick weeds which clung to the ship's bottom.

"Come on," Yancy said grimly. "I'm goin' to have a look around. We need food."

He strode back through the waist of the ship, with Miggs shuffling behind. Feeling his way to the towering stern, he found the fog thinner, less pungent.

The hatch leading down into the stern hold was open. It hung before his face like an uplifted hand, scarred, bloated, as if in mute warning. And out of the aperture at its base straggled a spidery thing that was strangely out of place here on this abandoned derelict—a curious, menacing, crawling vine with mottled triangular leaves and immense orange-hued blossoms. Like a living snake, intertwined about itself, it coiled out of the hold and wormed over the deck.

Yancy stepped closer, hesitantly. Bending down, he reached to grasp one of the blooms, only to turn his face away and fall back with an involuntary mutter. The flowers were sickly sweet, nauseating. They repelled him with their savage odor.

"Somethin'—" Miggs whispered sibilantly, "is watchin' us, Nels! I can feel it!"

Yancy peered all about him. He, too, felt a third presence close at hand. Something malignant, evil, unearthly. He could not name it.

"It's your imagination," he snapped. "Shut up, will you?"

"We ain't alone, Nels. This ain't no ship at all!"

"Shut *up!*"

"But the flowers there—they ain't right. Flowers don't grow aboard a Christian ship, Nels!"

"This hulk's been here long enough for trees to grow on it," Yancy said curtly. "The seeds probably took root in the filth below."

"Well, I don't like it."

"Go forward and see what you can find. I'm goin' below to look around."

Miggs shrugged helplessly and moved away. Alone, Yancy descended to the lower levels. It was dark down here, full of shadows and huge gaunt forms that lost their substance in the coils of thick, sinuous fog. He felt his way along the passage, pawing the wall with both hands. Deeper and deeper into the labyrinth he went, until he found the galley.

The galley was a dungeon, reeking of dead, decayed food, as if the stench had hung there for an eternity without being molested; as if the entire ship lay in an atmosphere of its own—an atmosphere of the grave—through which the clean outer air never broke.

But there was food here, canned food that stared down at him from the rotted shelves. The labels were blurred, illegible. Some of the cans crumbled in Yancy's fingers as he seized them—disintegrated into brown, dry dust and trickled to the floor. Others were in fair condition, airtight. He stuffed four of them into his pockets and turned away.

Eagerly now, he stumbled back along the passage. The prospects of food took some of those other thoughts out of his mind, and he was in better humor when he finally found the captain's cabin.

Here, too, the evident age of the place gripped him, The walls were gray with mold, falling into a broken, warped floor. A single table stood on the far side near the bunk, a blackened, grimy table bearing an upright oil lamp and a single black book.

He picked the lamp up timidly and shook it. The circular base was yet half full of oil, and he set it down carefully. It would come in handy later. Frowning, he peered at the book beside it.

It was a seaman's Bible, a small one, lying there, coated with cracked dust, dismal with age. Around it, as if some crawling slug had examined it on all sides, leaving a trail of excretion, lay a peculiar line of black pitch, irregular but unbroken.

Yancy picked the book up and flipped it open. The pages slid under his fingers, allowing a scrap of loose paper to flutter to the floor. He stooped to retrieve it, then, seeing that it bore a line of penciled script, he peered closely at it.

The writing was an apparently irrelevant scrawl—a meaningless memorandum which said crudely:

It's the bats and the crates. I know it now, but it is too late. God help me!

With a shrug, he replaced it and thrust the Bible into his belt, where it pressed comfortingly against his body. Then he continued his exploration.

In the wall cupboard he found two full bottles of liquor, which proved to be brandy. Leaving them there, he groped out of the cabin and returned to the upper deck in search of Miggs.

Miggs was leaning on the rail, watching something below. Yancy trudged toward him, calling out shrilly:

"Say, I got food, Miggs! Food and brand—"

He did not finish. Mechanically his eyes followed the direction of Miggs's stare, and he recoiled involuntarily as his words clipped into stifled silence. On the surface of the oily water below, huge sea snakes paddled against the ship's side—enormous slithering shapes, banded with streaks of black and red and yellow, vicious and repulsive.

"They're back," Miggs said quickly. "They know this ain't no proper ship. They come here out of their hell-hole, to wait for us."

Yancy glanced at him curiously. The inflection of Miggs's voice was peculiar—not at all the phlegmatic, guttural tone that usually grumbled through the little man's lips. It was almost eager!

"What did you find?" Yancy faltered.

"Nothin'. All the ship's boats are hangin' in their davits. Never been touched."

"I found food," Yancy said abruptly, gripping his arm. "We'll eat, then we'll feel better. What the hell are we, anyhow—a couple of fools? Soon as we eat, we'll stock the dory and get off this blasted death ship and clear out of this stinkin' fog. We got water in the tarpaulin."

"We'll clear out? Will we, Nels?"

"Yah. Let's eat."

Once again, Yancy led the way below decks to the galley. There, after a twenty-minute effort in building a fire in the rusty stove, he and Miggs prepared a meal, carrying the food into the captain's cabin, where Yancy lighted the lamp.

They ate slowly, sucking the taste hungrily out of every mouthful, reluctant to finish. The lamplight, flickering in their faces, made gaunt masks of features that were already haggard and full of anticipation.

The brandy, which Yancy fetched out of the cupboard, brought back strength and reason—and confidence. It brought back, too, that unnatural sheen to Miggs's twitching eyes.

"We'd be damned fools to clear out of here right off," Miggs said suddenly. "The fog's got to lift sooner or later. I ain't trustin' myself to no small boat again. Nels—not when we don't know where we're at."

Yancy looked at him sharply. The little man turned away with a guilty shrug. Then hesitantly:

"I—I kinda like it here, Nels."

Yancy caught the odd gleam in those small eyes. He bent forward quickly.

"Where'd you go when I left you alone?" he demanded.

"Me? I didn't go nowhere. I—I just looked around a bit, and I picked a couple of them flowers. See."

Miggs groped in his shirt pocket and held up one of the livid, orange-colored blooms. His face took on an unholy brilliance as he held the thing close to his lips and inhaled its deadly aroma. His eyes, glittering across the table, were on fire with sudden fanatic lust.

For an instant Yancy did not move. Then, with a savage oath, he lurched up and snatched the flower out of Miggs's fingers. Whirling, he flung it to the floor and ground it under his boot.

"You damned thick-headed fool!" he screeched. "You—God help you!"

Then he went limp, muttering incoherently. With faltering steps he stumbled out of the cabin and along the black passageway, and up on the abandoned deck. He staggered to the rail and stood there, holding himself erect with nerveless hands.

"God!" he whispered hoarsely. "God—what did I do that for? Am I goin' crazy?"

No answer came out of the silence. But he knew the answer. The thing he had done down there in the skipper's cabin—those mad words that had spewed from his mouth—had been involuntary. Something inside him, some sense of danger that was all about him, had hurled the words out of his mouth before he could control them. And his nerves were on edge, too. They felt as though they were ready to crack.

But he knew instinctively that Miggs had made a terrible mistake. There was something unearthly and wicked about those sickly sweet flowers. Flowers didn't grow aboard ship. Not real flowers. Real flowers had to take root somewhere, and, besides, they didn't have that drunken, etherish odor. Miggs should have left the vine alone. Clinging at the rail there, Yancy *knew* it, without knowing why.

He stayed there for a long time, trying to think and get his nerves back again. In a little while he began to feel frightened, being alone, and he returned belowdecks to the cabin.

He stopped in the doorway, and stared.

Miggs was still there, slumped grotesquely over the table. The bottle was empty. Miggs was drunk, unconscious, mercifully oblivious of his surroundings.

For a moment Yancy glared at him morosely. For a moment, too, a new fear tugged at Yancy's heart—fear of being left alone through the coming night. He yanked Miggs's arm and shook him savagely; but there was no response. It would be hours, long, dreary, sinister hours, before Miggs regained his senses.

Bitterly Yancy took the lamp and set about exploring the rest of the ship. If he could find the ship's papers, he considered, they might dispel his terror. He might learn the truth.

With this in mind, he sought the mate's quarters. The papers had not been in the captain's cabin where they belonged; therefore they might be here.

But they were not. There was nothing—nothing but a chronometer, sextant, and other nautical instruments lying in curious positions on the mate's table, rusted beyond repair. And there were flags, signal flags, thrown down as if they had been used at the last moment. And, lying in a distorted heap on the floor, was a human skeleton.

Avoiding this last horror, Yancy searched the room thoroughly. Evidently, he reasoned, the captain had died early in the *Golconda's* unknown plague. The mate had brought these instruments, these flags, to his own cabin, only to succumb before he could use them.

Only one thing Yancy took with him when he went out: a lantern, rusty and brittle, but still serviceable. It was empty, but he poured oil into it from the lamp. Then, returning the lamp to the captain's quarters where Miggs lay unconscious, he went on deck.

He climbed the bridge and set the lantern beside him. Night was coming. Already the fog was lifting, allowing darkness to creep in beneath it. And so Yancy stood there, alone and helpless, while blackness settled with uncanny quickness over the entire ship.

He was being watched. He felt it. Invisible eyes, hungry and menacing, were keeping check on his movements. On the deck beneath him were those inexplicable flowers, trailing out of the unexplored hold, glowing like phosphorescent faces in the gloom.

"By God," Yancy mumbled, "I'm goin' to get out of here!"

His own voice startled him and caused him to stiffen and peer about him, as if someone else had uttered the words. And then, very suddenly, his eyes became fixed on the far horizon to starboard. His lips twitched open, spitting out a shrill cry.

"Miggs! Miggs! A light! Look, Miggs—"

Frantically he stumbled down from the bridge and clawed his way below decks to the mate's cabin. Feverishly he seized the signal flags. Then, clutching them in his hand, he moaned helplessly and let them fall. He realized that they were no good, no good in the dark. Gibbering to himself, he searched for rockets. There were none.

Suddenly he remembered the lantern. Back again he raced through the passage, on deck, up on the bridge. In another moment, with the lantern dangling from his arm, he was clambering higher and higher into the black spars of the mainmast. Again and again he slipped and caught himself with outflung hands. And at length he stood high above the deck, feet braced, swinging the lantern back and forth . . .

Below him the deck was no longer silent, no longer abandoned. From bow to stern it was trembling, creaking, whispering up at him. He peered down fearfully. Blurred shadows seemed to be prowling through the darkness, coming out of nowhere, pacing dolefully back and forth through the gloom. They were watching him with a furtive interest.

He called out feebly. The muted echo of his own voice came back up to him. He was aware that the bell was tolling again, and the swish of the sea was louder, more persistent.

With an effort he caught a grip on himself.

"Damned fool," he rasped. "Drivin' yourself crazy—"

The moon was rising. It blurred the blinking light on the horizon and penetrated the darkness like a livid yellow finger. Yancy lowered the lantern with a sob. It was no good now. In the glare of the moonlight, this puny flame would be invisible to the men aboard that other ship. Slowly, cautiously, he climbed down to the deck.

He tried to think of something to do, to take his mind off the fear. Striding to the rail, he hauled up the water butts from the dory. Then he stretched the tarpaulin to catch the precipitation of the night dew. No telling how long he and Miggs would be forced to remain aboard the hulk.

He turned, then, to explore the forecastle. On his way across the deck, he stopped and held the light over the creeping vine. The curious flowers had become fragrant, heady, with the fumes of an intoxicating drug. He followed the coils to where they vanished into the hold, and he looked down. He saw only a tumbled pile of boxes and crates—barred boxes, which must have been cages at one time.

Again he turned away. The ship was trying to tell him something. He felt it—felt the movements of the deck planks beneath his feet. The moonlight, too, had made hideous white things of the scattered bones in the bow. Yancy stared at them with a shiver. He stared again, and grotesque thoughts obtruded into his consciousness. The bones were moving. Slithering, sliding over the deck, assembling themselves, gathering into definite shapes. He could have sworn it!

Cursing, he wrenched his eyes away. Damned fool, thinking such thoughts! With clenched fists he advanced to the forecastle; but before he reached it, he stopped again.

It was the sound of flapping wings that brought him about. Turning quickly with a jerk, he was aware that the sound emanated from the open hold. Hesitantly he stepped forward—and stood rigid with an involuntary scream.

Out of the aperture came two horrible shapes—two inhuman things with immense, clapping wings and glittering eyes. Hideous, enormous. *Bats!*

Instinctively he flung his arm up to protect himself. But the creatures did not attack. They hung for an instant, poised over the hatch, eyeing him with something that was fiendishly like intelligence. Then they flapped over the deck, over the rail, and away into the night. As they sped away towards the west, where he had seen the light of the other ship twinkling, they clung together like witches hell-bent on some evil mission. And below them, in the bloated sea, huge snakes weaved smoky, golden patterns—waiting! . . .

He stood fast, squinting after the bats. Like two hellish black eyes they grew smaller and smaller, became pinpoints in the moon-glow, and finally vanished. Still he did not stir. His lips were dry, his body stiff and unnatural. He licked his mouth. Then he was conscious of something more. From somewhere behind him came a thin, throbbing threat of harmony—a lovely, utterly sweet musical note that fascinated him.

He turned slowly. His heart was hammering, surging. His eyes went suddenly wide.

There, not five feet from him, stood a human form. Not his imagination. Real!

But he had never seen a girl like her before. She was too beautiful. She was wild, almost savage, with her great dark eyes boring into him. Her skin was white, smooth as alabaster. Her hair was jet black; and a waving coil of it, like a broken cobweb of pitch strings, framed her face. Grotesque hoops of gold dangled from her ears. In her hair, above them, gleamed two of those sinister flowers from the straggling vine.

He did not speak; he simply gaped. The girl was barefoot, bare-legged. A short, dark skirt covered her slender thighs. A ragged white waist, open at the throat, revealed the full curve of her breast. In one hand she held a long wooden reed, a flutelike instrument fashioned out of crude wood. And about her middle, dangling almost to the deck, twined a scarlet, silken sash, brilliant as the sun, but not so scarlet as her lips, which were parted in a faint, suggestive smile, showing teeth of marble whiteness!

"Who—who are you?" Yancy mumbled.

She shook her head. Yet she smiled with her eyes, and he felt, somehow, that she understood him. He tried again, in such tongues as he knew. Still, she shook her head, and still he felt that she was mocking him. Not until he chanced upon a scattered, faltering greeting in Serbian, did she nod her head.

"Dobra!" she replied, in a husky, rich voice which sounded, somehow, as if it were rarely used.

He stepped closer then. She was a gipsy evidently. A Tzany of the Serbian hills. She moved very close to him with a floating, almost ethereal movement of her slender body. Peering into his face, flashing her haunting smile at him, she lifted the flutelike instrument and, as if it were nothing at all unnatural or out of place, began to play again the song which had first attracted his attention.

He listened in silence until she had finished. Then, with a cunning smile, she touched her fingers to her lips and whispered softly:

"You—mine. Yes?"

He did not understand. She clutched his arm and glanced fearfully toward the west, out over the sea.

"You—mine!" she said again, fiercely. "Papa Bocito—Seraphino—they no have you. You—not go—to them!"

He thought he understood then. She turned away from him and went silently across the deck. He watched her disappear into the forecastle, and would have followed her, but once again the ship—the whole ship—seemed to be struggling to whisper a warning.

Presently she returned, holding in her white hand a battered silver goblet, very old and very tarnished, brimming with scarlet fluid. He took it silently. It was impossible to refuse her. Her eyes had grown into lakes of night, lit by the burning moon. Her lips were soft, searching, undeniable.

"Who are you?" he whispered.

"Stragella," she smiled.

"Stragella . . . Stragella . . . "

The name itself was compelling. He drank the liquid slowly, without taking his eyes from her lovely face. The stuff had the taste of wine—strong, sweet wine. It was intoxicating, with the same weird effect that was contained in the orange blooms which she wore in her hair and which groveled over the deck behind her.

Yancy's hands groped up weakly. He rubbed his eyes, feeling suddenly weak, powerless, as if the very blood had been drained from his veins. Struggling futilely, he staggered back, moaning half inaudibly.

Stragella's arms went about him, caressing him with sensuous touch. He felt them, and they were powerful, irresistible. The girl's smile maddened him. Her crimson lips hung before his face, drawing nearer, mocking him. Then, all at once, she was seeking his throat. Those warm, passionate, deliriously pleasant lips were searching to touch him.

He sensed his danger. Frantically he strove to lift his arms and push her away. Deep in his mind some struggling intuition, some half-alive idea, warned him that he was in terrible peril. This girl, Stragella, was not of his kind; she was a creature of the darkness, a denizen of a different, frightful world of her own! Those lips, wanting his flesh, were inhuman, too fervid—

Suddenly she shrank away from him, releasing him with a jerk. A snarling animal-like sound surged through her flaming mouth. Her hand lashed out, rigid, pointing to the thing that hung in his belt. Talonic fingers pointed to the Bible that defied her!

But the scarlet fluid had taken its full effect. Yancy stumped down, unable to cry out. In a heap he lay there, paralyzed, powerless to stir.

He knew that she was commanding him to rise. Her lips, moving in pantomime, forming soundless words. Her glittering eyes were fixed upon him, hypnotic. The Bible—she wanted him to cast it over the rail! She wanted him to stand up and go into her arms. Then her lips would find a hold . . .

But he could not obey. He could not raise his arms to support himself. She, in turn, stood at bay and refused to advance. Then, whirling about, her lips drawn into a diabolical curve, beautiful but bestial, she retreated. He saw her dart back, saw her tapering body whip about, with the crimson sash outflung behind her as she raced across the deck.

Yancy closed his eyes to blot out the sight. When he opened them again, they opened to a new, more intense horror. On the *Golconda's* deck, Stragella was darting erratically among those piles of gleaming bones. But they were bones no longer. They had gathered into shapes, taken on flesh, blood. Before his very eyes they assumed substance, men and beasts alike. And then began an orgy such as Nels Yancy had never before looked upon—an orgy of the undead.

Monkeys, giant apes, lunged about the deck. A huge python reared its sinuous head to glare. On the hatch cover a snow-leopard, snarling furiously, crouched to spring. Tigers, tapirs, crocodiles— fought together in the bow. A great brown bear, of the type found in the lofty plateaus of the Pamirs, clawed at the rail.

And the men! Most of them were dark-skinned—dark enough to have come from the same region, from Madras. With them crouched Chinamen, and some Anglo Saxons. Starved, all of them. Lean, gaunt, mad!

Pandemonium raged then. Animals and men alike were insane with hunger. In a little struggling knot, the men were gathered about the number-two hatch, defending themselves. They were wielding firearms—firing point-blank with desperation into the writhing mass that confronted them. And always, between them and around them and among, darted the girl who called herself Stragella.

They cast no shadows, those ghost shapes. Not even the girl, whose arms he had felt about him only a moment ago. There was nothing real in the scene, nothing human. Even the sounds of the shots and the screams of the cornered men, even the roaring growls of the big cats, were smothered as if they came to him through heavy glass windows, from a sealed chamber.

He was powerless to move. He lay in a cataleptic condition, conscious of the entire pantomime, yet unable to flee from it. And his senses were horribly acute—so acute that he turned his eyes upward with an abrupt twitch, instinctively, and then shrank into himself with a new fear as he discerned the two huge bats which had winged their way across the sea. . . .

They were returning now. Circling above him, they flapped down one after the other and settled with heavy, sullen thuds upon the hatch, close to that weird vine of flowers. They seemed to have lost their shape, these nocturnal monstrosities, to have become fantastic blurs, enveloped in an unearthly bluish radiance. Even as he stared at them, they vanished altogether for a moment; and then the strange vapor cleared to reveal the two creatures who stood there!

Not bats! Humans! Inhumans! They were gypsies, attired in moldy, decayed garments which stamped them as Balkans. Man and woman. Lean, emaciated, ancient man with fierce white mustache, plump old woman with black, rat-like eyes that seemed unused to the light of day. And they spoke to Stragella—spoke to her eagerly. She, in turn, swung about with enraged face and pointed to the Bible in Yancy's belt.

But the pantomime was not finished. On the deck the men and animals lay moaning, sobbing. Stragella turned noiselessly, calling the old man and woman after her. Calling them by name.

"Come—Papa Bocito, Seraphino!"

The tragedy of the ghost ship was being reenacted. Yancy knew it, and shuddered at the thought. Starvation, cholera had driven the *Golconda's* crew mad. The jungle beasts, unfed, hideously savage, had escaped out of their confinement. And now—now that the final conflict was over—Stragella and Papa Bocito and Seraphino were proceeding about their ghastly work.

Stragella was leading them. Her charm, her beauty, gave her a hold on the men. They were in love with her. She had *made* them love her, madly and without reason. Now she was moving from one to another, loving them and holding them close to her. And as she stepped away from each man, he went limp, faint, while she laughed terribly and passed on to the next. Her lips were parted. She licked them hungrily—licked the blood from them with a sharp, crimson tongue.

How long it lasted, Yancy did not know. Hours, hours on end. He was aware, suddenly, that a high wind was screeching and wailing in the upper reaches of the ship; and, peering up, he saw that the spars were no longer bare and rotten with age. Great gray sails stood out against the black sky—fantastic things without any definite form or outline. And the moon above them had vanished utterly. The howling wind was bringing a storm with it, filling the sails to bulging proportions. Beneath the decks the ship was groaning like a creature in agony. The seas were lashing her, slashing her, carrying her forward with amazing speed.

Of a sudden came a mighty grinding sound. The *Golconda* hurtled back, as if a huge, jagged reef of submerged rock had bored into her bottom. She listed. Her stern rose high in the air. And Stragella, with her two fellow fiends, was standing in the bow, screaming in mad laughter in the teeth of the wind. The other two laughed with her.

Yancy saw them turn toward him, but they did not stop. Somehow, he did not expect them to stop. This scene, this mad pantomime, was not the present; it was the past. He was not here at all. All this had happened years ago! Forgotten, buried in the past!

But he heard them talking, in a mongrel dialect full of Serbian words.

"It is done, Papa Bocito! We shall stay here forever now. There is land within an hour's flight, where fresh blood abounds and will always abound. And here, on this wretched hulk, they will never find our graves to destroy us!"

The horrible trio passed close. Stragella turned, to stare out across the water, and raised her hand in silent warning. Yancy, turning wearily to stare in the same direction, saw that the first streaks of daylight were beginning to filter over the sea.

With a curious floating, drifting movement the three undead creatures moved toward the open hatch. They descended out of sight. Yancy, jerking himself erect and surprised to find that the effects of the drug had worn off with the coming of dawn, crept to the hatch and peered down—in time to see those fiendish forms enter their coffins. He knew then what the crates were. In the dim light, now that he was staring directly into the aperture, he saw what he had not noticed before. Three of those oblong boxes were filled with dank grave-earth!

He knew then the secret of the unnatural flowers. They *had* roots! They were rooted in the soil which harbored those undead bodies!

Then, like a groping finger, the dawn came out of the sea. Yancy walked to the rail, dazed. It was over now—all over. The orgy was ended. The *Golconda* was once more an abandoned, rotted hulk.

For an hour he stood at the rail, sucking in the warmth and glory of the sunlight. Once again that wall of unsightly mist was rising out of the water on all sides. Presently it would bury the ship, and Yancy shuddered.

He thought of Miggs. With quick steps he paced to the companionway and descended to the lower passage. Hesitantly he prowled through the thickening layers of dank fog. A queer sense of foreboding crept over him.

He called out even before he reached the door. There was no answer. Thrusting the barrier open, he stepped across the sill—and then he stood still while a sudden harsh cry broke from his lips.

Miggs was lying there, half across the table, his arms flung out, his head turned grotesquely on its side, staring up at the ceiling.

"Miggs! Miggs!" The sound came choking through Yancy's lips. "Oh, God, Miggs—what's happened?"

He reeled forward. Miggs was cold and stiff, and quite dead. All the blood was gone out of his face and arms. His eyes were glassy, wide open. He was as white as marble, shrunken horribly. In his throat were two parallel marks, as if a sharp-pointed staple had been hammered into the flesh and then withdrawn. The marks of the vampire.

For a long time Yancy did not retreat. The room swayed and lurched before him. He was alone. Alone! The whole ghastly thing was too sudden, too unexpected.

Then he stumbled forward and went down on his knees, clawing at Miggs's dangling arm.

"Oh God, Miggs," he mumbled incoherently. "You got to help me. I can't stand it!"

He clung there, white-faced, staring, sobbing thickly, and presently slumped in a pitiful heap, dragging Miggs over on top of him.

It was late afternoon when he regained consciousness. He stood up, fighting away the fear that overwhelmed him. He had to get away, get away! The thought hammered into his head with monotonous force. Get away!

He found his way to the upper deck. There was nothing he could do for Miggs. He would have to leave him here. Stumbling, he moved along the rail and reached down to draw the small boat closer, where he could provision it and make it ready for his departure.

His fingers clutched emptiness. The ropes were gone. The dory was gone. He hung limp, staring down at a flat expanse of oily sea.

For an hour he did not move. He fought to throw off his fear long enough to think of a way out. Then he stiffened with a sudden jerk and pushed himself away from the rail.

The ship's boats offered the only chance. He groped to the nearest one and labored feverishly over it.

But the task was hopeless. The life boats were of metal, rusted through and through, wedged in their davits. The wire cables were knotted and immovable. He tore his hands on them, wringing blood from his scarred fingers. Even while he worked, he knew that the boats would not float. They were rotten, through and through.

He had to stop, at last, from exhaustion.

After that, knowing that there was no escape, he had to do something, anything, to keep sane. First he would clear those horrible bones from the deck, then explore the rest of the ship . . .

It was a repulsive task, but he drove himself to it. If he could get rid of the bones, perhaps Stragella and the other two creatures would not return. He did not know. It was merely a faint hope, something to cling to.

With grim, tight-pressed lips he dragged the bleached skeletons over the deck and kicked them over the side, and stood watching them as they sank from sight. Then he went to the hold, smothering his terror, and descended into the gloomy belly of the vessel. He avoided the crates with a shudder of revulsion. Ripping up that evil vine-thing by the roots, he carried it to the rail and flung it away, with the mold of grave earth still clinging to it.

After that he went over the entire ship, end to end, but found nothing.

He slipped the anchor chains then, in the hopes that the ship would drift away from that vindictive bank of fog. Then he paced back and forth, muttering to himself and trying to force courage for the most hideous task of all.

The sea was growing dark, and with dusk came increasing terror. He knew the *Golconda* was drifting. Knew, too, that the undead inhabitants of the vessel were furious with him for allowing the boat to drift away from their source of food. Or they *would* be furious when they came alive again after their interim of forced sleep.

And there was only one method of defeating them. It was a horrible method, and he was already frightened. Nevertheless he searched the deck for a marlin spike and found one; and, turning sluggishly, he went back to the hold.

A stake, driven through the heart of each of the horrible trio . . .

The rickety stairs were steep in shadow. Already the dying sun, buried behind its wreath of evil fog, was a ring of bloody mist. He glanced at it and realized that he must hurry. He cursed himself for having waited so long. It was hard, lowering himself into the pitch-black hold when he could only feel his footing and trust to fate. His boots scraped ominously on the steps. He held his hands above him, gripping the deck timbers.

And suddenly he slipped.

His foot caught on the edge of a lower step, twisted abruptly, and pitched him forward. He cried out. The marlin spike dropped from his hand and clattered on one of the crates below. He tumbled in a heap, clawing for support. The impact knocked something out of his belt. And he realized, even as his head came in sharp contact with the foremost oblong box, that the Bible, which had heretofore protected him, was no longer a part of him.

He did not lose complete control of his senses. Frantically he sought to regain his knees and grope for the black book in the gloom of the hold. A sobbing, choking sound came pitifully from his lips.

A soft, triumphant laugh came out of the darkness close to him. He swung about heavily—so heavily that the movement sent him sprawling again in an inert heap.

He was too late. She was already there on her knees, glaring at him hungrily. A peculiar bluish glow welled about her face. She was ghastly beautiful as she reached behind her into the oblong crate and began to trace a circle about the Bible with a chunk of soft, tarry, pitch-like substance clutched in her white fingers.

Yancy stumbled toward her, finding strength in desperation. She straightened to meet him. Her lips, curled back, exposed white teeth. Her arms coiled out, enveloping him, stifling his struggles. God, they were strong. He could not resist them. The same languid, resigned feeling came over him. He would have fallen, but she held him erect.

She did not touch him with her lips. Behind her he saw two other shapes take form in the darkness. The savage features of Papa Bocito glowered at him; and Seraphino's ratty, smoldering eyes, full of hunger, bored into him. Stragella was obviously afraid of them.

Yancy was lifted from his feet. He was carried out on deck and borne swiftly, easily, down the companionway, along the lower passage, through a swirling blanket of hellish fog and darkness, to the cabin where Miggs lay dead. And he lost consciousness while they carried him.

HE COULD NOT TELL, when he opened his eyes, how long he had been asleep. It seemed a long, long interlude. Stragella was sitting beside him. He lay on the bunk in the cabin, and the lamp was burning on the table, revealing Miggs's limp body in full detail.

Yancy reached up fearfully to touch his throat. There were no marks there, not yet.

He was aware of voices, then. Papa Bocito and the ferret-faced woman were arguing with the girl beside him. The savage old man in particular was being angered by her cool, possessive smile.

"We are drifting away from the prison isles," Papa Bocito snarled, glancing at Yancy with unmasked hate. "It is his work, lifting the anchor. Unless you share him with us until we drift ashore, we shall perish!"

"He is mine," Stragella shrugged, modulating her voice to a persuasive whisper. "You had the other. This one is mine. I shall have him!"

"He belongs to us all!"

"Why?" Stragella smiled. "Because he has looked upon the resurrection night? Ah, he is the first to learn our secret."

Seraphino's eyes narrowed at that, almost to pinpoints. She jerked forward, clutching the girl's shoulder.

"We have quarreled enough," she hissed. "Soon it will be daylight. He belongs to us all because he has taken us away from the isles and learned our secrets."

The words drilled their way into Yancy's brain. "The resurrection night!" There was an ominous significance in it, and he thought he knew its meaning. His eyes, or his face, must have revealed his thoughts, for Papa Bocito drew near to him and pointed into his face with a long, bony forefinger, muttering triumphantly.

"You have seen what no other eyes have seen," the ancient man growled bitterly. "Now, for that, you shall become one of us. Stragella wants you. She shall have you for eternity—for a life without death. Do you know what that means?"

Yancy shook his head dumbly, fearfully.

"We are the undead," Bocito leered. "Our victims become creatures of the blood, like us. At night we are free. During the day we must return to our graves. That is why"—he cast his arm toward the upper deck in a hideous gesture—"those other victims of ours have not yet become like us, they were never buried; they have no graves to return to. Each night we give them life for our own amusement, but they are not of the brotherhood—yet."

Yancy licked his lips and said nothing. he understood then. Every night it happened. A nightly pantomime, when the dead became alive again, reenacting the events of the night when the Golconda had become a ship of hell.

"We are gypsies," the old man gloated. "Once we were human, living in our pleasant little camp in the shadow of Pobyezdin

Potok's crusty peaks, in the Morava Valley of Serbia. That was in the time of Milutin, six hundreds of years ago. Then the vampires of the hills came for us and took us to them. We lived the undead life until there was no more blood in the valley. So we went to the coast, we three, transporting our grave earth with us. And we lived there, alive by night and dead by day, in the coastal villages of the Black Sea, until the time came when we wished to go to the far places."

Seraphino's guttural voice interrupted him, saying harshly:

"Hurry. It is nearly dawn!"

"And we obtained passage on this *Golconda*, arranging to have our crates of grave earth carried secretly to the hold. And the ship fell into cholera and starvation and storm. She went aground. And— here we are. Ah, but there is blood upon the islands, my pretty one, and so we anchored the *Golconda* on the reef, where life was close at hand!"

Yancy closed his eyes with a shudder. He did not understand all of the words. They were a jargon of gipsy tongue. But he knew enough to horrify him.

Then the old man ceased gloating. He fell back, glowering at Stragella. And the girl laughed, a mad, cackling, triumphant laugh of possession. She leaned forward, and the movement brought her out of the line of the lamplight, so that the feeble glow fell full over Yancy's prostrate body.

At that, with an angry snarl, she recoiled. Her eyes went wide with abhorrence. Upon his chest gleamed the crucifix—the tattooed cross and savior which had been indelibly printed there. Stragella held her face away, shielding her eyes. She cursed him horribly. Backing away, she seized the arms of her companions and pointed with trembling finger to the thing which had repulsed her.

The fog seemed to seep deeper and deeper into the cabin during the ensuing silence. Yancy struggled to a sitting posture and cringed back against the wall, waiting for them to attack him. It would be finished in a moment, he knew. Then he would join Miggs, with those awful marks on his throat and Stragella's lips crimson with his sucked blood.

But they held their distance. The fog enveloped them, made them almost indistinct. He could see only three pairs of glaring, staring, phosphorescent eyes that grew larger and wider and more intensely terrible.

He buried his face in his hands, waiting. They did not come. He heard them mumbling, whispering. Vaguely he was conscious of another sound, far off and barely audible. The howl of wolves.

Beneath him the bunk was swaying from side to side with the movement of the ship. The *Golconda* was drifting swiftly. A storm had risen out of nowhere, and the wind was singing its dead dirge in the rotten spars high above decks. He could hear it moaning, wheezing, like a human being in torment.

Then the three pairs of glittering orbs moved nearer. The whispered voices ceased, and a cunning smile passed over Stragella's features. Yancy screamed, and flattened against the wall. He watched her in fascination as she crept upon him. One arm was flung across her eyes to protect them from the sight of the crucifix. In the other hand, outstretched, groping ever nearer, she clutched that hellish chunk of pitchlike substance with which she had encircled the Bible!

He knew what she would do. The thought struck him like an icy blast, full of fear and madness. She would slink closer, closer, until her hand touched his flesh. Then she would place the black substance around the tattooed cross and kill its powers. His defense would be gone. Then—those cruel lips on his throat . . .

There was no avenue of escape. Papa Bocito and the plump old woman, grinning malignantly, had slid to one side, between him and the doorway. And Stragella writhed forward with one alabaster arm feeling . . . feeling . . .

He was conscious of the roar of surf, very close, very loud, outside the walls of the fog-filled enclosure. The ship was lurching, reeling heavily, pitching in the swell. Hours must have passed. Hours and hours of darkness and horror.

Then she touched him. The sticky stuff was hot on his chest, moving in a slow circle. He hurled himself back, stumbled, went down, and she fell upon him.

Under his tormented body the floor of the cabin split asunder. The ship buckled from top to bottom with a grinding, roaring impact. A terrific shock burst through the ancient hulk, shattering its rotted timbers.

The lamp caromed off the table, plunging the cabin in semi-darkness. Through the port-holes filtered a gray glare. Stragella's face, thrust into Yancy's, became a mask of beautiful fury. She whirled back. She stood rigid, screaming lividly to Papa Bocito and the old hag.

"Go back! Go back!" she riled. "We have waited too long! It is dawn!"

She ran across the floor, grappling with them. Her lips were distorted. Her body trembled. She hurled her companions to the door. Then, as she followed them into the gloom of the passage, she turned upon Yancy with a last unholy snarl of defeated rage. And she was gone.

Yancy lay limp. When he struggled to his feet at last and went on deck, the sun was high in the sky, bloated and crimson, struggling to penetrate the cone of fog which swirled about the ship.

The ship lay far over, careened on her side. A hundred yards distant over the port rail lay the heaven-sent sight of land—a bleak, vacant expanse of jungle-rimmed shore line.

He went deliberately to work—a task that had to be finished quickly, lest he be discovered by the inhabitants of the shore and be considered stark mad. Returning to the cabin, he took the oil lamp and carried it to the open hold. There, sprinkling the liquid over the ancient wood, he set fire to it.

Turning, he stepped to the rail. A scream of agony, unearthly and prolonged, rose up behind him. Then he was over the rail, battling in the surf.

When he staggered up on the beach, twenty minutes later, the *Golconda* was a roaring furnace. On all sides of her the flames snarled skyward, spewing through that hellish cone of vapor. Grimly Yancy turned away and trudged along the beach.

He looked back after an hour of steady plodding. The lagoon was empty. The fog had vanished. The sun gleamed down with warm brilliance on a broad, empty expanse of sea.

Hours later he reached a settlement. Men came and talked to him, and asked curious questions. They pointed to his hair, which was stark white. They told him he had reached Port Blair, on the southern island of the Andamans. After that, noticing the peculiar gleam of his blood-shot eyes, they took him to the home of the governor.

There he told his story—told it hesitantly, because he expected to be disbelieved, mocked.

The governor looked at him critically.

"You don't expect me to understand?" the governor said. "I am not so sure, sir. This is a penal colony, a prison isle. During the past few years, more than two hundred of our convicts have died in the most curious way. Two tiny punctures in the throat. Loss of blood."

"You—you must destroy the graves," Yancy muttered.

The governor nodded silently, significantly.

After that, Yancy returned to the world, alone. Always alone. Men peered into his face and shrank away from the haunted stare of his eyes. They saw the crucifix upon his chest and wondered why, day and night, he wore his shirt flapping open, so that the brilliant design glared forth.

But their curiosity was never appeased. Only Yancy knew; and Yancy was silent.

WE ARE DEAD TOGETHER

Charles de Lint

> *The ideal condition be right*
> *Would be, I admit, that men should be right*
> *by instinct;*
> *But since we are all likely to go astray,*
> *The reasonable thing is to learn from those*
> *who can teach.*
>
> —Sophocles

Let it be recounted in the *swato*—the stories of my people that chronicle our history and keep it alive—that while Kata Petalo was first and foremost a fool, she meant well. I truly believed there was a road I could walk between the world of the Rom and the *shilmullo*.

We have always been an adaptable people. We'd already lived side by side with the *Gaje* for ten times a hundred years, a part of their society, and yet apart from it. The undead were just another kind of non-Gypsy; why shouldn't we be able to coexist with them as well?

I knew now. I had always known. We didn't call them the *shilmullo*—the cold dead—simply for the touch of their pale flesh, cold as marble. Their hearts were cold too—cold and black as the hoarfrost that rimmed the hedges by which my ancestors had camped in gentler times.

I had always known, but I had chosen to forget. I had let the chance for survival seduce me.

"*Yekka buliasa nashti beshes pe done gratsende,*" was what Bebee Yula used to tell us when we were children. With one behind you cannot sit on two horses. It was an old saying, a warning to those Rom who thought they could be both Rom and *Gaje*, but instead were neither.

I had ridden two horses these past few years, but all my cleverness served me ill in the end, for they took Budo from me all the same; took him, stole his life, and left me with his cold, pale corpse that would rise from its death tonight to be forever a part of their world and lost to mine.

For see, the *shilmullo* have no art.

The muses that inspire the living can't find lodging in their dead flesh, can't spark the fires of genius in their cold hearts. The *shilmullo* can mimic, but they can't create. There are no Rembrandts counted in their ranks, no Picassos. No Yeatses, no Steinbecks. No Mozarts, no Dylans. For artwork, for music, for plays and films and poetry and books, they need the living—Rom or *Gaje*.

I'm not the best musician in this new world that the *shilmullo* tore from the grave of the old, but I have something not one of them can ever possess, except vicariously: I have the talent to compose. I have written hundreds of manuscripts in honor of my patron, Brian Stansford—yes, *that* Stansford, the president of Stansford Chemicals—in every style of music. There are sonatas bearing his name and various music hall songs; jazz improvisations, three concertos, one symphony, and numerous airs in the traditional style of the Rom; rap music, pop songs, heavy metal anthems.

I have accompanied him to dinners and galas and openings where my performances and music have always gained him the envy of his peers.

In return, like any pet, I was given safety—both for myself and my family. Every member of the Petalo clan has the Stansford tattoo on their left brow, an ornate capital S, decorated with flowered vines with a tiny wolf's paw print enclosed in the lower curve of the letter. Sixteen Petalos could walk freely in the city and countryside with that mark on their brow.

Only Bebee Yula, my aunt, refused the tattoo.

"You do this for us," she told me, "but I will not be an obligation on any member of my clan. What you do is wrong. We must forget the boundaries that lie between ourselves and the *Gaje* and be united against our common enemy. To look out only for yourself, your family, makes you no better than the *shilmullo* themselves."

"There is no other way," I had explained. "Either I do this, or we die."

"There are worse things than death," she told me. "What you mean to do is one of them. You will lose your soul, Kata. You will become as cold in your heart as those you serve."

I tried to explain it better, but she would not argue further with me at that time. She had the final word. She was an old woman—in her eighties, Papa said—but she killed three *shilmullo* before she herself was slain. We all knew she was brave, but not one of us learned the lesson she'd given her life to tell us.

Sixteen Petalos allowed the bloodred Stansford tattoo to be placed on their brows.

But now there are only fifteen of us, for protected though he was, three *shilmullo* stole Budo from me. Stansford himself spoke to me, explaining how it was an unfortunate accident. They were young, Budo's murderers, they hadn't seen the tattoo until it was too late. Perhaps I would now do as he had previously suggested and bring my family to live in one of his protected enclaves.

"We are Rom," I had said. He gave me a blank look. "I'm a busy man, Kathy," he said, calling me by my *nav gajikano*—my non-Gypsy name. "Would you get to the point?"

It should have explained everything. To be Rom was to live in all places; without freedom of movement, we might as well be dead. I wanted to explain it to him, but the words wouldn't come.

Stansford regarded me, his flesh white in the fluorescent light that lit his office, small sparks of red fire deep in his pupils. If I had thought he would have any sympathy, I was sorely mistaken.

"Let Taylor know when you've picked a new mate," was all he said, "and we'll have him—or her—tattooed."

Then he bent down to his paperwork as though I were no longer present.

I had been dismissed. I sat for a long moment, ignored, finally learning to hate him, before I left his office and went back downtown to the small apartment in a deserted tenement where Budo and I had been staying this week.

Budo lay stretched out on newspapers before the large window in the living room where Taylor and another of Stansford's men had left him two days ago. I knelt beside the corpse and looked down at what had been my husband. His throat had been savaged, but otherwise he looked as peaceful as though he were sleeping. His eyes were closed. A lock of his dark hair fell across his brow. I pushed it aside, laid a hand on his cold flesh.

He was dead, but not dead. He had been killed at 3:00 A.M. Tonight at the same time, three days after his death, his eyes would open and if I was still here, he would not remember me. They never remember anything until that initial thirst is slaked.

His skin was almost translucent. Pale, far too pale. Where was the dark-skinned Budo I had married?

Gone. Dead. All that remained of him was this bitter memory of pale flesh.

"I was wrong," I said.

I spoke neither to myself, nor to the corpse. My voice was for the ghost of my aunt, Bebee Yula, gone to the land of shadows. Budo would never take that journey—not if I let him wake.

I lifted my gaze to look out through the window at the street below. Night lay dark on its pavement. *Shilmullo* don't need streetlights and what humans remain in the city know better than to walk out-of-doors once the sun has gone down. The emptiness I saw below echoed endlessly inside me.

I rose to my feet and crossed the room to where our two canvas backpacks lay against the wall. My fiddle case lay between them. I opened it and took out the fiddle. When I ran my thumb across the strings, the notes seemed to be swallowed by the room. They had no ring, no echo.

Budo's death had stolen their music.

For a long moment I held the fiddle against my chest, then I took the instrument by its neck and smashed it against the wall. The strings popped free as the body shattered, the end of one of them licking out to sting my cheek. It drew blood.

I took the fiddle's neck back to where Budo's corpse lay and knelt beside him again. Raising it high above my head, I brought the jagged end down, plunging it into his chest—

There!

The corpse bucked as though I'd struck it with an electric current. Its eyes flared open, gaze locking on mine. It was a stranger's gaze. The corpse's hands scrabbled weakly against my arms, but my leather jacket kept me safe from its nails. It was too soon for him to have reached the full power of a *shilmullo*. His hands were weak. His eyes could glare, but not bend me to his will.

It took longer for the corpse to die than I had thought it would.

When it finally lay still, I leaned back on my heels, leaving the fiddle's neck sticking up out of the corpse's chest. I tried to summon tears—my sorrow ran deep; I had yet to cry—but the emptiness just gathered more thickly inside me. So I simply stared at my handiwork, sickened by what I saw, but forcing myself to look so that I would have the courage to finish the night's work.

Bebee Yula had been a wealth of old sayings. "Where you see Rom," she had said once, "there is freedom. Where you do not, there is no freedom."

I had traded our freedom for tattoos. Those tattoos did not mean safety, but *prikaza*—misfortune. Bad luck. We were no longer Rom, my family and I, but only Bebee Yula had seen that.

Until now.

I HAD A RECITAL the following night—at a gala of Stansford's at the Brewer Theatre. There was a seating capacity of five hundred and, knowing Stansford, he would make certain that every seat was filled.

I walked from the tenement with my fiddle case in hand. A new piece I'd composed for Stansford last week was to be the finale, so I didn't have to be at the theater until late, but I was going early. I stopped only once along the way, to meet my brother Vedel. I had explained my needs to him the day before.

"It's about time," had been his only response.

I remembered Bebee Yula telling me she would not be an obligation on any member of her clan and wondered if the rest of my family agreed with her the way that Vedel seemed to. I had always told myself I did what I did for them; now I had learned that it had been for myself.

I wanted to live. I could not bear to have my family unprotected.

Many of the legends that tell of the *shilmullo* are false or embroidered, but this was true: There are only three ways to kill them. By beheading. By a stake in the heart. And by fire.

What Vedel brought me was an explosive device he'd gotten from a member of the local Gaje freedom fighters. It was small enough to fit in my empty fiddle case, but with a firepower large enough to bring down the house. Five hundred would burn in the ensuing inferno. It would not be enough, but it was all I could do.

I embraced Vedel, there on the street, death lying in its case at my feet.

"We are Rom," he whispered into my hair. "We were meant to be free."

I nodded. Slowly stepping back from him, I picked up the case and went on alone to the theater.

I would not return.

LET IT BE RECOUNTED in the *swato* that while Kata Petalo was first and foremost a fool, she meant well.

Even a fool can learn wisdom, but oh, the lesson is hard.

ŦHis Ŧowп Aiп'ŧ Biɢ EпovɢH

Tanya Huff

Ow! Vicki, be careful!"

"Sorry. Sometimes I forget how sharp they are."

"Terrific." He wove his fingers through her hair and pulled just hard enough to make his point. "Don't."

"Don't what?" She grinned up at him, teeth gleaming ivory in the moonlight spilling across the bed. "Don't forget or don't . . . "

The sudden demand of the telephone for attention buried the last of her question.

Detective-Sergeant Michael Celluci sighed. "Hold that thought," he said, rolled over, and reached for the phone. "Celluci."

"Fifty-two division just called. They've found a body down at Richmond and Peter they think we might want to have a look at."

"Dave, it's . . . " He squinted at the clock, " . . . one twenty-nine in the A.M. and I'm off duty."

On the other end of the line, his partner, theoretically off duty as well, refused to take the hint. "Ask me who the stiff is?"

Celluci sighed again. "Who's the stiff?"

"Mac Eisler."

"Shit."

"Funny, that's exactly what I said." Nothing in Dave Graham's voice indicated he appreciated the joke. "I'll be there in ten."

"Make it fifteen."

"You in the middle of something?"

Celluci watched as Vicki sat up and glared at him. "I was."

"Welcome to the wonderful world of law enforcement."

Vicki's hand shot out and caught Celluci's wrist before he could heave the phone across the room. "Who's Mac Eisler?" she asked as, scowling, he dropped the receiver back in its cradle and swung his legs off the bed.

"You heard that?"

"I can hear the beating of your heart, the movement of your blood, the song of your life." She scratched the back of her leg with one bare foot. "I should think I can overhear a lousy phone conversation."

"Eisler's a pimp." Celluci reached for the light switch, changed his mind, and began pulling on his clothes. Given the full moon riding just outside the window, it wasn't exactly dark and given Vicki's sensitivity to bright light, not to mention her temper, he figured it was safer to cope. "We're pretty sure he offed one of his girls a couple of weeks ago."

Vicki scooped her shirt up off the floor. "Irene MacDonald?"

"What? You overheard that, too?"

"I get around. How sure's pretty sure?"

"Personally positive. But we had nothing solid to hold him on."

"And now he's dead." Skimming her jeans up over her hips, she dipped her brows in a parody of deep thought. "Golly, I wonder if there's a connection."

"Golly yourself," Celluci snarled. "You're not coming with me."

"Did I ask?"

"I recognized the tone of voice. I know you, Vicki. I knew you when you were a cop, I knew you when you were a P.I. and I don't care how much you've changed physically, I know you now you're a . . . a . . . "

"Vampire." Her pale eyes seemed more silver than gray. "You can say it, Mike. It won't hurt my feelings. Bloodsucker. Night-walker. Creature of Darkness."

"Pain in the butt." Carefully avoiding her gaze, he shrugged into his shoulder holster and slipped a jacket on over it. "This is police business, Vicki, stay out of it. Please." He didn't wait for a response but crossed the shadows to the bedroom door. Then he paused, one foot over the threshold. "I doubt I'll be back by dawn. Don't wait up."

Vicki Nelson, ex of the Metropolitan Toronto Police Force, ex-private investigator, recent vampire, decided to let him go. If he could joke about the change, he accepted it. And besides, it was always more fun to make him pay for smart-ass remarks when he least expected it.

She watched from the darkness as Celluci climbed into Dave Graham's car. Then, with the taillights disappearing in the distance, she dug out his spare set of car keys and proceeded to leave tangled entrails of Highway Traffic Act strewn from Downsview to the heart of Toronto.

It took no supernatural ability to find the scene of the crime. What with the police, the press, and the morbidly curious, the area seethed with people. Vicki slipped past the constable stationed at the far end of the alley and followed the paths of shadow until she stood just outside the circle of police around the body.

Mac Eisler had been a somewhat attractive, not very tall, white male Caucasian. Eschewing the traditional clothing excesses of his profession, he was dressed simply in designer jeans and an olive-green raw silk jacket. At the moment, he wasn't looking his best. A pair of rusty nails had been shoved through each manicured hand, securing his body upright across the back entrance of a trendy restaurant. Although the pointed toes of his tooled leather cowboy boots indented the wood of the door, Eisler's head had been turned completely around so that he stared, in apparent astonishment, out into the alley.

The smell of death fought with the stink of urine and garbage. Vicki frowned. There was another scent, a pungent predator scent that raised the hair on the back of her neck and drew her lips up off her teeth. Surprised by the strength of her reaction, she stepped silently into a deeper patch of night lest she give herself away.

"Why the hell would I have a comment?"

Preoccupied with an inexplicable rage, she hadn't heard Celluci arrive until he greeted the press. Shifting position slightly, she watched as he and his partner moved in off the street and got their first look at the body.

"Jesus H. Christ."

"On crutches," agreed the younger of the two detectives already on the scene.

"Who found him?"

"Dishwasher, coming out with the trash. He was obviously meant to be found; they nailed the bastard right across the door."

"The kitchen's on the other side and no one heard hammering?"

"I'll go you one better than that. Look at the rust on the head of those nails—they haven't been hammered."

"What? Someone just pushed the nails through Eisler's hands and into solid wood?"

"Looks like."

Celluci snorted. "You trying to tell me that Superman's gone bad?"

Under the cover of their laughter, Vicki bent and picked up a piece of planking. There were four holes in the unbroken end and two remaining three-inch spikes. She pulled a spike out of the wood and pressed it into the wall of the building by her side. A smut of rust marked the ball of her thumb, but the nail looked no different.

She remembered the scent.

Vampire.

" . . . UNABLE TO COME TO the phone. Please leave a message after the long beep."

"Henry? It's Vicki. If you're there, pick up." She stared across the dark kitchen, twisting the phone cord between her fingers. "Come on, Fitzroy, I don't care what you're doing, this is important." Why wasn't he home writing? Or chewing on Tony. Or something. "Look, Henry, I need some information. There's another one of, of us, hunting my territory and I don't know what I should do. I know what I want to do . . . " The rage remained, interlaced with the knowledge of *another*. " . . . but I'm new at this bloodsucking undead stuff, maybe I'm overreacting. Call me. I'm still at Mike's."

She hung up and sighed. Vampires didn't share territory.

Which was why Henry had stayed in Vancouver and she'd come back to Toronto.

Well, all right, it's not the only reason I came back. She tossed Celluci's spare car keys into the drawer in the phone table and wondered if she should write him a note to explain the mysterious emptying of his gas tank. "Nah. He's a detective, let him figure it out."

Sunrise was at five twelve. Vicki didn't need a clock to tell her that it was almost time. She could feel the sun stroking the edges of her awareness.

"It's like that final instant, just before someone hits you from behind, when you know it's going to happen, but you can't do a damn thing about it." She crossed her arms on Celluci's chest and pillowed her head on them, adding, *"Only it lasts longer."*

"And this happens every morning?"

"Just before dawn."

"And you're going to live forever?"

"That's what they tell me."

Celluci snorted. *"You can have it."*

Although Celluci had offered to light-proof one of the two unused bedrooms, Vicki had been uneasy about the concept. At four and a half centuries, maybe Henry Fitzroy could afford to be blasé about immolation, but Vicki still found the whole idea terrifying and had no intention of being both helpless and exposed. Anyone could walk into a bedroom.

No one would accidentally walk into an enclosed plywood box, covered in a blackout curtain, at the far end of a five-foot-high crawl space—but just to be on the safe side, Vicki dropped two by fours into iron brackets over the entrance. Folded nearly in half, she hurried to her sanctuary, feeling the sun drawing closer, closer. Somehow she resisted the urge to turn.

"There's nothing behind me," she muttered, awkwardly stripping off her clothes. Her heart slamming against her ribs, she crawled under the front flap of the box, latched it behind her, and squirmed into her sleeping bag, stretched out ready for dawn.

"Jesus H. Christ, Vicki," Celluci had said squatting at one end while she'd wrestled the twin bed mattress inside. *"At least a coffin would have a bit of historical dignity."*

"You know where I can get one?"

"I'm not having a coffin in my basement."

"Then quit flapping your mouth."

She wondered, as she lay there waiting for oblivion, where the other was. Did they feel the same near panic knowing that they had no control over the hours from dawn to dusk? Or had they, like Henry, come to accept the daily death that governed an immortal life? There should, she supposed, be a sense of kinship between them, but all she could feel was a possessive fury. No one hunted in her territory.

"Pleasant dreams," she said as the sun teetered on the edge of the horizon. "And when I find you, you're toast."

Celluci had been and gone by the time the darkness returned. The note he'd left about the car was profane and to the point. Vicki added a couple of words he'd missed and stuck it under a refrigerator magnet in case he got home before she did.

She'd pick up the scent and follow it, the hunter becoming the hunted and, by dawn, the streets would be hers again.

The yellow police tape still stretched across the mouth of the alley. Vicki ignored it. Wrapping the night around her like a cloak, she stood outside the restaurant door and sifted the air.

Apparently, a pimp crucified over the fire exit hadn't been enough to close the place and Tex Mex had nearly obliterated the scent of a death not yet twenty-four hours old. Instead of the predator, all she could smell was fajitas.

"Goddamn it," she muttered, stepping closer and sniffing the wood. "How the hell am I supposed to find . . . ?"

She sensed his life the moment before he spoke.

"What are you doing?"

Vicki sighed and turned. "I'm sniffing the door frame. What's it look like I'm doing?"

"Let me be more specific," Celluci snarled. "What are you doing *here*?"

"I'm looking for the person who offed Mac Eisler," Vicki began. She wasn't sure how much more explanation she was willing to offer.

"No, you're not. You are not a cop. You aren't even a P.I. anymore. And how the hell am I going to explain you if Dave sees you?"

Her eyes narrowed. "You don't have to explain me, Mike."

"Yeah? He thinks you're in Vancouver."

"Tell him I came back."

"And do I tell him that you spend your days in a box in my basement? And that you combust in sunlight? And what do I tell him about your eyes?"

Vicki's hand rose to push at the bridge of her glasses but her fingers touched only air. The retinitis pigmentosa that had forced her from the Metro Police and denied her the night had been reversed when Henry'd changed her. The darkness held no secrets from her now. "Tell him they got better."

"RP doesn't get better."

"Mine did."

"Vicki, I know what you're doing." He dragged both hands up through his hair. "You've done it before. You had to quit the force.

You were half-blind. So what? Your life may have changed, but you were still going to prove that you were 'Victory' Nelson. And it wasn't enough to be a private investigator. You threw yourself into stupidly dangerous situations just to prove you were still who you wanted to be. And now your life has changed again and you're playing the same game."

She could hear his heart pounding, see a vein pulsing framed in the white vee of his open collar, feel the blood surging just below the surface in reach of her teeth. The Hunger rose and she had to use every bit of control Henry had taught her to force it back down. This wasn't about that.

Since she'd returned to Toronto, she'd been drifting; feeding, hunting, relearning the night, relearning her relationship with Michael Celluci. The early morning phone call had crystallized a subconscious discontent and, as Celluci pointed out, there was really only one thing she knew how to do.

Part of his diatribe was based on concern. After all their years together playing cops and lovers, she knew how he thought; if something as basic as sunlight could kill her, what else waited to strike her down. It was only human nature for him to want to protect the people he loved—for him to want to protect her.

But that was only the basis for *part* of the diatribe.

"You can't have been happy with me lazing around your house. I can't cook and I don't do windows." She stepped toward him. "I should think you'd be thrilled that I'm finding my feet again."

"Vicki."

"I wonder," she mused, holding tight to the Hunger, "how you'd feel about me being involved in this if it wasn't your case. I am, after all, better equipped to hunt the night than, oh, detective-sergeants."

"Vicki . . . " Her name had become a nearly inarticulate growl.

She leaned forward until her lips brushed his ear. "Bet you I solve this one first." Then she was gone, moving into shadow too quickly for mortal eyes to track.

"Who you talking to, Mike?" Dave Graham glanced around the empty alley. " I thought I heard . . . " Then he caught sight of the expression on his partner's face. "Never mind."

VICKI COULDN'T REMEMBER THE last time she felt so alive. *Which, as I'm now a card-carrying member of the bloodsucking undead, makes for an interesting feeling.* She strode down Queen Street West, almost intoxicated by the lives surrounding her, fully aware of crowds parting to let her through and the admiring glances that traced her path. A connection had been made between her old life and her new one.

"*You must surrender the day,*" Henry had told her, "*but you need not surrender anything else.*"

"So what you're trying to tell me," she'd snarled, "*is that we're just normal people who drink blood?*"

Henry had smiled. "*How many* normal *people do you know?*"

She hated it when he answered a question with a question, but now she recognized his point. Honesty forced her to admit that Celluci had a point as well. She did need to prove to herself that she was still herself. She always had. The more things changed, the more they stayed the same.

"Well, now we've got that settled," She looked around for a place to sit and think. In her old life, that would have meant a donut shop or the window seat in a cheap restaurant and as many cups of coffee as it took. In this new life, being enclosed with humanity did not encourage contemplation. Besides, coffee, a major component of the old equation, made her violently ill, a fact she deeply resented.

A few years back, CITY TV, a local Toronto station, had renovated a deco building on the corner of Queen and John. They'd done a beautiful job and the six-story, white building with its ornately molded modern windows, had become a focal point of the neighborhood. Vicki slid into the narrow walkway that separated it from its more down-at-the-heels neighbor and swarmed up what effectively amounted to a staircase for one of her kind.

When she reached the roof a few seconds later, she perched on one crenelated corner and looked out over the downtown core. These were her streets; not Celluci's and not some out-of-town bloodsucker's. It was time she took them back. She grinned and fought the urge to strike a dramatic pose.

All things considered, it wasn't likely that the Metropolitan Toronto Police Department—in the person of Detective-Sergeant Michael Celluci—would be willing to share information. Briefly, she regretted issuing the challenge, then she shrugged it off. As Henry said, the night was too long for regrets.

She sat and watched the crowds jostling about on the sidewalks below, clumps of color indicating tourists among the Queen Street regulars. On a Friday night in August, this was the place to be as the

Toronto artistic community rubbed elbows with wanna-bes and neverwoulds.

Vicki frowned. Mac Eisler had been killed before midnight on a Thursday night in an area that never completely slept. Someone had to have seen or heard something. Something they probably didn't believe and were busy denying. Murder was one thing, creatures of the night were something else again.

"Now then," she murmured, "where would a person like that—and considering the time of day we're assuming a regular not a tourist—where would that person be tonight?"

She found him in the third bar she checked, tucked back in a corner, trying desperately to get drunk, and failing. His eyes darted from side to side, both hands were locked around his glass, and his body language screamed *I'm dealing with some bad shit here, leave me alone.*

Vicki sat down beside him and for an instant let the Hunter show. His reaction was everything she could have hoped for.

He stared at her, frozen in terror, his mouth working but no sound coming out.

"Breathe," she suggested.

The ragged intake of air did little to calm him, but it did break the paralysis. He shoved his chair back from the table and started to stand.

Vicki closed her fingers around his wrist. "Stay."

He swallowed and sat down again.

His skin was so hot it nearly burned and she could feel his pulse beating against it like a small wild creature struggling to be free. The Hunger clawed at her and her own breathing became a little ragged. "What's your name?"

"Ph . . . Phil."

She caught his gaze with hers and held it. "You saw something last night."

"Yes." Stretched almost to the breaking point, he began to tremble.

"Do you live around here?"

"Yes."

Vicki stood and pulled him to his feet, her tone half command-half caress. "Take me there. We have to talk."

Phil stared at her. "Talk?"

She could barely hear the question over the call of his blood. "Well, talk first."

"It was a woman. Dressed all in black. Hair like a thousand strands of shadow, skin like snow, eyes like black ice. She chuckled, deep in her throat, when she saw me and licked her lips. They were painfully red. Then she vanished, so quickly that she left an image on the night."

"Did you see what she was doing?"

"No. But then, she didn't have to be doing anything to be terrifying. I've spent the last twenty-four hours feeling like I met my death."

Phil had turned out to be a bit of a poet. And a bit of an athlete. All in all, Vicki considered their time together well spent. Working carefully after he fell asleep, she took away his memory of her and muted the meeting in the alley. It was the least she could do for him.

Description sounds like someone escaped from a Hammer film; The Bride of Dracula Kills a Pimp.

She paused, key in the lock, and cocked her head. Celluci was home, she could feel his life and if she listened very hard, she could hear the regular rhythm of breathing that told her he was asleep. Hardly surprising as it was only three hours to dawn.

There was no reason to wake him as she had no intention of sharing what she'd discovered and no need to feed, but after a long, hot shower, she found herself standing at the door of his room. And then at the side of his bed.

Mike Celluci was thirty-seven. There were strands of gray in his hair and although sleep had smoothed out many of the lines, the deeper creases around his eyes remained. He would grow older. In time, he would die. What would she do then?

She lifted the sheet and tucked herself up close to his side. He sighed and without completely waking scooped her closer still.

"Hair's wet," he muttered.

Vicki twisted, reached up, and brushed the long curl back off his forehead. "I had a shower."

"Where'd you leave the towel?"

"In a sopping pile on the floor."

Celluci grunted inarticulately and surrendered to sleep again.

Vicki smiled and kissed his eyelids. "I love you, too."

She stayed beside him until the threat of sunrise drove her away.

"Irene MacDonald."

Vicki lay in the darkness and stared unseeing up at the plywood. The sun was down and she was free to leave her sanctuary, but she remained a moment longer, turning over the name that had been on her tongue when she woke. She remembered facetiously wondering if the deaths of Irene MacDonald and her pimp were connected.

Irene had been found beaten nearly to death in the bathroom of her apartment. She'd died two hours later in the hospital.

Celluci said that he was personally certain Mac Eisler was responsible. That was good enough for Vicki.

Eisler could've been unlucky enough to run into a vampire who fed on terror as well as blood—Vicki had tasted terror once or twice during her first year when the Hunger occasionally slipped from her control and she knew how addictive it could be—or he could've been killed in revenge for Irene.

Vicki could think of one sure way to find out.

"BRANDON? IT'S VICKI NELSON."

"Victoria?" Surprise lifted most of the Oxford accent off Dr. Brandon Singh's voice. "I thought you'd relocated to British Columbia."

"Yeah, well, I came back."

"I suppose that might account for the improvement over the last month or so in a certain detective we both know."

She couldn't resist asking. "Was he really bad while I was gone?"

Brandon laughed. "He was unbearable and, as you know, I am able to bear a great deal. So, are you still in the same line of work?"

"Yes, I am." Yes, she was. God, it felt good. "Are you still the Assistant Coroner?"

"Yes, I am. As I think I can safely assume you didn't call me, at home, long after office hours, just to inform me that you're back on the job, what do you want?"

Vicki winced. "I was wondering if you'd had a look at Mac Eisler."

"Yes, Victoria, I have. And I'm wondering why you can't call me during regular business hours. You must know how much I enjoy discussing autopsies in front of my children."

"Oh, God, I'm sorry, Brandon, but it's important."

"Yes. It always is." His tone was so dry it crumbled. "But since you've already interrupted my evening, try to keep my part of the conversation to a simple yes or no."

"Did you do a blood volume check on Eisler?"

"Yes."

"Was there any missing?"

"No. Fortunately, in spite of the trauma to the neck, the integrity of the blood vessels had not been breached."

So much for yes or no; she knew he couldn't keep to it. "You've been a big help, Brandon, thanks."

"I'd say *any time*, but you'd likely hold me to it." He hung up abruptly.

Vicki replaced the receiver and frowned. She—the *other*—hadn't fed. The odds moved in favor of Eisler killed because he murdered Irene.

"WELL, IF IT ISN'T Andrew P." Vicki leaned back against the black Trans Am and adjusted the pair of nonprescription glasses she'd picked up just after sunset. With her hair brushed off her face and the window-glass lenses in front of her eyes, she didn't look much different than she had a year ago. Until she smiled.

The pimp stopped dead in his tracks, bluster fading before he could get the first obscenity out. He swallowed, audibly. "Nelson. I heard you were gone."

Listening to his heart race, Vicki's smile broadened. "I came back. I need some information. I need the name of one of Eisler's other girls."

"I don't know." Unable to look away, he started to shake. "I didn't have anything to do with him. I don't remember."

Vicki straightened and took a slow step toward him. "Try, Andrew."

There was a sudden smell of urine and a darkening stain down the front of the pimp's cotton drawstring pants. "Uh, D . . . D . . . Debbie Ho. That's all I can remember. Really."

"And she works?"

"Middle of the track." His tongue tripped over the words in the rush to spit them at her. "Jarvis and Carlton."

"Thank you." Sweeping a hand toward his car, Vicki stepped aside.

He dove past her and into the driver's seat, jabbing the key into the ignition. The powerful engine roared to life and with one last panicked look into the shadows, he screamed out of the driveway, ground his way through three gear changes, and hit eighty before he reached the corner.

The two cops, quietly sitting in the parking lot of the donut shop on that same corner, hit their siren and took off after him.

Vicki slipped the glasses into the inner pocket of the tweed jacket she'd borrowed from Celluci's closet and grinned. To paraphrase a certain adolescent crimefighting amphibian, I *love* being a vampire."

"I NEED TO TALK to you, Debbie."

The young woman started and whirled around, glaring suspiciously at Vicki. "You a cop?"

Vicki sighed. "Not any more." Apparently, it was easier to hide the vampire than the detective. "I'm a private investigator and I want to ask you some questions about Irene MacDonald."

"If you're looking for the shithead who killed her, you're too late. Someone already found him."

"And that's who I'm looking for."

"Why?" Debbie shifted her weight to one hip.

"Maybe I want to give him a medal."

The hooker's laugh held little humor. "You got that right. Mac got everything he deserved."

"Did Irene ever do women?"

Debbie snorted. "Not for free," she said pointedly.

Vicki handed her a twenty.

"Yeah, sometimes. It's safer, medically, you know?"

Editing out Phil's more ornate phrases, Vicki repeated his description of the woman in the alley.

Debbie snorted again. "Who the hell looks at their faces?"

"You'd remember this one if you saw her. She's . . . " Vicki weighed and discarded several possibilities and finally settled on, " . . . powerful."

"Powerful." Debbie hesitated, frowned, and continued in a rush. "There was this person Irene was seeing a lot of, but she wasn't charging. That's one of the things that set Mac off, not that the shithead needed much encouragement. We knew it was gonna happen, I mean we've all felt Mac's temper, but Irene wouldn't stop. She said that just being with this person was a high better than drugs. I guess it could've been a woman. And since she was sort of the reason Irene died, well, I know they used to meet in this bar on Queen West. Why are you hissing?"

"Hissing?" Vicki quickly yanked a mask of composure down over her rage. The other hadn't come into her territory only to kill

Eisler—she was definitely hunting it. "I'm not hissing. I'm just having a little trouble breathing."

"Yeah, tell me about it." Debbie waved a hand ending in three-inch scarlet nails at the traffic on Jarvis. "You should try standing here sucking carbon monoxide all night."

In another mood, Vicki might have reapplied the verb to a different object, but she was still too angry. "Do you know which bar?"

"What, now I'm her social director? No, I don't know which bar." Apparently they'd come to the end of the information twenty dollars could buy as Debbie turned her attention to a prospective client in a gray sedan. The interview was clearly over.

Vicki sucked the humid air past her teeth. There weren't that many bars on Queen West. Last night she'd found Phil in one. Tonight, who knew.

NOW THAT SHE KNEW enough to search for it, minute traces of the other predator hung in the air—diffused and scattered by the paths of prey. With so many lives masking the trail, it would be impossible to track her. Vicki snarled. A pair of teenagers, noses pierced, heads shaved, and Doc Martens laced to the knee, decided against asking for change and hastily crossed the street.

It was Saturday night, minutes to Sunday. The bars would be closing soon. If the *other* was hunting, she would have already chosen her prey.

I wish Henry had called back. Maybe over the centuries they've— we've—evolved ways to deal with this. Maybe we're supposed to talk first. Maybe it's considered bad manners to rip her face off and feed it to her if she doesn't agree to leave.

Standing in the shadow of a recessed storefront, just beyond the edge of the artificial safety the streetlight offered to the children of the sun, she extended her senses the way she'd been taught and touched death within the maelstrom of life.

She found Phil, moments later, lying in yet another of the alleys that serviced the business of the day and provided a safe haven for the darker business of the night. His body was still warm, but his heart had stopped beating and his blood no longer sang. Vicki touched the tiny, nearly closed wound she'd made in his wrist the night before and then the fresh wound in the bend of his elbow. She didn't know how he had died, but she knew who had done it. He stank of the *other*.

Vicki no longer cared what was traditionally "done" in these instances. There would be no talking. No negotiating. It had gone one life beyond that.

"I rather thought that if I killed him you'd come and save me the trouble of tracking you down. And here you are, charging in without taking the slightest of precautions." Her voice was low, not so much threatening as in itself a threat. "You're hunting in my territory, child."

Still kneeling by Phil's side, Vicki lifted her head. Ten feet away, only her face and hands clearly visible, the other vampire stood. Without thinking—unable to think clearly through the red rage that shrieked for release—Vicki launched herself at the snow-white column of throat, finger hooked to talons, teeth bared.

The Beast Henry had spent a year teaching her to control, was loose. She felt herself lost in its raw power and she reveled in it.

The *other* made no move until the last possible second then she lithely twisted and slammed Vicki to one side.

Pain eventually brought reason back. Vicki lay panting in the fetid damp at the base of a dumpster, one eye swollen shut, a gash across her forehead still sluggishly bleeding. Her right arm was broken.

"You're strong," the *other* told her, a contemptuous gaze pinning her to the ground. "In another hundred years you might have stood a chance. But you're an infant. A child. You haven't the experience to control what you are. This will be your only warning. Get out of my territory. If we meet again, I *will* kill you."

VICKI SAGGED AGAINST THE inside of the door and tried to lift her arm. During the two and a half hours it had taken her to get back to Celluci's house, the bone had begun to set. By tomorrow night, provided she fed in the hours remaining until dawn, she should be able to use it.

"Vicki?"

She started. Although she'd known he was home, she'd assumed—without checking—that because of the hour he'd be asleep. She squinted as the hall light came on and wondered, listening to him pad down the stairs in bare feet, whether she had the energy to make it into the basement bathroom before he saw her.

He came into the kitchen, tying his bathrobe belt around him, and flicked on the overhead light. "We need to talk," he said grimly as the shadows that might have hidden her fled. "Jesus H. Christ. What the hell happened to you?"

"Nothing much." Eyes squinted nearly shut, Vicki gingerly probed the swelling on her forehead. "You should see the other guy."

Without speaking, Celluci reached over and hit the play button on the telephone answering machine.

"Vicki? Henry. If someone's hunting your territory, whatever you do, don't challenge. Do you hear me? *Don't* challenge. You can't win. They're going to be older, able to overcome the instinctive rage and remain in full command of their power. If you won't surrender the territory . . . " The sigh the tape played back gave a clear opinion of how likely he thought that was to occur. " . . . you're going to have to negotiate. If you can agree on boundaries, there's no reason why you can't share the city." His voice suddenly belonged again to the lover she'd lost with the change. "Call me, please, before you do anything."

It was the only message on the tape.

"Why," Celluci asked as it rewound, his gaze taking in the cuts and the bruising and the filth, "do I get the impression that it's 'the other guy' Fitzroy's talking about?"

Vicki tried to shrug. Her shoulders refused to cooperate. "It's my city, Mike. It always has been. I'm going to take it back."

He stared at her for a long moment then he shook his head. "You heard what Henry said. You can't win. You haven't been . . . what you are, long enough. It's only been fourteen months."

"I know." The rich scent of his life prodded the Hunger and she moved to put a little distance between them.

He closed it up again. "Come on." Laying his hand in the center of her back, he steered her toward the stairs. *Put it aside for now*, his tone told her. *We'll argue about it later.* "You need a bath."

"I need . . . "

"I know. But you need a bath first. I just changed the sheets."

THE DARKNESS WAKES ALL *in different ways*, Henry had told her. *We were all human once and we carried our differences through the change.*

For Vicki, it was like the flicking of a switch; one moment she wasn't, the next she was. This time, when she returned from the little death of the day, an idea returned with her.

Four-hundred-and-fifty-odd years a vampire, Henry had been seventeen when he changed. The other had walked the night for

perhaps as long—her gaze had carried the weight of several lifetimes—but her physical appearance suggested that her mortal life
had lasted even less time than Henry's had. Vicki allowed that it
made sense. Disaster may have precipitated her change, but passion
was the usual cause.

And no one does that kind of never-say-die passion like a teenager.

It would be difficult for either Henry or the other to imagine a
response that came out of a mortal rather than a vampiric experience. They'd both had centuries of the latter and not enough of the
former to count.

Vicki had been only fourteen months a vampire, but she'd been
human thirty-two years when Henry'd saved her by drawing her to
his blood to feed. During those thirty-two years, she'd been nine
years a cop—two accelerated promotions, three citations, and the
best arrest record on the force.

There was no chance of negotiation.

She couldn't win if she fought.

She'd be damned if she'd flee.

"Besides . . . " For all she realized where her strength had to lie,
Vicki's expression held no humanity. she owes me for Phil."

CELLUCI HAD LEFT HER a note on the fridge.

Does this have anything to do with Mac Eisler?

Vicki stared at it for a moment then scribbled her answer under-
neath.

Not anymore.

It took three weeks to find where the *other* spent her days. Vicki
used old contacts where she could and made new ones where she
had to. Any modern Van Helsing could have done the same.

For the next three weeks, Vicki hired someone to watch the *other*
come and go, giving reinforced instructions to stay in the car with the
windows closed and the air-conditioning running. Life had an infinite
number of variations, but one piece of machinery smelled pretty much
like any other. It irritated her that she couldn't sit stakeout herself, but
the information she needed would've kept her out after sunrise.

"HOW THE HELL DID you burn your hand?"

Vicki continued to smear ointment over the blister. Unlike the
injuries she'd taken in the alley, this would heal slowly and painfully.
"Accident in a tanning salon."

"That's not funny."

She picked up the roll of gauze from the counter. "You're losing your sense of humor, Mike."

Celluci snorted and handed her the scissors. "I never had one."

"MIKE, I WANTED TO warn you, I won't be back by sunrise."

Celluci turned slowly, the TV dinner he'd just taken from the microwave held in both hands. "What do you mean?"

She read the fear in his voice and lifted the edge of the tray so that the gravy didn't pour out and over his shoes. "I mean I'll be spending the day somewhere else."

"Where?"

"I can't tell you."

"Why? Never mind." He raised a hand as her eyes narrowed. "Don't tell me. I don't want to know. You're going after that other vampire aren't you? The one Fitzroy told you to leave alone."

"I thought you didn't want to know."

"I already know," he grunted. "I can read you like a book. With large type. And pictures."

Vicki pulled the tray from his grip and set it on the counter. "She's killed two people. Eisler was a scumbag who may have deserved it, but the other . . . "

"Other?" Celluci exploded. "Jesus H. Christ, Vicki, in case you've forgotten, murder's against the law! Who the hell painted a big vee on your long johns and made you the vampire vigilante?"

"Don't you remember?" Vicki snapped. "You were there. I didn't make this decision, Mike. You and Henry made it for me. You'd just better learn to live with it." She fought her way back to calm. "Look, you can't stop her, but I can. I know that galls, but that's the way it is."

They glared at each other, toe to toe. Finally Celluci looked away.

"I can't stop you, can I?" he asked bitterly. "I'm only human after all."

"Don't sell yourself short," Vicki snarled. "You're quintessentially human. If you want to stop me, you face me and ask me not to go and *then* you remember it every time *you* go into a situation that could get your ass shot off."

After a long moment, he swallowed, lifted his head, and met her eyes. "Don't die. I thought I lost you once and I'm not strong enough to go through that again."

"Are you asking me not to go?"

He snorted. "I'm asking you to be careful. Not that you ever listen."

She took a step forward and rested her head against his shoulder, wrapping herself in the beating of his heart.

"This time, I'm listening."

* * *

THE STUDIOS IN THE converted warehouse on King Street were not supposed to be live-in. A good 75 percent of the tenants ignored that. The studio Vicki wanted was at the back on the third floor. The heavy steel door—an obvious upgrade by the occupant—had been secured by the best lock money could buy.

New senses and old skills got through it in record time.

Vicki pushed open the door with her foot and began carrying boxes inside. She had a lot to do before dawn.

"She goes out every night between ten and eleven, then she comes home every morning between four and five. You could set your watch by her."

Vicki handed him an envelope.

He looked inside, thumbed through the money, then grinned up at her. "Pleasure doing business for you. Any time you need my services, you know where to call."

"Forget it," she told him.

And he did.

BECAUSE SHE EXPECTED HER, Vicki knew the moment the *other* entered the building. The Beast stirred and she tightened her grip on it. To lose control now would be disaster.

She heard the elevator, then footsteps in the hall.

"You know I'm in here," she said silently, *"and you know you can take me. Be overconfident, believe I'm a fool, and walk right in."*

"I thought you were smarter than this." The *other* stepped into the apartment, then casually turned to lock the door. "I told you when I saw you again I'd kill you."

Vicki shrugged, the motion masking her fight to remain calm. "Don't you even want to know why I'm here?"

"I assume you've come to negotiate." She raised ivory hands and released thick, black hair from its bindings. "We went past that when you attacked me." Crossing the room, she preened before a large ornate mirror that dominated one wall of the studio.

"I attacked you because you murdered Phil."

"Was that his name?" The other laughed. The sound had razored edges. "I didn't bother to ask it."

"Before you murdered him."

"Murdered? You are a child. They are prey, we are predators— their deaths are ours if we desire them. You'd have learned that in time." She turned, the patina of civilization stripped away. "Too bad you haven't any time left."

Vicki snarled but somehow managed to stop herself from attacking. Years of training whispered, *Not yet.* She had to stay exactly where she was.

"Oh, yes." The sibilants flayed the air between them. "I almost forgot. You wanted me to ask you why you came. Very well. Why?"

Given the address and the reason, Celluci could've come to the studio during the day and slammed a stake through the *other's* heart. The vampire's strongest protection, would be of no use against him. Mike Celluci believed in vampires.

"I came," Vicki told her, "because some things you have to do yourself."

The wire ran up the wall, tucked beside the surface-mounted cable of a cheap renovation, and disappeared into the shadows that clung to a ceiling sixteen feet from the floor. The switch had been stapled down beside her foot. A tiny motion, too small to evoke attack, flipped it.

Vicki had realized from the beginning that there were a number of problems with her plan. The first involved placement. Every living space included an area where the occupant felt secure—a favorite chair, a window . . . a mirror. The second problem was how to mask what she'd done. While the other would not be able to sense the various bits of wiring and equipment, she'd be fully aware of Vicki's scent *on* the wiring and equipment. Only if Vicki remained in the studio, could that smaller trace be lost in the larger.

The third problem was directly connected with the second. Given that Vicki had to remain, how was she to survive?

Attached to the ceiling by sheer brute strength, positioned so that they shone directly down into the space in front of the mirror, were a double bank of lights cannibalized from a tanning bed. The sun held a double menace for the vampire—its return to the sky brought complete vulnerability and its rays burned.

Henry had a round scar on the back of one hand from too close an encounter with the sun. When her burn healed, Vicki would have a matching one from a deliberate encounter with an imitation.

The *other* screamed as the lights came on, the sound pure rage and so inhuman that those who heard it would have to deny it for sanity's sake.

Vicki dove forward, ripped the heavy brocade off the back of the couch, and burrowed frantically into its depths. Even that instant of light had bathed her skin in flame and she moaned as, for a moment, the searing pain became all she was. After a time, when it grew no worse, she managed to open her eyes.

The light couldn't reach her, but neither could she reach the switch to turn it off. She could see it, three feet away just beyond the shadow of the couch. She shifted her weight and a line of blister rose across one leg. Biting back a shriek, she curled into a fetal position, realizing her refuge was not entirely secure.

Okay, genius, now what?

Moving very, very carefully, Vicki wrapped her hand around the one by two that braced the lower edge of the couch. From the tension running along it, she suspected that breaking it off would result in at least a partial collapse of the piece of furniture.

And if it goes, I very well may go with it.

And then she heard the sound of something dragging itself across the floor.

Oh, shit! She's not dead!

The wood broke, the couch began to fall in on itself, and Vicki, realizing that luck would have a large part to play in her survival, smacked the switch and rolled clear in the same motion.

The room plunged into darkness.

Vicki froze as her eyes slowly readjusted to the night. Which was when she finally became conscious of the smell. It had been there all along, but her senses had refused to acknowledge it until they had to.

Sunlight burned.

Vicki gagged.

The dragging sound continued.

The hell with this! She didn't have time to wait for her eyes to repair the damage they'd obviously taken. She needed to see *now*.

Fortunately, although it hadn't seemed fortunate at the time, she'd learned to maneuver without sight.

She threw herself across the room.

The light switch was where they always were, to the right of the door.

The thing on the floor pushed itself up on fingerless hands and glared at her out of the blackened ruin of a face. Laboriously it turned, hate radiating off it in palpable waves and began to pull itself toward her again.

Vicki stepped forward to meet it.

While the part of her that remembered being human writhed in revulsion, she wrapped her hands around its skull and twisted it in a full circle. The spine snapped. Another full twist and what was left of the head came off in her hands.

She'd been human for thirty-two years, but she'd been fourteen months a vampire.

"No one hunts in *my* territory," she snarled as the *other* crumbled to dust.

She limped over to the wall and pulled the plug supplying power to the lights. Later, she'd remove them completely—the whole concept of sunlamps gave her the creeps.

When she turned, she was facing the mirror.

The woman who stared out at her through bloodshot eyes, exposed skin blistered and red, was a hunter. Always had been really. The question became, who was she to hunt?

Vicki smiled. Before the sun drove her to use her inherited sanctuary, she had a few quick phone calls to make. The first to Celluci; she owed him the knowledge that she'd survived the night. The second to Henry for much the same reason.

The third call would be to the 800 line that covered the classifieds of Toronto's largest alternative newspaper. This ad was going to be a little different than the one she'd placed upon leaving the force. Back then, she'd been incredibly depressed about leaving a job she loved for a life she saw as only marginally useful. This time, she had no regrets.

Victory Nelson, Investigator: Otherworldly Crimes a Specialty.

DUTY

Ed Gorman

Earlier this morning, just as the sun had begun to burn the dew off the farm fields, Keller got out his old Schwinn and set off. In less than a minute, he'd left behind the tarpaper shack where he lived with a goat, three chickens he'd never had the heart to eat, four cats, and a hamster. The hamster had been Timmy's.

Today he traveled the old two-lane highway. The sun hot on his back, he thought of how it used to be on this stretch of asphalt, the bright red convertibles with the bright pink blondes in them and the sound of rock and roll waving like a banner in the wind. Or the green John Deere tractors moving snail-slow, trailing infuriated city drivers behind.

The old days. Before the change. He used to sit in a chair in front of his shack and talk to his wife, Martha, and his son, Timmy, till Timmy went to sleep in Martha's lap. Then Keller would take the boy inside and lay him gently in bed and kiss his boy-moist brow good night. The Kellers had always been referred to locally, and not unkindly, as "that hippie family." Keller had worn the tag as a badge of honor. In a world obsessed with money and power, he'd wanted to spend his days discovering again and again the simple pleasures of starry nights, of clear quick country streams, of mountain music strummed on an old six-string and accompanied by owls and kitties and crocuses. Somehow back in time he'd managed to get himself an advanced degree in business and finance. But after meeting

Martha, the happiest and most contented person he'd ever known, he'd followed her out here and he never once yearned for the treacherous world he'd deserted.

He thought of these things as he angled the Schwinn down the center of the highway, his golden collie, Andy, running alongside, appreciative of the exercise. Across Keller's shoulder was strapped his ancient backpack, the one he'd carried twenty years ago in college. You could see faintly where the word *Adidas* had been.

He rode on. The Schwinn's chain was loose and banged noisily sometimes, and on a particularly hard bump the front fender sometimes rubbed the tire. He fixed the bike methodically, patiently, at least once a week, but the Schwinn was like a wild boy and would never quite be tamed. Timmy had been that way.

The trip took two hours. By that time, Andy was tired of running, his pink tongue lolling out of his mouth, exhausted, and Keller was tired of pedaling.

The farmhouse was up a high sloping hill, east of the highway.

From his backpack Keller took his binoculars. He spent ten minutes scanning the place. He had no idea what he was looking for. He just wanted to reassure himself that the couple who'd sent the message with Conroy—a pig farmer ten miles to the west of Keller's—were who and what they claimed to be.

He saw a stout woman in a faded housedress hanging laundry on a backyard clothesline. He saw a sun-reddened man in blue overalls moving among a waving carpet of white hungry chickens, throwing them golden kernels of corn. He saw a windmill turning with rusty dignity in the southern wind.

After returning his binoculars to his backpack, he mounted the Schwinn again, patted Andy on the head, and set off up the steep gravel hill.

THE WOMAN SAW KELLER FIRST. He had come around the edge of the big two-story frame house when she was just finishing with her laundry.

She looked almost angry when she saw who he was.

She didn't speak to him; instead, she called out in a weary voice for her husband. Somehow, the man managed to hear her above the squawking chickens. He set down the tin pan that held the kernels of corn, then walked over and stood by his wife.

"You're a little early," the farmer said. His name was Dodds—

Alcie Dodds—and his wife was Myrna. Keller used to see them at
the potluck dinners the community held back before the change.

"I wasn't sure how long it would take. Guess I left a little before
I needed to."

"You enjoy what you do, Mr. Keller? Does it give you pleasure?"
Myrna Dodds said.

"Now, Myrna, don't be—"

"I just want him to answer the question. I just want him to
answer honestly."

By now, Keller was used to being treated this way. It was, he
knew, a natural reaction.

Alcie Dodds said, "She hasn't had much sleep the last couple of
nights, Keller. You know what I'm saying."

Keller nodded.

"You want a cup of coffee?" Alcie Dodds said.

"I'd appreciate it."

Suddenly the woman started crying. She put her hands to her
face and simply began wailing, her fleshy body shaking beneath the
loose-fitting housedress.

Keller saw such grief everywhere he went. He wished there was
something he could do about it.

Dodds went over and slid his arm around his wife. "Why don't
you go in and see Beth, honey?"

Mention of the name only caused the woman to begin sobbing
even more uncontrollably.

She took her hands from her face and glared at Keller. "I hope
you rot in hell, Mr. Keller. I hope you rot in hell."

SHADOWS COOLED THE KITCHEN. The air smelled of the stew bubbling on the stove, of beef and tomatoes and onions and paprika.

The two men sat at a small kitchen table beneath a funeral home
calendar that had a picture of Jesus as a young and very handsome
bearded man. By now, they were on their second cup of coffee.

"Sorry about the missus."

"I understand. I'd feel the same way."

"We always assume it won't happen to us."

"Ordinarily, they don't get out this far. It isn't worth it for them.
They stick to cities, or at least areas where the population is heavy."

"But they do get out here," Dodds said. "More often than people
like to admit."

Keller sighed. He stared down into his coffee cup. "I guess that's true."

"I hear it happened to you."

"Yes."

"Your boy."

"Right."

"The fucking bastards. The fucking bastards." Dodds made a large fist and brought it down thunderously on the table that smelled of the red-and-white-checkered oilcloth. In the window above the sink the sky was very blue and the blooming trees very green.

After a time, Dodds said, "You ever seen one? In person, I mean?"

"No."

"We did once. We were in Chicago. We were supposed to get back to our hotel room before dusk, before they came out into the streets but we got lost. Anybody ever tell you about their smell?"

"Yes."

"It's like rotting meat. You can't believe it. Especially when a lot of them are in one place at the same time. And they've got these sores all over them. Like leprosy. We made it back to the hotel all right, but before we did we saw these two young children—they'd turned already—they found this old lady and they started chasing her, having a good time with her, really prolonging it, and then she tripped in the street and one of them knelt beside her and went to work. You heard about how they puke afterward?"

"Yes. The shock to their digestive systems. All the blood."

"Never saw anybody puke like this. And the noise they made when they were puking. Sickening. Then the old lady got up and let out this cry. I've never heard anything even close to it. Just this loud animal noise. She was already starting to turn."

Keller finished his coffee.

"You want more?"

"No, thanks, Mr. Dodds."

"You want a Pepsi? Got a six-pack we save for special occasions." He shrugged. "I'm not much of a liquor drinker."

"No, thanks, Mr. Dodds."

Dodds drained his own coffee. "Can I ask you something?"

"Sure."

It was time to get it over with. Dodds was stalling. Keller didn't blame him.

"You ever find that you're wrong?"

"How so, Mr. Dodds?"

"You know, that you think they've turned but they really haven't?"

Keller knew what Dodds was trying to say, of course. He was trying to say—to whatever God existed—please let it be a mistake. Please let it not be what it seems to be.

"Not so far, I haven't, Mr. Dodds. I'm sorry."

"You know how it's going to be on her, don't you, on my wife?"

"Yes, I'm afraid I do, Mr. Dodds."

"She won't ever be the same."

"No, I don't suppose she will."

Dodds stared down at his hands and turned them into fists again. Under his breath, he said, "Fucking bastards."

"Maybe we'd better go have a look, Mr. Dodds."

"You sure you don't want another cup of coffee?"

"No, thanks, Mr. Dodds. I appreciate the offer, though."

DODDS LED THEM THROUGH the cool, shadowy house. The place was old. You could tell that by all the mahogany trim and the height of the ceilings and the curve of the time-swollen floor. But even given its age it was a pleasant and comfortable place, a nook of sweet shade on a hot day.

Down the hall Keller could hear Mrs. Dodds singing, humming really, soft noises rather than words.

"Forgive her if she acts up again, Mr. Keller."

Keller nodded.

And it was then the rock came sailing through the window in the front room. The smashing glass had an almost musical quality to it on the hot silent afternoon.

"What the hell was that?" Dodds wondered.

He turned around and ran back down the pink wallpapered hall and right out the front door, almost slamming the screen door in Keller's face.

There were ten of them on the lawn, in the shade of the elm, six men, four women. Two of the men held carbines.

"There he is," one of the men said.

"That sonofabitch Keller," another man said.

"You people get out of here, and now," Dodds said, coming down off the porch steps. "This is my land."

"You really gonna let him do it, Alcie?" a man said.

"That's my business," Dodds said, pawing at the front of his coveralls.

A pretty woman leaned forward. "I'm sorry we came, Alcie. The men just wouldn't have it any other way. Us women just came along to make sure there wasn't no violence."

"Speak for yourself, honey," a plump woman in a man's checkered shirt and jeans said. "Personally, I'd like to cut Keller's balls off and feed 'em to my pigs."

Two of the men laughed at her. She'd said it to impress them and she'd achieved her end.

"Go on, now, before somethin' is said or done that can't be unsaid or undone," Dodds said.

"Your wife want this done?" the man with the second carbine said. He answered his own question: "Bet she don't. Bet she fought you on it all the way."

A soft breeze came. It was an afternoon for drinking lemonade and watching monarch butterflies and seeing the foals in the pasture running up and down the summer green hills. It was not an afternoon for angry men with carbines.

"You heard me now," Dodds said.

"How 'bout you, chickenshit? You got anything to say for yourself, Keller?"

"Goddamnit, Davey—" Dodds started to say.

"Won't use my gun, Alcie. Don't need it."

And with that the man named Davey tossed his carbine to one of the other men and then stepped up near the steps where Dodds and Keller stood.

Keller recognized Davey. He ran the feed and grain in town and was a legendary tavern bully. God forbid you should ever beat him at snooker. He had freckles like a pox and fists like anvils.

"You hear what I asked you, chickenshit?"

"Davey—" Dodds started to say again.

Keller stepped down off the steps. He was close enough to smell the afternoon beer on Davey's breath.

"This wasn't easy for Mr. Dodds, Davey," Keller said. He spoke so softly Davey's friends had to lean forward to hear. "But it's his decision to make. His and his wife's."

"You enjoy it, don't you, chickenshit?" Davey said. "You're some kind of pervert who gets his kicks that way, aren't you?"

Behind him, his friends started cursing Keller, and that only emboldened Davey all the more.

He threw a big roundhouse right and got Keller right in the mouth.

Keller started to drop to the ground, black spots alternating with yellow spots before his eyes, and then Davey raised his right foot and kicked Keller square in the chest.

"Kill that fucker, Davey! Kill that fucker!" one of the men with the carbines shouted.

And then, on the sinking afternoon, the shotgun was fired.

The bird shot got so close to Davey that it tore tiny holes in his right sleeve, like something that had been gnawed on by a puppy.

"You heard my husband," Mrs. Dodds said, standing on the porch with a sawed-off double barrel that looked to be one mean and serious weapon. "You get off our land."

Davey said, "We was only tryin' to help you, missus. We knew you didn't want—"

But she silenced him. "I was wrong about Keller here. If he didn't care about them, he couldn't do it. He had to do it to his own wife and son, or are you forgetting that?"

Davey said, "But—"

And Mrs. Dodds leveled the shotgun right at his chest. "You think I won't kill you, Davey, you're wrong."

Davey's wife took him by the sleeve. "C'mon, honey; you can see she's serious."

But Davey had one last thing to say. "It ain't right what he does. Don't you know that, Mrs. Dodds? It ain't right!"

But Mrs. Dodds could only sadly shake her head. "You know what'd become of 'em if he didn't do it, don't you? Go into the city sometime and watch 'em. Then tell me you'd want one of your own to be that way."

Davey's wife tugged on his sleeve again. Then she looked up at Mrs. Dodds and said, "I'm sorry for this, Mrs. Dodds. I really am. The boys here just had too much to drink and—" She shook her head. "I'm sorry."

And in ones and twos they started drifting back to the pickup trucks they'd parked on the downslope side of the gravel drive.

"It's a nice room," Keller said twenty minutes later. And it was. The wallpaper was blue. Teddy bears and unicorns cavorted across it. There was a tiny table and chairs and a globe and a set of junior encyclopedias, things she would grow up to use someday. Or would have, anyway.

In the corner was the baby's bed. Mrs. Keller stood in front of it, protecting it. "I'm sorry how I treated you when you first came."

"I know."

"And I'm sorry Davey hit you."

"Not your fault."

By now he realized that she was not only stalling. She was also doing something else—pleading. "You look at little Beth and you be sure."

"I will."

"I've heard tales of how sometimes you think they've turned but it's just some other illness with the same symptoms."

"I'll be very careful."

Mr. Dodds said, "You want us to leave the room?"

"It'd be better for your wife."

And then she spun around and looked down into the baby's bed where her seven-month-old daughter lay discolored and breathing as if she could not catch her breath, both primary symptoms of the turning.

She picked the infant up and clutched it to her chest. And began sobbing so loudly, all Keller could do was put his head down.

It fell to Mr. Dodds to pry the baby from his wife's grip and to lead Mrs. Dodds from the baby's room.

On his way out, starting to cry a man's hard, embarrassed tears, Mr. Dodds looked straight at Keller and said, "Just be sure, Mr. Keller. Just be sure."

Keller nodded that he'd be sure.

The room smelled of sunlight and shade and baby powder.

The bed had the sort of slatted sides you could pull up or down. He put it down and leaned over to the baby. She was very pretty, chunky, blond, with a cute little mouth. She wore diapers. They looked very white compared to the blue, asphyxiated color of her skin.

His examination was simple. The Dodds could easily have done it themselves, but of course they didn't want to. It would only have confirmed their worst fears.

He opened her mouth. She started to cry. He first examined her gums and then her teeth. The tissue on the former had started to harden and scab; the latter had started to elongate.

The seven-month-old child was in the process of turning.

Sometimes they roamed out here from the cities and took what they could find. One of them had broken into the Dodds's two weeks ago and had stumbled on the baby's room.

He worked quickly, as he always did, as he'd done with his wife and son when they'd been ambushed in the woods one day and had then started to turn.

All that was left of civilization was in the outlands such as these. Even though you loved them, you could not let them turn because the life ahead for them was so unimaginably terrible. The endless hunt for new bodies, the feeding frenzies, the constant illness that was a part of the condition and the condition was forever—

No, if you loved them, you had only one choice.

In this farming community, no one but Keller could bring himself to do what was necessary. They always deluded themselves that their loved ones hadn't really been infected, hadn't really begun turning—

And so it fell to Keller.

He rummaged quickly through his Adidas backpack now, finding hammer and wooden stake.

He returned to the bed and leaned over and kissed the little girl on the forehead. "You'll be with God, honey," he said. "You'll be with God."

He stood up straight, took the stake in his left hand and set it against her heart, and then with great sad weariness raised the hammer.

He killed her as he killed them all, clean and quick, hot infected blood splattering his face and shirt, her final cry one more wound in his soul.

ON THE PORCH, MRS. DODDS inside in her bedroom, Mr. Dodds put his hand on Keller's shoulder and said, "I'll pray for you, Mr. Keller."

"I'll be needing your prayers, Mr. Dodds," Keller said, and then nodded good-bye and left.

IN HALF AN HOUR, he was well down the highway again, Andy getting another good run for the day, pink tongue lolling.

In his backpack he could feel the sticky hammer and stake, the same tools he used over and over again as the sickness of the cities spread constantly outward.

In a while it began to rain. He was still thinking of the little Dodds girl, of her innocent eyes there at the very last.

Midnight Mass

F. Paul Wilson

It had been almost a full minute since he'd slammed the brass knocker against the heavy oak door. That should have been proof enough. After all, wasn't the knocker in the shape of a cross? But no, they had to squint through their peephole and peer through the sidelights that framed the door.

Rabbi Zev Wolpin sighed and resigned himself to the scrutiny. He couldn't blame people for being cautious, but this seemed a bit overly so. The sun was in the west and shining full on his back; he was all but silhouetted in it. What more did they want?

I should maybe take off my clothes, and dance naked?

He gave a mental shrug and savored the damp sea air. At least it was cool here. He'd bicycled from Lakewood, which was only ten miles inland from this same ocean but at least twenty degrees warmer. The bulk of the huge Tudor retreat house stood between him and the Atlantic, but the ocean's briny scent and rhythmic rumble were everywhere.

Spring Lake. An Irish Catholic seaside resort since before the turn of the century. He looked around at its carefully restored Victorian houses, the huge mansions arrayed here along the beach front, the smaller homes set in neat rows running straight back from the ocean. Many of them were still occupied. Not like Lakewood. Lakewood was an empty shell.

Not such a bad place for a retreat, he thought. He wondered how many houses like this the Catholic Church owned.

A series of clicks and clacks drew his attention back to the door as numerous bolts were pulled in rapid succession. The door swung inward revealing a nervous-looking young man in a long black cassock. As he looked at Zev his mouth twisted and he rubbed the back of his wrist across it to hide a smile.

"And what should be so funny?" Zev asked.

"I'm sorry. It's just—!"

"I know," Zev said, waving off any explanation as he glanced down at the wooden cross slung on a cord around his neck. "I know."

A bearded Jew in a baggy black serge suit wearing a yarmulke and a cross. Hilarious, no?

So, *nu?* This was what the times demanded, this was what it had come to if he wanted to survive. And Zev did want to survive. Someone had to live to carry on the traditions of the Talmud and the Torah, even if there were hardly any Jews left alive in the world.

Zev stood on the sunny porch, waiting. The priest watched him in silence.

Finally Zev said, "Well, may a wandering Jew come in?"

"I won't stop you," the priest said, "but surely you don't expect me to invite you."

Ah, yes. Another precaution. The vampire couldn't cross the threshold of a home unless he was invited in, so don't invite. A good habit to cultivate, he supposed.

He stepped inside and the priest immediately closed the door behind him, relatching all the locks one by one. When he turned around Zev held out his hand.

"Rabbi Zev Wolpin, Father. I thank you for allowing me in."

"Brother Christopher, sir," he said, smiling and shaking Zev's hand. His suspicions seemed to have been completely allayed. "I'm not a priest yet. We can't offer you much here, but—"

"Oh, I won't be staying long. I just came to talk to Father Joseph Cahill."

Brother Christopher frowned. "Father Cahill isn't here at the moment."

"When will he be back?"

"I—I'm not sure. You see—"

"Father Cahill is on another bender," said a stentorian voice behind Zev.

He turned to see an elderly priest facing him from the far end of the foyer. White-haired, heavy set, wearing a black cassock.

"I'm Rabbi Wolpin."

"Father Adams," the priest said, stepping forward and extending his hand.

As they shook Zev said, "Did you say he was on 'another' bender? I never knew Father Cahill to be much of a drinker."

"Apparently there was a lot we never knew about Father Cahill," the priest said stiffly.

"If you're referring to that nastiness last year," Zev said, feeling the old anger rise in him, "I for one never believed it for a minute. I'm surprised anyone gave it the slightest credence."

"The veracity of the accusation was irrelevant in the final analysis. The damage to Father Cahill's reputation was a fait accompli. Father Palmeri was forced to request his removal for the good of Saint Anthony's parish."

Zev was sure that sort of attitude had something to do with Father Joe being on "another bender."

"Where can I find Father Cahill?"

"He's in town somewhere, I suppose, making a spectacle of himself. If there's any way you can talk some sense into him, please do. Not only is he killing himself with drink but he's become quite an embarrassment to the priesthood and to the Church."

Which bothers you more? Zev wanted to ask but held his tongue.

"I'll try."

He waited for Brother Christopher to undo all the locks, then stepped toward the sunlight.

"Try Morton's down on Seventy-one," the younger man whispered as Zev passed.

ZEV RODE HIS BICYCLE south on 71. It was almost strange to see people on the streets. Not many, but more than he'd ever see in Lakewood again. Yet he knew that as the vampires consolidated their grip on the world and infiltrated the Catholic communities, there'd be fewer and fewer day people here as well.

He thought he remembered passing a place named Morton's on his way to Spring Lake. And then up ahead he saw it, by the railroad track crossing, a white stucco one-story box of a building with "Morton's Liquors" painted in big black letters along the side.

Father Adams's words echoed back to him: . . . *on another bender* . . .

Zev pushed his bicycle to the front door and tried the knob. Locked up tight. A look inside showed a litter of trash and empty shelves. The windows were barred; the back door was steel and locked as securely as the front. So where was Father Joe?

Then he spotted the basement window at ground level by the overflowing trash dumpster. It wasn't latched. Zev went down on his knees and pushed it open.

Cool, damp, musty air wafted against his face as he peered into the Stygian blackness. It occurred to him that he might be asking for trouble by sticking his head inside, but he had to give it a try. If Father Cahill wasn't here, Zev would begin the return trek to Lakewood and write this whole trip off as wasted effort.

"Father Joe?" he called. "Father Cahill?"

"That you again, Chris?" said a slightly slurred voice. "Go home, will you? I'll be all right. I'll be back later."

"It's me, Joe. Zev. From Lakewood."

He heard shoes scraping on the floor and then a familiar face appeared in the shaft of light from the window.

"Well I'll be damned. It *is* you! Thought you were Brother Chris come to drag me back to the retreat house. Gets scared I'm gonna get stuck out after dark. So how ya doin', Reb? Glad to see you're still alive. Come on in!"

Zev saw that Father Cahill's eyes were glassy and he swayed ever so slightly, like a skyscraper in the wind. He wore faded jeans and a black Bruce Springsteen *Tunnel of Love* Tour sweatshirt.

Zev's heart twisted at the sight of his friend in such condition. Such a mensch like Father Joe shouldn't be acting like a *shikker*. Maybe it was a mistake coming here. Zev didn't like seeing him like this.

"I don't have that much time, Joe. I came to tell you—"

"Get your bearded ass down here and have a drink or I'll come up and drag you down."

"All right," Zev said. "I'll come in but I won't have a drink."

He hid his bike behind the dumpster, then squeezed through the window. Father Joe helped him to the floor. They embraced, slapping each other on the back. Father Joe was a taller man, a giant from Zev's perspective. At six-four he was ten inches taller, at thirty-five he was a quarter-century younger; he had a muscular frame, thick brown hair, and—on better days—clear blue eyes.

"You're grayer, Zev, and you've lost weight."

"Kosher food is not so easily come by these days."

"All kinds of food is getting scarce." He touched the cross slung from Zev's neck and smiled. "Nice touch. Goes well with your zizith."

Zev fingered the fringe protruding from under his shirt. Old habits didn't die easily.

"Actually, I've grown rather fond of it."

"So what can I pour you?" the priest said, waving an arm at the crates of liquor stacked around him. "My own private reserve. Name your poison."

"I don't want a drink."

"Come on, Reb. I've got some nice hundred-proof Stoly here. You've got to have at least *one* drink—"

"Why? Because you think maybe you shouldn't drink alone?"

Father Joe smiled. "Touché."

"All right," Zev said. *"Bissel.* I'll have *one* drink on the condition that you *don't* have one. Because I wish to talk to you."

The priest considered that a moment, then reached for the vodka bottle.

"Deal."

He poured a generous amount into a paper cup and handed it over. Zev took a sip. He was not a drinker and when he did imbibe he preferred his vodka ice cold from a freezer. But this was tasty. Father Cahill sat back on a crate of Jack Daniel's and folded his arms.

"Nu?" the priest said with a Jackie Mason shrug.

Zev had to laugh. "Joe, I still say that somewhere in your family tree is Jewish blood."

For a moment he felt light, almost happy. When was the last time he had laughed? Probably more than a year now, probably at their table near the back of Horovitz's deli, shortly before the Saint Anthony's nastiness began, well before the vampires came.

Zev thought of the day they'd met. He'd been standing at the counter at Horovitz's waiting for Yussel to wrap up the stuffed derma he had ordered when this young giant walked in. He towered over the other rabbis in the place, looked as Irish as Paddy's pig, and wore a Roman collar. He said he'd heard this was the only place on the whole Jersey Shore where you could get a decent corned beef sandwich. He ordered one and cheerfully warned that it better be good. Yussel asked him what could he know about good corned beef and the priest replied that he grew up in Bensonhurst. Well, about half the people in Horovitz's on that day—and on any other day for that matter—grew up in Bensonhurst and before you knew it they were all asking him if he knew such-and-such a store and so-and-so's deli.

Zev then informed the priest—with all due respect to Yussel Horovitz behind the counter—that the best corned beef sandwich in the world was to be had at Shmuel Rosenberg's Jerusalem Deli in Bensonhurst. Father Cahill said he'd been there and agreed 100 percent.

Yussel served him his sandwich then. As he took a huge bite out of the corned beef on rye, the normal *tummel* of a deli at lunchtime died away until Horovitz's was as quiet as a *shoul* on Sunday morning. Everyone watched him chew, watched him swallow. Then they waited. Suddenly his face broke into this big Irish grin.

"I'm afraid I'm going to have to change my vote," he said. "Horovitz's of Lakewood makes the best corned beef sandwich in the world."

Amid cheers and warm laughter, Zev led Father Cahill to the rear table that would become theirs and sat with this canny and charming gentile who had so easily won over a roomful of strangers and provided such a *mechaieh* for Yussel. He learned that the young priest was the new assistant to Father Palmeri, the pastor at Saint Anthony's Catholic church at the northern end of Lakewood. Father Palmeri had been there for years but Zev had never so much as seen his face. He asked Father Cahill—who wanted to be called Joe—about life in Brooklyn these days and they talked for an hour.

During the following months they would run into each other so often at Horovitz's that they decided to meet regularly for lunch, on Mondays and Thursdays. They did so for years, discussing religion—Oy, the religious discussions!—politics, economics, philosophy, life in general. During those lunchtimes they solved most of the world's problems. Zev was sure they'd have solved them all if the scandal at Saint Anthony's hadn't resulted in Father Joe's removal from the parish.

But that was in another time, another world. The world before the vampires took over.

Zev shook his head as he considered the current state of Father Joe in the dusty basement of Morton's Liquors.

"It's about the vampires, Joe," he said, taking another sip of the Stoly. "They've taken over Saint Anthony's."

Father Joe snorted and shrugged.

"They're in the majority, now, Zev, remember? They've taken over everything. Why should Saint Anthony's be different from any other parish in the world?"

"I didn't mean the parish. I meant the church."

The priest's eyes widened slightly. "The church? They've taken over the building itself?"

"Every night," Zev said. "Every night they are there."

"That's a holy place. How do they manage that?"

"They've desecrated the altar, destroyed all the crosses. Saint Anthony's is no longer a holy place."

"Too bad," Father Joe said, looking down and shaking his head sadly. "It was a fine old church." He looked up again, at Zev. "How do you know about what's going on at Saint Anthony's? It's not exactly in your neighborhood."

"A neighborhood I don't exactly have anymore."

Father Joe reached over and gripped his shoulder with a huge hand.

"I'm sorry, Zev. I heard how your people got hit pretty hard over there. Sitting ducks, huh? I'm really sorry."

Sitting ducks. An appropriate description. Oh, they'd been smart, those bloodsuckers. They knew their easiest targets. Whenever they swooped into an area they singled out Jews as their first victims, and among Jews they picked the Orthodox first of the first. Smart. Where else would they be less likely to run up against a cross? It worked for them in Brooklyn, and so when they came south into New Jersey, spreading like a plague, they headed straight for the town with one of the largest collections of yeshivas in North America.

But after the Bensonhurst holocaust the people in the Lakewood communities did not take quite so long to figure out what was happening. The Reformed and Conservative synagogues started handing out crosses at Shabbes—too late for many but it saved a few. Did the Orthodox congregations follow suit? No. They hid in their homes and shules and yeshivas and read and prayed.

And were liquidated.

A cross, a crucifix—they held power over the vampires, drove them away. His fellow rabbis did not want to accept that simple fact because they could not face its devastating ramifications. To hold up a cross was to negate two thousand years of Jewish history, it was to say that the Messiah had come and they had missed him.

Did it say that? Zev didn't know. Argue about it later. Right now, people were dying. But the rabbis had to argue it now. And as they argued, their people were slaughtered like cattle.

How Zev railed at them, how he pleaded with them! Blind, stubborn fools! If a fire was consuming your house, would you refuse to throw water on it just because you'd always been taught not to believe in water? Zev had arrived at the rabbinical council wearing a cross and had been thrown out—literally sent hurtling through the front door. But at least he had managed to save a few of his own people. Too few.

He remembered his fellow Orthodox rabbis, though. All the ones who had refused to face the reality of the vampires' fear of crosses, who had forbidden their students and their congregations to wear crosses, who had watched those same students and congregations die en masse only to rise again and come for them. And soon those very same rabbis were roaming their own community, hunting the survivors, preying on other yeshivas, other congregations, until the entire community was liquidated and incorporated into the brotherhood of the vampire. The great fear had come to pass: they'd been assimilated.

The rabbis could have saved themselves, could have saved their people, but they would not bend to the reality of what was happening around them. Which, when Zev thought about it, was not at all out of character. Hadn't they spent generations learning to turn away from the rest of the world?

Those early days of anarchic slaughter were over. Now that the vampires held the ruling hand, the bloodletting had become more organized. But the damage to Zev's people had been done—and it was irreparable. Hitler would have been proud. His Nazi "final solution" was an afternoon picnic compared to the work of the vampires. They did in months what Hitler's Reich could not do in all the years of the Second World War.

There's only a few of us now. So few and so scattered. A final Diaspora.

For a moment Zev was almost overwhelmed by grief, but he pushed it down, locked it back into that place where he kept his sorrows, and thought of how fortunate it was for his wife Chana that she died of natural causes before the horror began. Her soul had been too gentle to weather what had happened to their community.

"Not as sorry as I, Joe," Zev said, dragging himself back to the present. "But since my neighborhood is gone, and since I have hardly any friends left, I use the daylight hours to wander. So call me the Wandering Jew. And in my wanderings I meet some of your old parishioners."

The priest's face hardened. His voice became acid.

"Do you, now? And how fares the remnant of my devoted flock?"

"They've lost all hope, Joe. They wish you were back."

He laughed. "Sure they do! Just like they rallied behind me when my name and honor were being dragged through the muck last year. Yeah, they want me back. I'll bet!"

"Such anger, Joe. It doesn't become you."

"Bullshit. That was the old Joe Cahill, the naive turkey who believed all his faithful parishioners would back him up. But no. Palmeri tells the bishop the heat is getting too much for him, the bishop removes me, and the people I dedicated my life to all stand by in silence as I'm railroaded out of my parish."

"It's hard for the commonfolk to buck a bishop."

"Maybe. But I can't forget how they stood quietly by while I was stripped of my position, my dignity, my integrity, of everything I wanted to be . . . "

Zev thought Joe's voice was going to break. He was about to reach out to him when the priest coughed and squared his shoulders.

"Meanwhile, I'm a pariah over here in the retreat house. A god-damn leper. Some of them actually believe—" He broke off in a growl. "Ah, what's the use? It's over and done. Most of the parish is dead anyway, I suppose. And if I'd stayed there I'd probably be dead too. So maybe it worked out for the best. And who gives a shit anyway."

He reached for the bottle of Glenlivet next to him.

"No-no!" Zev said. "You promised!"

Father Joe drew his hand back and crossed his arms across his chest.

"Talk on, oh, bearded one. I'm listening."

Father Joe had certainly changed for the worse. Morose, bitter, apathetic, self-pitying. Zev was beginning to wonder how he could have called this man a friend.

"They've taken over your church, desecrated it. Each night they further defile it with butchery and blasphemy. Doesn't that mean anything to you?"

"It's Palmeri's parish. I've been benched. Let him take care of it."

"Father Palmeri is their leader."

"He should be. He's their pastor."

"No. He leads the vampires in the obscenities they perform in the church."

Father Joe stiffened and the glassiness cleared from his eyes.

"Palmeri? He's one of them?"

Zev nodded. "More than that. He's the local leader. He orchestrates their rituals."

Zev saw rage flare in the priest's eyes, saw his hands ball into fists, and for a moment he thought the old Father Joe was going to burst through.

Come on, Joe. Show me that old fire.

But then he slumped back onto the crate.

"Is that all you came to tell me?"

Zev hid his disappointment and nodded. "Yes."

"Good." He grabbed the scotch bottle. "Because I need a drink."

Zev wanted to leave, yet he had to stay, had to probe a little bit deeper and see how much of his old friend was left, and how much had been replaced by this new, bitter, alien Joe Cahill. Maybe there was still hope. So they talked on.

Suddenly he noticed it was dark.

"Gevalt!" Zev said. "I didn't notice the time!"

Father Joe seemed surprised too. He ran to the window and peered out.

"Damn! Sun's gone down!" He turned to Zev. "Lakewood's out of the question for you, Reb. Even the retreat house is too far to risk now. Looks like we're stuck here for the night."

"We'll be safe?"

He shrugged. "Why not? As far as I can tell I'm the only one who's been in here for months, and only in the daytime. Be pretty odd if one of those human leeches should decide to wander in here tonight."

"I hope so."

"Don't worry. We're okay if we don't attract attention. I've got a flashlight if we need it, but we're better off sitting here in the dark and shooting the breeze till sunrise." Father Joe smiled and picked up a huge silver cross, at least a foot in length, from atop one of the crates. "Besides, we're armed. And frankly, I can think of worse places to spend the night."

He stepped over to the case of Glenlivet and opened a fresh bottle. His capacity for alcohol was enormous.

Zev could think of worse places too. In fact he had spent a number of nights in much worse places since the holocaust. He decided to put the time to good use.

"So, Joe. Maybe I should tell you some more about what's happening in Lakewood."

After a few hours their talk died of fatigue. Father Joe gave Zev the flashlight to hold and stretched out across a couple of crates to sleep. Zev tried to get comfortable enough to doze but found sleep impossible. So he listened to his friend snore in the darkness of the cellar.

Poor Joe. Such anger in the man. But more than that—hurt. He felt betrayed, wronged. And with good reason. But with everything falling apart as it was, the wrong done to him would never be righted. He should forget about it already and go on with his life, but apparently he couldn't. Such a shame. He needed something to pull him out of his funk. Zev had thought news of what had happened to his old parish might rouse him, but it seemed only to make him want to drink more. Father Joe Cahill, he feared, was a hopeless case.

Zev closed his eyes and tried to rest. It was hard to get comfortable with the cross dangling in front of him so he took it off but laid it within easy reach. He was drifting toward a doze when he heard a noise outside. By the dumpster. Metal on metal.

My bicycle!

He slipped to the floor and tiptoed over to where Father Joe slept. He shook his shoulder and whispered.

"Someone's found my bicycle!"

The priest snorted but remained sleeping. A louder clatter outside made Zev turn, and as he moved his elbow struck a bottle. He grabbed for it in the darkness but missed. The sound of smashing glass echoed through the basement like a cannon shot. As the odor of scotch whiskey replaced the musty ambiance, Zev listened for further sounds from outside. None came.

Maybe it had been an animal. He remembered how raccoons used to raid his garbage at home . . . when he'd had a home . . . when he'd had garbage . . .

Zev stepped to the window and looked out. Probably an animal. He pulled the window open a few inches and felt cool night air wash across his face. He pulled the flashlight from his coat pocket and aimed it through the opening.

Zev almost dropped the light as the beam illuminated a pale, snarling demonic face, baring its fangs and hissing. He fell back as the thing's head and shoulders lunged through the window, its curved fingers clawing at him, missing. Then it launched itself the rest of the way through, hurtling toward Zev.

He tried to dodge but he was too slow. The impact knocked the flashlight from his grasp and it went rolling across the floor. Zev cried out as he went down under the snarling thing. Its ferocity was overpowering, irresistible. It straddled him and lashed at him, batting his fending arms aside, its clawed fingers tearing at his collar to free his throat, stretching his neck to expose the vulnerable flesh, its foul breath gagging him as it bent its fangs toward him. Zev screamed out his helplessness.

II

FATHER JOE AWOKE TO the cries of a terrified voice.

He shook his head to clear it and instantly regretted the move. His head weighed at least two hundred pounds, and his mouth was stuffed with foul-tasting cotton. Why did he keep doing this to himself? Not only did it leave him feeling lousy, it gave him bad dreams. Like now.

Another terrified shout, only a few feet away.

He looked toward the sound. In the faint light from the flashlight rolling across the floor he saw Zev on his back, fighting for his life against—

Damn! This was no dream. One of those bloodsuckers had got in here!

He leaped over to where the creature was lowering its fangs toward Zev's throat. He grabbed it by the back of the neck and lifted it clear of the floor. It was surprisingly heavy but that didn't slow him. Joe could feel the anger rising in him, surging into his muscles.

"Rotten piece of filth!"

He swung the vampire by its neck and let it fly against the cinderblock wall. It impacted with what should have been bone-crushing force, but it bounced off, rolled on the floor, and regained its feet in one motion, ready to attack again. Strong as he was, Joe knew he was no match for a vampire's power. He turned, grabbed his big silver crucifix, and charged the creature.

"Hungry? Eat this!"

As the creature bared its fangs and hissed at him, Joe shoved the long lower end of the cross into its open mouth. Blue-white light flickered along the silver length of the crucifix, reflecting in the creature's startled, agonized eyes as its flesh sizzled and crackled. The vampire let out a strangled cry and tried to turn away but Joe wasn't through with it yet. He was literally seeing red as rage poured out of a hidden well and swirled through him. He rammed the cross deeper down the thing's gullet. Light flashed deep in its throat, illuminating the pale tissues from within. It tried to grab the cross and pull it out but the flesh of its fingers burned and smoked wherever they came in contact with the cross.

Finally Joe stepped back and let the thing squirm and scrabble up the wall and out the window into the night. Then he turned to Zev. If anything had happened—

"Hey, Reb!" he said, kneeling beside the older man. "You all right?"

"Yes," Zev said, struggling to his feet. "Thanks to you."

Joe slumped onto a crate, momentarily weak as his rage dissipated. *This is not what I'm about*, he thought. But it had felt so damn good to let it loose on that vampire. Too good. And that worried him.

I'm falling apart . . . like everything else in the world.

"That was too close," he said to Zev, giving the older man's shoulder a fond squeeze.

"Too close for that vampire for sure," Zev said, replacing his yarmulke. "And would you please remind me, Father Joe, that in the future if ever I should maybe get my blood sucked and become a vampire that I should stay far away from you."

Joe laughed for the first time in too long. It felt good.

THEY CLIMBED OUT AT first light. Joe stretched his cramped muscles in the fresh air while Zev checked on his hidden bicycle.

"Oy," Zev said as he pulled it from behind the dumpster. The front wheel had been bent so far out of shape that half the spokes were broken. "Look what he did. Looks like I'll be walking back to Lakewood."

But Joe was less interested in the bike than in the whereabouts of their visitor from last night. He knew it couldn't have got far. And

it hadn't. They found the vampire—or rather what was left of it—
on the far side of the dumpster: a rotting, twisted corpse, blackened
to a crisp and steaming in the morning sunlight. The silver crucifix
still protruded from between its teeth.

Joe approached and gingerly yanked his cross free of the foul
remains.

"Looks like you've sucked your last pint of blood," he said and
immediately felt foolish.

Who was he putting on the macho act for? Zev certainly wasn't
going to buy it. Too out of character. But then, what *was* his character these days? He used to be a parish priest. Now he was a nothing.
A less than nothing.

He straightened up and turned to Zev.

"Come on back to the retreat house, Reb. I'll buy you breakfast."

But as Joe turned and began walking away, Zev stayed and
stared down at the corpse.

"They say they don't wander far from where they spent their
lives," Zev said. "Which means it's unlikely this fellow was Jewish
if he lived around here. Probably Catholic. Irish Catholic, I'd
imagine.

Joe stopped and turned. He stared at his long shadow. The
hazy rising sun at his back cast a huge hulking shape before him,
with a dark cross in one shadow hand and a smudge of amber
light where it poured through the unopened bottle of Scotch in
the other.

"What are you getting at?" he said.

"The Kaddish would probably not be so appropriate so I'm just
wondering if maybe someone should give him the last rites or whatever it is you people do when one of you dies."

"He wasn't one of us," Joe said, feeling the bitterness rise in him.
"He wasn't even human."

"Ah, but he used to be before he was killed and became one of
them. So maybe now he could use a little help."

Joe didn't like the way this was going. He sensed he was being
maneuvered.

"He doesn't deserve it," he said and knew in that instant he'd
been trapped.

"I thought even the worst sinner deserved it," Zev said.

Joe knew when he was beaten. Zev was right. He shoved the
cross and bottle into Zev's hands—a bit roughly, perhaps—then

went and knelt by the twisted cadaver. He administered a form of the final sacrament. When he was through he returned to Zev and snatched back his belongings.

"You're a better man than I am, Gunga Din," he said as he passed.

"You act as if they're responsible for what they do after they become vampires," Zev said as he hurried along beside him, panting as he matched Joe's pace.

"Aren't they?"

"No."

"You're sure of that?"

"Well, not exactly. But they certainly aren't human anymore, so maybe we shouldn't hold them accountable on human terms."

Zev's reasoning tone flashed Joe back to the conversations they used to have in Horovitz's deli.

"But Zev, we know there's some of the old personality left. I mean, they stay in their hometowns, usually in the basements of their old houses. They go after people they knew when they were alive. They're not just dumb predators, Zev. They've got the old consciousness they had when they were alive. Why can't they rise above it? Why can't they . . . resist?"

"I don't know. To tell the truth, the question has never occurred to me. A fascinating concept: an undead refusing to feed. Leave it to Father Joe to come up with something like that. We should discuss this on the trip back to Lakewood."

Joe had to smile. So *that* was what this was all about.

"I'm not going back to Lakewood."

"Fine. Then we'll discuss it now. Maybe the urge to feed is too strong to overcome."

"Maybe. And maybe they just don't try hard enough."

"This is a hard line you're taking, my friend."

"I'm a hard-line kind of guy."

"Well, you've become one."

Joe gave him a sharp look. "You don't know what I've become."

Zev shrugged. "Maybe true, maybe not. But do you truly think you'd be able to resist?"

"Damn straight."

Joe didn't know whether he was serious or not. Maybe he was just mentally preparing himself for the day when he might actually find himself in that situation.

"Interesting," Zev said as they climbed the front steps of the retreat house. "Well, I'd better be going. I've a long walk ahead of me. A long, *lonely* walk all the way back to Lakewood. A long, lonely, possibly *dangerous* walk back for a poor old man who—"

"All right, Zev! All *right!*" Joe said, biting back a laugh. "I get the point. You want me to go back to Lakewood. Why?"

"I just want the company," Zev said with pure innocence.

"No, really. What's going on in that Talmudic mind of yours? What are you cooking?"

"Nothing, Father Joe. Nothing at all."

Joe stared at him. Damn it all if his interest wasn't piqued. What was Zev up to? And what the hell? Why not go? He had nothing better to do.

All right, Zev. You win. I'll come back to Lakewood with you. But just for today. Just to keep you company. And I'm not going anywhere near Saint Anthony's, okay? Understood?"

"Understood, Joe. Perfectly understood."

"Good. Now wipe that smile off your face and we'll get something to eat."

III

UNDER THE CLIMBING SUN they walked south along the deserted beach, barefooting through the wet sand at the edge of the surf. Zev had never done this. He liked the feel of the sand between his toes, the coolness of the water as it sloshed over his ankles.

"Know what day it is?" Father Joe said. He had his sneakers slung over his shoulder. "Believe it or not, it's the Fourth of July."

"Oh, yes. Your Independence Day. We never made much of secular holidays. Too many religious ones to observe. Why should I not believe it's this date?"

Father Joe shook his head in dismay. "This is Manasquan Beach. You know what this place used to look like on the Fourth before the vampires took over? Wall-to-wall bodies."

"Really? I guess maybe sun-bathing is not the fad it used to be."

"Ah, Zev! Still the master of the understatement. I'll say one thing, though: the beach is cleaner than I've ever seen it. No beer cans or hypodermics." He pointed ahead. "But what's that up there?"

As they approached the spot, Zev saw a pair of naked bodies

stretched out on the sand, one male, one female, both young and short-haired. Their skin was bronzed and glistened in the sun. The man lifted his head and stared at them. A blue crucifix was tattooed in the center of his forehead. He reached into the knapsack beside him and withdrew a huge, gleaming, nickel-plated revolver.

"Just keep walking," he said.

"Will do," Father Joe said. "Just passing through."

As they passed the couple, Zev noticed a similar tattoo on the girl's forehead. He noticed the rest of her too. He felt an almost forgotten stirring deep inside him.

"A very popular tattoo," he said.

"Clever idea. That's one cross you can't drop or lose. Probably won't help you in the dark, but if there's a light on it might give you an edge."

They turned west and made their way inland, finding Route 70 and following it into Ocean County via the Brielle Bridge.

"I remember nightmare traffic jams right here every summer," Father Joe said as they trod the bridge's empty span. "Never thought I'd miss traffic jams."

They cut over to Route 88 and followed it all the way into Lakewood. Along the way they found a few people out and about in Bricktown and picking berries in Ocean County Park, but in the heart of Lakewood . . .

"A real ghost town," the priest said as they walked Forest Avenue's deserted length.

"Ghosts," Zev said, nodding sadly. It had been a long walk and he was tired. "Yes. Full of ghosts."

In his mind's eye he saw the shades of his fallen brother rabbis and all the yeshiva students, beards, black suits, black hats, crisscrossing back and forth at a determined pace on weekdays, strolling with their wives on Shabbes, their children trailing behind like ducklings.

Gone. All gone. Victims of the vampires. Vampires themselves now, most of them. It made him sick at heart to think of those good, gentle men, women, and children curled up in their basements now to avoid the light of day, venturing out in the dark to feed on others, spreading the disease . . .

He fingered the cross slung from his neck. *If only they had listened!*

"I know a place near Saint Anthony's where we can hide," he told the priest.

"You've traveled enough today, Reb. And I told you, I don't care about Saint Anthony's."

"Stay the night, Joe," Zev said, gripping the young priest's arm. He'd coaxed him this far; he couldn't let him get away now. "See what Father Palmeri's done."

"If he's one of them he's not a priest anymore. Don't call him Father."

"*They* still call him Father."

"Who?"

"The vampires."

Zev watched Father Joe's jaw muscles bunch.

Joe said, "Maybe I'll just take a quick trip over to Saint Anthony's myself—"

"No. It's different here. The area is thick with them—maybe twenty times as many as in Spring Lake. They'll get you if your timing isn't just right. I'll take you."

"You need rest, pal."

Father Joe's expression showed genuine concern. Zev was detecting increasingly softer emotions in the man since their reunion last night. A good sign perhaps?

"And rest I'll get when we get to where I'm taking you."

IV

Father Joe Cahill watched the moon rise over his old church and wondered at the wisdom of coming back. The casual decision made this morning in the full light of day seemed reckless and foolhardy now at the approach of midnight.

But there was no turning back. He'd followed Zev to the second floor of this two-story office building across the street from Saint Anthony's, and here they'd waited for dark. Must have been a law office once. The place had been vandalized, the windows broken, the furniture trashed, but there was an old Temple University Law School degree on the wall, and the couch was still in one piece. So while Zev caught some Z's, Joe sat and sipped a little of his scotch and did some heavy thinking.

Mostly he thought about his drinking. He'd done too much of that lately, he knew; so much so that he was afraid to stop cold. So he was taking just a touch now, barely enough to take the edge off. He'd finish the rest later, after he came back from that church over there.

He'd stared at Saint Anthony's since they'd arrived. It too had been extensively vandalized. Once it had been a beautiful little stone church, a miniature cathedral, really; very Gothic with all its pointed arches, steep roofs, crocketed spires, and multifoil stained glass windows. Now the windows were smashed, the crosses which had topped the steeple and each gable were gone, and anything resembling a cross in its granite exterior had been defaced beyond recognition.

As he'd known it would, the sight of Saint Anthony's brought back memories of Gloria Sullivan, the young, pretty church volunteer whose husband worked for United Chemical International in New York, commuting in every day and trekking off overseas a little too often. Joe and Gloria had seen a lot of each other around the church offices and had become good friends. But Gloria had somehow got the idea that what they had went beyond friendship, so she showed up at the rectory one night when Joe was there alone. He tried to explain that as attractive as she was, she was not for him. He had taken certain vows and meant to stick by them. He did his best to let her down easy but she'd been hurt. And angry.

That might have been that, but then her six-year-old son Kevin had come home from altar boy practice with a story about a priest making him pull down his pants and touching him. Kevin was never clear on who the priest had been, but Gloria Sullivan was. Obviously it had been Father Cahill. Any man who could turn down the heartfelt offer of her love and her body had to be either a queer or worse. And a child molester was worse.

She took it to the police and to the papers.

Joe groaned softly at the memory of how swiftly his life had become hell. But he had been determined to weather the storm, sure that the real culprit eventually would be revealed. He had no proof—still didn't—but if one of the priests at Saint Anthony's was a pederast, he knew it wasn't him. That left Father Alberto Palmeri, Saint Anthony's fifty-five-year-old pastor. Before Joe could get to the truth, however, Father Palmeri requested that Father Cahill be removed from the parish, and the bishop complied. Joe had left under a cloud that had followed him to the retreat house in the next county and hovered over him till this day. The only place he'd found even brief respite from the impotent anger and bitterness that roiled under his skin and soured his gut every minute of every day was in the bottle—and that was sure as hell a dead end.

So why had he agreed to come back here? To torture himself? Or to get a look at Palmeri and see how low he had sunk?

Maybe that was it. Maybe seeing Palmeri wallowing in his true element would give him the impetus to put the whole Saint Anthony's incident behind him and rejoin what was left of the human race—which needed him now more than ever.

And maybe it wouldn't.

Getting back on track was a nice thought, but over the past few months Joe had found it increasingly difficult to give much of a damn about anyone or anything.

Except maybe Zev. He'd stuck by Joe through the worst of it, defending him to anyone who would listen. But an endorsement from an Orthodox rabbi had meant diddly in Saint Anthony's. And yesterday Zev had biked all the way to Spring Lake to see him. Old Zev was all right.

And he'd been right about the number of vampires here too. Lakewood was *crawling* with the things. Fascinated and repelled, Joe had watched the streets fill with them shortly after sundown.

But what had disturbed him more were the creatures who'd come out *before* sundown.

The humans. Live ones.

The collaborators.

If there was anything lower, anything that deserved true death more than the vampires themselves, it was the still-living humans who worked for them.

Someone touched his shoulder and he jumped. It was Zev. He was holding something out to him. Joe took it and held it up in the moonlight: a tiny crescent moon dangling from a chain on a ring.

"What's this?"

"An earring. The local Vichy wear them."

"Vichy? Like the Vichy French?"

"Yes. Very good. I'm glad to see that you're not as culturally illiterate as the rest of your generation. Vichy humans—that's what I call the collaborators. These earrings identify them to the local nest of vampires. They are spared."

"Where'd you get them?"

Zev's face was hidden in the shadows. "Their previous owners . . . lost them. Put it on."

"My ear's not pierced."

A gnarled hand moved into the moonlight. Joe saw a long needle clasped between the thumb and index finger.

"That I can fix," Zev said.

"MAYBE YOU SHOULDN'T SEE this," Zev whispered as they crouched in the deep shadows on Saint Anthony's western flank.

Joe squinted at him in the darkness, puzzled.

"You lay a guilt trip on me to get me here, now you're having second thoughts?"

"It is horrible like I can't tell you."

Joe thought about that. There was enough horror in the world outside Saint Anthony's. What purpose did it serve to see what was going on inside?"

Because it used to be my church.

Even though he'd only been an associate pastor, never fully in charge, and even though he'd been unceremoniously yanked from the post, Saint Anthony's had been his first parish. He was here. He might as well know what they were doing inside.

"Show me."

Zev led him to a pile of rubble under a smashed stained glass window. He pointed up to where faint light flickered from inside.

"Look in there."

"You're not coming?"

"Once was enough, thank you."

Joe climbed as carefully, as quietly as he could, all the while becoming increasingly aware of a growing stench like putrid, rotting meat. It was coming from inside, wafting through the broken window. Steeling himself, he straightened up and peered over the sill.

For a moment he was disoriented, like someone peering out the window of a city apartment and seeing the rolling hills of a Kansas farm. This could not be the interior of Saint Anthony's.

In the flickering light of hundreds of sacramental candles he saw that the walls were bare, stripped of all their ornaments, of the plaques for the stations of the cross; the dark wood along the wall was scarred and gouged wherever there had been anything remotely resembling a cross. The floor too was mostly bare, the pews ripped from their neat rows and hacked to pieces, their splintered remains piled high at the rear under the choir balcony.

And the giant crucifix that had dominated the space behind the altar—only a portion of it remained. The cross-pieces on each side had been sawed off and so now an armless, life-size Christ hung upside down against the rear wall of the sanctuary.

Joe took in all that in a flash, then his attention was drawn to the unholy congregation that peopled Saint Anthony's this night. The collaborators—the Vichy humans, as Zev called them—made up the periphery of the group. They looked like normal, everyday people but each was wearing a crescent moon earring.

But the others, the group gathered in the sanctuary—Joe felt his hackles rise at the sight of them. They surrounded the altar in a tight knot. Their pale, bestial faces, bereft of the slightest trace of human warmth, compassion, or decency, were turned upward. His gorge rose when he saw the object of their rapt attention.

A naked teenage boy—his hands tied behind his back, was suspended over the altar by his ankles. He was sobbing and choking, his eyes wide and vacant with shock, his mind all but gone. The skin had been flayed from his forehead—apparently the Vichy had found an expedient solution to the cross tattoo—and blood ran in a slow stream down his abdomen and chest from his freshly truncated genitals. And beside him, standing atop the altar, a bloody-mouthed creature dressed in a long cassock. Joe recognized the thin shoulders, the graying hair trailing from the balding crown, but was shocked at the crimson vulpine grin he flashed to the things clustered below him.

"Now," said the creature in a lightly accented voice Joe had heard hundreds of times from Saint Anthony's pulpit.

Father Alberto Palmeri.

And from the group a hand reached up with a straight razor and drew it across the boy's throat. As the blood flowed down over his face, those below squeezed and struggled forward like hatchling vultures to catch the falling drops and scarlet trickles in their open mouths.

Joe fell away from the window and vomited. He felt Zev grab his arm and lead him away. He was vaguely aware of crossing the street and heading toward the ruined legal office.

V

Why in God's name did you want me to see that?"

Zev looked across the office toward the source of the words. He could see a vague outline where Father Joe sat on the floor, his back against the wall, the open bottle of scotch in his hand. The priest had taken one drink since their return, no more.

"I thought you should know what they were doing to your church."

"So you've said. But what's the reason behind that one?"

Zev shrugged in the darkness. "I'd heard you weren't doing well, that even before everything else began falling apart, you had already fallen apart. So when I felt it safe to get away, I came to see you. Just as I expected, I found a man who was angry at everything and letting it eat up his *guderim*. I thought maybe it would be good to give that man something very specific to be angry at."

"You bastard!" Father Joe whispered. "Who gave you the right?"

"Friendship gave me the right, Joe. I should hear that you are rotting away and do nothing? I have no congregation of my own anymore so I turned my attention on you. Always I was a somewhat meddlesome rabbi."

"Still are. Out to save my soul, ay?"

"We rabbis don't save souls. Guide them maybe, hopefully give them direction. But only you can save your soul, Joe."

Silence hung in the air for awhile. Suddenly the crescent-moon earring Zev had given Father Joe landed in the puddle of moonlight on the floor between them.

"Why do they do it?" the priest said. "The Vichy—why do they collaborate?"

"The first were quite unwilling, believe me. They cooperated because their wives and children were held hostage by the vampire. But before too long the dregs of humanity began to slither out from under their rocks and offer their services in exchange for the immortality of vampirism."

"Why bother working for them? Why not just bare your throat to the nearest bloodsucker?"

"That's what I thought at first," Zev said. "But as I witnessed the Lakewood holocaust I detected the vampires' pattern. They can choose who joins their ranks, so after they've fully infiltrated a population, they change their tactics. You see, they don't want too many of their kind concentrated in one area. It's like too many carnivores in one forest—when the herds of prey are wiped out, the predators starve. So they start to employ a different style of killing. For only when the vampire draws the life's blood from the throat with its fangs does the victim become one of them. Anyone drained as in the manner of that boy in the church tonight dies a true death. He's as dead now as someone run over by a truck. He will not rise tomorrow night."

"I get it," Father Joe said. "The Vichy trade their daylight services and dirty work to the vampires now for immortality later on."

"Correct."

There was no humor in the soft laugh that echoed across the room from Father Joe.

"Swell. I never cease to be amazed at our fellow human beings. Their capacity for good is exceeded only by their ability to debase themselves."

"Hopelessness does strange things, Joe. The vampires know that. So they rob us of hope. That's how they beat us. They transform our friends and neighbors and leaders into their own, leaving us feeling alone, completely cut off. Some of us can't take the despair and kill ourselves."

"Hopelessness," Joe said. "A potent weapon."

After a long silence, Zev said "So what are you going to do now, Father Joe?"

Another bitter laugh from across the room.

"I suppose this is the place where I declare that I've found new purpose in life and will now go forth into the world as a fearless vampire killer."

"Such a thing would be nice."

"Well screw that. I'm only going as far as across the street."

"To Saint Anthony's?"

Zev saw Father Joe take a swig from the Scotch bottle and then screw the cap on tight.

"Yeah. To see if there's anything I can do over there."

"Father Palmeri and his nest might not like that."

"I told you, don't call him Father. And screw *him*. Nobody can do what he's done and get away with it. I'm taking my church back."

In the dark, behind his beard, Zev smiled.

VI

JOE STAYED UP THE rest of the night and let Zev sleep. The old guy needed his rest. Sleep would have been impossible for Joe anyway. He was too wired. He sat up and watched Saint Anthony's.

They left before first light, dark shapes drifting out the front doors and down the stone steps like parishioners leaving a predawn service. Joe felt his back teeth grind as he scanned the group for Palmeri, but he couldn't make him out in the dimness. By the time the sun began to peek over the rooftops and through the trees to the east, the street outside was deserted.

He woke Zev and together they approached the church. The heavy oak and iron front doors, each forming half of a pointed arch, were closed. He pulled them open and fastened the hooks to keep them open. Then he walked through the vestibule and into the nave.

Even though he was ready for it, the stench backed him up a few steps. When his stomach settled, he forced himself ahead, treading a path between the two piles of shattered and splintered pews. Zev walked beside him, a handkerchief pressed over his mouth.

Last night he had thought the place a shambles. He saw now that it was worse. The light of day poked into all the corners, revealing everything that had been hidden by the warm glow of the candles. Half a dozen rotting corpses hung from the ceiling he hadn't noticed them last night—and others were sprawled on the floor against the walls. Some of the bodies were in pieces. Behind the chancel rail a headless female torso was draped over the front of the pulpit. To the left stood the statue of Mary. Someone had fitted her with foam rubber breasts and a huge dildo. And at the rear of the sanctuary was the armless Christ hanging head down on the upright of his cross.

"My church," he whispered as he moved along the path that had once been the center aisle, the aisle brides used to walk down with their fathers. "Look what they've done to my church!"

Joe approached the huge block of the altar. Once it had been backed against the far wall of the sanctuary, but he'd had it moved to the front so that he could celebrate Mass facing his parishioners. Solid Carrara marble, but you'd never know it now. So caked with dried blood, semen, and feces it could have been made of styrofoam.

His revulsion was fading, melting away in the growing heat of his rage, drawing the nausea with it. He had intended to clean up the place but there was so much to be done, too much for two men.

It was hopeless.

"Fadda Joe?"

He spun at the sound of the strange voice. A thin figure stood uncertainly in the open doorway. A man of about fifty edged forward timidly.

"Fadda Joe, izat you?"

Joe recognized him now. Carl Edwards. A twitchy little man who used to help pass the collection basket at 10:30 Mass on Sundays. A transplantee from Jersey City—hardly anyone around here was originally from around here. His face was sunken, his eyes feverish as he stared at Joe.

"Yes, Carl. It's me."

"Oh, tank God!" He ran forward and dropped to his knees before Joe. He began to sob. "You come back! Tank God, you come back!"

Joe pulled him to his feet.

"Come on now, Carl. Get a grip."

"You come back ta save us, ain'tcha? God sent ya here to punish him, din't He?"

"Punish whom?"

"Fadda Palmeri! He's one a dem! He's da woist a alla dem! He—"

"I know," Joe said. "I know."

"Oh, it's so good to have ya back, Fadda Joe! We ain't knowed what to do since da suckers took ova. We been prayin fa someone like youse an now ya here. It's a freakin' miracle!"

Joe wanted to ask Carl where he and all these people who seemed to think they needed him now had been when he was being railroaded out of the parish. But that was ancient history.

"Not a miracle, Carl," Joe said, glancing at Zev. Rabbi Wolpin brought me back." As Carl and Zev shook hands, Joe said, "And I'm just passing through."

"Passing t'rough? No. Dat can't be! Ya gotta stay!"

Joe saw the light of hope fading in the little man's eyes. Something twisted within him, tugging him.

"What can I do here, Carl? I'm just one man."

"I'll help! I'll do whatever ya want! Jes tell me!"

"Will you help me clean up?"

Carl looked around and seemed to see the cadavers for the first time. He cringed and turned a few shades paler.

"Yeah . . . sure. Anything."

Joe looked at Zev. "Well? What do you think?"

Zev shrugged. "I should tell you what to do? My parish it's not."

"Not mine either."

Zev jutted his beard at Carl. "I think maybe he'd tell you differently."

Joe did a slow turn. The vaulted nave was utterly silent except for the buzzing of the flies around the cadavers. A massive clean-up job. But if they worked all day they could make a decent dent in it. And then—

And then what?

Joe didn't know. He was playing this by ear. He'd wait and see what the night brought.

"Can you get us some food, Carl? I'd sell my soul for a cup of coffee."

Carl gave him a strange look.

"Just a figure of speech, Carl. We'll need some food if we're going to keep working."

The man's eyes lit again.

"Dat means ya staying?"

"For a while."

"I'll getcha some food," he said excitedly as he ran for the door. "An' coffee. I know someone who's still got coffee. She'll part wit' some of it for Fadda Joe." He stopped at the door and turned. "Ay, an' Fadda, I neva believed any a dem tings dat was said aboutcha. Neva."

Joe tried but he couldn't hold it back.

"It would have meant a lot to have heard that from you last year, Carl."

The man lowered his eyes. "Yeah. I guess it woulda. But I'll make it up to ya, Fadda. I will. You can take dat to da bank."

Then he was out the door and gone. Joe turned to Zev and saw the old man rolling up his sleeves.

"*Nu?*" Zev said. "The bodies. Before we do anything else, I think maybe we should move the bodies."

VII

BY EARLY AFTERNOON, ZEV was exhausted. The heat and the heavy work had taken their toll. He had to stop and rest. He sat on the chancel rail and looked around. Nearly eight hours' work and they'd barely scratched the surface. But the place did look and smell better.

Removing the flyblown corpses and scattered body parts had been the worst of it. A foul, gut-roiling task that had taken most of the morning. They'd carried the corpses out to the small graveyard behind the church and left them there. Those people deserved a decent burial but there was no time for it today.

Once the corpses were gone, Father Joe had torn the defilements from the statue of Mary and then they'd turned their attention to the huge crucifix. It took a while but they finally found Christ's plaster arms in the pile of ruined pews. They were still nailed to the sawn-off cross-piece of the crucifix. While Zev and Father Joe worked at jury-rigging a series of braces to reattach the arms, Carl found a mop and bucket and began the long, slow process of washing the fouled floor of the nave.

Now the crucifix was intact again—the life-size plaster Jesus had his arms reattached and was once again nailed to his refurbished cross. Father Joe and Carl had restored him to his former position of dominance. The poor man was upright again, hanging over the center of the sanctuary in all his tortured splendor.

A grisly sight. Zev could never understand the Catholic attachment to these gruesome statues. But if the vampires loathed them, then Zev was for them all the way.

His stomach rumbled with hunger. At least they'd had a good breakfast. Carl had returned from his food run this morning with bread, cheese, and two thermoses of hot coffee. He wished now they'd saved some. Maybe there was a crust of bread left in the sack. He headed back to the vestibule to check and found an aluminum pot and a paper bag sitting by the door. The pot was full of beef stew and the sack contained three cans of Pepsi.

He poked his head out the doors but no one was in sight on the street outside. It had been that way all day—he'd spy a figure or two peeking in the front doors; they'd hover there for a moment as if to confirm that what they had heard was true, then they'd scurry away. He looked at the meal that had been left. A group of the locals must have donated from their hoard of canned stew and precious soft drinks to fix this. Zev was touched.

He called Father Joe and Carl.

"Tastes like Dinty Moore," Father Joe said around a mouthful of the stew.

"It is," Carl said. "I recognize da little potatoes. Da ladies of the parish must really be excited about youse comin' back to break inta deir canned goods like dis."

They were feasting in the sacristy, the small room off the sanctuary where the priests had kept their vestments—a clerical Green Room, so to speak. Zev found the stew palatable but much too salty. He wasn't about to complain, though.

"I don't believe I've ever had anything like this before."

"I'd be real surprised if you had," said Father Joe. "I doubt very much that something that calls itself Dinty Moore is kosher."

Zev smiled but inside he was suddenly filled with a great sadness. Kosher . . . how meaningless now seemed all the observances which he had allowed to rule and circumscribe his life. Such a fierce proponent of strict dietary laws he'd been in the days before the Lakewood holocaust. But those days were gone, just as the Lakewood community was gone. And Zev was a changed man. If he hadn't changed, if he were still observing, he couldn't sit here and sup with these two men. He'd have to be elsewhere, eating special classes of specially prepared foods off separate sets of dishes. But really, wasn't division what holding to the dietary laws in modern times was all about? They served a purpose beyond mere observance of tradition. They placed another wall between observant Jews and outsiders, keeping them separate even from other Jews who didn't observe.

Zev forced himself to take a big bite of the stew. Time to break down all the walls between people . . . while there was still enough time and people left alive to make it matter.

"You okay, Zev?" Father Joe asked.

Zev nodded silently, afraid to speak for fear of sobbing. Despite all its anachronisms, he missed his life in the good old days of last year. Gone. It was all gone. The rich traditions, the culture, the friends, the prayers. He felt adrift—in time and in space. Nowhere was home.

"You sure?" The young priest seemed genuinely concerned.

"Yes, I'm okay. As okay as you could expect me to feel after spending the better part of the day repairing a crucifix and eating nonkosher food. And let me tell you, that's not so okay."

He put his bowl aside and straightened from his chair.

"Come on, already. Let's get back to work. There's much yet to do."

VIII

SUN'S ALMOST DOWN," CARL said.

Joe straightened from scrubbing the altar and stared west through one of the smashed windows. The sun was out of sight behind the houses there.

"You can go now, Carl," he said to the little man. "Thanks for your help."

"Where youse gonna go, Fadda?"

"I'll be staying right here."

Carl's prominent Adam's apple bobbed convulsively as he swallowed.

"Yeah? Well den, I'm staying too. I tol' ya I'd make it up ta ya, din't I? An besides, I don't tink the suckas'll like da new, improved Saint Ant'ny's too much when dey come back tonight, d'you? I don't even tink dey'll get t'rough da doors."

Joe smiled at the man and looked around. Luckily it was July when the days were long. They'd had time to make a difference here. The floors were clean, the crucifix was restored and back in its proper position, as were most of the Stations of the Cross plaques. Zev had found them under the pews and had taken the ones not shattered beyond recognition and rehung them on the walls. Lots of new crosses littered those walls. Carl had found a hammer and nails and had made dozens of them from the remains of the pews.

"No. I don't think they'll like the new decor one bit. But there's something you can get us if you can, Carl. Guns. Pistols, rifles, shotguns, anything that shoots."

Carl nodded slowly. "I know a few guys who can help in dat department."

"And some wine. A little red wine if anybody's saved some."

"You got it."

He hurried off.

"You're planning Custer's last stand, maybe?" Zev said from where he was tacking the last of Carl's crude crosses to the east wall.

"More like the Alamo."

"Same result," Zev said with one of his shrugs.

Joe turned back to scrubbing the altar. He'd been at it for over an hour now. He was drenched with sweat and knew he smelled like a bear, but he couldn't stop until it was clean.

An hour later he was forced to give up. No use. It wouldn't come clean. The vampires must have done something to the blood and foulness to make the mixture seep into the surface of the marble like it had.

He sat on the floor with his back against the altar and rested. He didn't like resting because it gave him time to think. And when he started to think he realized that the odds were pretty high against his seeing tomorrow morning.

At least he'd die well fed. Their secret supplier had left them a dinner of fresh fried chicken by the front doors. Even the memory of it made his mouth water. Apparently someone was *really* glad he was back.

To tell the truth, though, as miserable as he'd been, he wasn't ready to die. Not tonight, not any night. He wasn't looking for an Alamo or a Little Big Horn. All he wanted to do was hold off the vampires till dawn. Keep them out of Saint Anthony's for one night. That was all. That would be a statement—*his* statement. If he found an opportunity to ram a stake through Palmeri's rotten heart, so much the better, but he wasn't counting on that. One night. Just to let them know they couldn't have their way every where With everybody whenever they felt like it. He had surprise on his side tonight, so maybe it would work. One night. Then he'd be on his way.

"What the fuck have you *done?*"

Joe looked up at the shout. A burly, long-haired man in jeans and a flannel shirt stood in the vestibule staring at the partially restored nave. As he approached, Joe noticed his crescent moon earring.

A Vichy.

Joe balled his fists but didn't move.

"Hey, I'm talking to you, mister. Are you responsible for this?'"

When all he got from Joe was a cold stare, he turned to Zev.

"Hey, you! Jew! What the hell do you think *you're* doing?" He started toward Zev. "You get those fucking crosses off—"

"Touch him and I'll break you in half," Joe said in a low voice.

The Vichy skidded to a halt and stared at him.

"Hey, asshole! Are you crazy? Do you know what Father Palmeri will do to you when he arrives?"

"*Father* Palmeri? Why do you still call him that?"

"It's what he wants to be called. And he's going to call you *dog meat* when he gets here!"

Joe pulled himself to his feet and looked down at the Vichy. The man took two steps back. Suddenly he didn't seem so sure of himself.

"Tell him I'll be waiting. Tell him Father Cahill is back."

"You're a priest? You don't look like one."

"Shut up and listen. Tell him Father Joe Cahill is back—and he's pissed. Tell him that. Now get out of here while you still can."

The man turned and hurried out into the growing darkness. Joe turned to Zev and found him grinning through his beard.

" 'Father Joe Cahill is back—and he's pissed.' I like that."

"We'll make it into a bumper sticker. Meanwhile let's close those doors. The criminal element is starting to wander in. I'll see if we can find some more candles. It's getting dark in here."

IX

HE WORE THE NIGHT like a tuxedo.

Dressed in a fresh cassock, Father Alberto Palmeri turned off County Line Road and strolled toward Saint Anthony's. The night was lovely, especially when you owned it. And he owned the night in this area of Lakewood now. He loved the night. He felt at one with it, attuned to its harmonies and its discords. The darkness made him feel so alive. Strange to have to lose your life before you could really feel alive. But this was it. He'd found his niche, his métier.

Such a shame it had taken him so long. All those years trying to deny his appetites, trying to be a member of the other side, cursing himself when he allowed his appetites to win, as he had with in increasing frequency toward the end of his mortal life. He should have given in to them completely long ago.

It had taken undeath to free him.

And to think he had been afraid of undeath, had cowered in fear each night in the cellar of the church, surrounded by crosses. Fortunately he had not been as safe as he'd thought and one of the beings he now called brother was able to slip in on him in the dark while he dozed. He saw now that he had lost nothing but his blood by that encounter.

And in trade he'd gained a world.

For now it was his world, at least this little corner of it, one in which he was completely free to indulge himself in any way he wished. Except for the blood. He had no choice about the blood. That was a new appetite, stronger than all the rest, one that would not be denied. But he did not mind the new appetite in the least. He'd found interesting ways to sate it.

Up ahead he spotted dear, defiled Saint Anthony's. He wondered what his servants had prepared for him tonight. They were
quite imaginative. They'd yet to bore him.

But as he drew nearer the church, Palmeri slowed. His skin prick-
led. The building had changed. Something was very wrong there,
wrong inside. Something amiss with the light that beamed from the
windows. This wasn't the old familiar candlelight, this was something
else, something more. Something that made his insides tremble.

Figures raced up the street toward him. Live ones. His night
vision picked out the earrings and familiar faces of some of his servants. As they neared he sensed the warmth of the blood coursing
just beneath their skins. The hunger rose in him and he fought the
urge to rip into one of their throats. He couldn't allow himself that
pleasure. He had to keep the servants dangling, keep them working
for him and the nest. They needed the services of the indentured
living to remove whatever obstacles the cattle might put in their way.

"Father! Father!" they cried.

He loved it when they called him Father, loved being one of the
undead and dressing like one of the enemy.

"Yes, my children. What sort of victim do you have for us
tonight?"

"No victim, father—trouble!"

The edges of Palmeri's vision darkened with rage as he heard of
the young priest and the Jew who had dared to try to turn Saint
Anthony's into a holy place again. When he heard the name of the
priest, he nearly exploded.

"Cahill? Joseph Cahill is back in my church?"

"He was cleaning the altar!" one of the servants said.

Palmeri strode toward the church with the servants trailing
behind. He knew that neither Cahill nor the Pope himself could
clean that altar. Palmeri had desecrated it himself, he had learned
how to do that when he became nest leader. But what else had the
young pup dared to do?

Whatever it was, it would be undone. *Now!*

Palmeri strode up the steps and pulled the right door open—
and screamed in agony.

The light! The *light!* The LIGHT! White agony lanced through
Palmeri's eyes and seared his brain like two hot pokers. He retched
and threw his arms across his face as he staggered back into the
cool, comforting darkness.

It took a few minutes for the pain to drain off, for the nausea to pass, for vision to return.

He'd never understand it. He'd spent his entire life in the presence of crosses and crucifixes, surrounded by them. And yet as he'd become undead, he was unable to bear the sight of one. As a matter of fact, since he'd become undead, he'd never even *seen* one. A cross was no longer an object. It was a light, a light so excruciatingly bright, so blazingly white that it was sheer agony to look at it. As a child in Naples he'd been told by his mother not to look at the sun, but when there'd been talk of an eclipse, he'd stared directly into its eye. The pain of looking at a cross was a hundred, no, a thousand times worse than that. And the bigger the cross or crucifix, the worse the pain.

He'd experienced monumental pain upon looking into Saint Anthony's tonight. That could only mean that Joseph, that young bastard, had refurbished the giant crucifix. It was the only possible explanation.

He swung on his servants.

"Get in there! Get that crucifix down!"

"They've got guns!"

"Then get help. But get it *down!*"

"We'll get guns too! We can—"

"*No!* I want him! I want that priest alive! I want him for myself! Anyone who kills him will suffer a very painful, very long and lingering true death! Is that clear?"

It was clear. They scurried away without answering.

Palmeri went to gather the other members of the nest.

X

DRESSED IN A CASSOCK and a surplice, Joe came out of the sacristy and approached the altar. He noticed Zev keeping watch at one of the windows. He didn't tell him how ridiculous he looked carrying the shotgun Carl had brought back. He held it so gingerly, like it was full of nitroglycerine and would explode if he jiggled it.

Zev turned, and smiled when he saw him.

"*Now* you look like the old Father Joe we all used to know."

Joe gave him a little bow and proceeded toward the altar.

All right: He had everything he needed. He had the Missal they'd found in among the pew debris earlier today. He had the wine; Carl had brought back about four ounces of sour red babarone. He'd found a smudged surplice and a dusty cassock on the floor of one of the closets in the sacristy, and he wore them now. No hosts, though. A crust of bread left over from breakfast would have to do. No chalice, either. If he'd known he was going to be saying Mass he'd have come prepared. As a last resort he'd used the can opener in the rectory to remove the top from one of the Pepsi cans from lunch. Quite a stretch from the gold chalice he'd used since his ordination, but probably more in line with what Jesus had used at that first Mass—the Last Supper.

He was uncomfortable with the idea of weapons in Saint Anthony's but he saw no alternative. He and Zev knew nothing about guns, and Carl knew little more; they'd probably do more damage to themselves than to the Vichy if they tried to use them. But maybe the sight of them would make the Vichy hesitate, slow them down. All he needed was a little time here, enough to get to the consecration.

This is going to be the most unusual Mass in history, he thought.

But he was going to get through it if it killed him. And that was a real possibility. This might well be his last Mass. But he wasn't afraid. He was too excited to be afraid. He'd had a slug of the Scotch—just enough to ward off the DTs—but it had done nothing to quell the buzz of the adrenaline humming along every nerve in his body.

He spread everything out on the white tablecloth he'd taken from the rectory and used to cover the filthy altar. He looked at Carl.

"Ready?"

Carl nodded and stuck the .38 caliber pistol he'd been examining in his belt.

"Been a while, Fadda. We did it in Latin when I was a kid, but I tink I can swing it."

"Just do your best and don't worry about any mistakes."

Some Mass. A defiled altar, a crust for a host, a Pepsi can for a chalice, a fifty-year-old, pistol-packing altar boy, and a congregation consisting of a lone, shotgun-carrying Orthodox Jew.

Joe looked heavenward.

You do understand, don't you, Lord, that this was arranged on short notice?

Time to begin.

He read the Gospel but dispensed with the homily. He tried to remember the Mass as it used to be said, to fit in better with Carl's outdated responses. As he was starting the Offertory the front doors flew open and a group of men entered—ten of them, all with crescent moons dangling from their ears. Out of the corner of his eye he saw Zev move away from the window toward the altar, pointing his shotgun at them.

As soon as they entered the nave and got past the broken pews, the Vichy fanned out toward the sides. They began pulling down the Stations of the Cross, ripping Carl's makeshift crosses from the walls and tearing them apart. Carl looked up at Joe from where he knelt, his eyes questioning, his hand reaching for the pistol in his belt.

Joe shook his head and kept up with the Offertory.

When all the little crosses were down, the Vichy swarmed behind the altar. Joe chanced a quick glance over his shoulder and saw them begin their attack on the newly repaired crucifix.

"Zev!" Carl said in a low voice, cocking his head toward the Vichy. "Stop 'em!"

Zev worked the pump on the shotgun. The sound echoed through the church. Joe heard the activity behind him come to a sudden halt. He braced himself for the shot . . .

But it never came.

He looked at Zev. The old man met his gaze and sadly shook his head. He couldn't do it. To the accompaniment of the sound of renewed activity and derisive laughter behind him, Joe gave Zev a tiny nod of reassurance and understanding, then hurried the Mass toward the Consecration.

As he held the crust of bread aloft, he started at the sound of the life-sized crucifix crashing to the floor, cringed as he heard the freshly buttressed arms and crosspiece being torn away again.

As he held the wine aloft in the Pepsi can, the swaggering, grinning Vichy surrounded the altar and brazenly tore the cross from around his neck. Zev and Carl put up a struggle to keep theirs but were overpowered.

And then Joe's skin began to crawl as a new group entered the nave. There had to be at least forty of them, all of them vampires.

And Palmeri was leading them.

XI

PALMERI HID HIS HESITANCY as he approached the altar. The crucifix and its intolerable whiteness were gone, yet something was not right. Something repellent here, something that urged him to flee. What?

Perhaps it was just the residual effect of the crucifix and all the crosses they had used to line the walls. That had to be it. The unsettling aftertaste would fade as the night wore on. Oh, yes. His night-brothers and sisters from the nest would see to that.

He focused his attention on the man behind the altar and laughed when he realized what he held in his hands.

"Pepsi, Joseph? You're trying to consecrate Pepsi?" He turned to his nest siblings. "Do you see this, my brothers and sisters? Is this the man we are to fear? And look who he has with him! An old Jew and a parish hanger-on!"

He heard their hissing laughter as they fanned out around him, sweeping toward the altar in a wide phalanx. The Jew and Carl—he recognized Carl and wondered how he'd avoided capture for so long—retreated to the other side of the altar where they flanked Joseph. And Joseph . . . Joseph's handsome Irish face so pale and drawn, his mouth drawn into such a tight, grim line. He looked scared to death. And well he should be.

Palmeri put down his rage at Joseph's audacity. He was glad he had returned. He'd always hated the young priest for his easy manner with people, for the way the parishioners had flocked to him with their problems despite the fact that he had nowhere near the experience of their older and wiser pastor. But that was over now. That world was gone, replaced by a nightworld—Palmeri's world. And no one would be flocking to Father Joe for anything when Palmeri was through with him. "Father Joe"—how he'd hated it when the parishioners had started calling him that. Well, their Father Joe would provide superior entertainment tonight. This was going to be *fun.*

"Joseph, Joseph, Joseph," he said as he stopped and smiled at the young priest across the altar. "This futile gesture is so typical of your arrogance."

But Joseph only stared back at him, his expression a mixture of defiance and repugnance. And that only fueled Palmeri's rage.

"Do I repel you, Joseph? Does my new form offend your precious shanty-Irish sensibilities? Does my undeath disgust you?"

"You managed to do all that while you were still alive, Alberto."

Palmeri allowed himself to smile. Joseph probably thought he was putting on a brave front, but the tremor in his voice betrayed his fear.

"Always good with the quick retort, weren't you, Joseph. Always thinking you were better than me, always putting yourself above me."

"Not much of a climb where a child molester is concerned."

Palmeri's anger mounted.

"So superior. So self-righteous. What about *your* appetites, Joseph? The secret ones? What are they? Do you always hold them in check? Are you so far above the rest of us that you never give in to an improper impulse? I'll bet you think that even if we made you one of us you could resist the blood hunger."

He saw by the startled look in Joseph's face that he had struck a nerve. He stepped closer, almost touching the altar.

"You do, don't you? You really think you could resist it! Well, we shall see about that, Joseph. By dawn you'll be drained—we'll each take a turn at you—and when the sun rises you'll have to hide from its light. When the night comes you'll be one of us. And then all the rules will be off. The night will be yours. You'll be able to do anything and everything you've ever wanted. But the blood hunger will be on you too. You won't be sipping your god's blood, as you've done so often, but *human* blood. You'll thirst for hot, human blood, Joseph. And you'll have to sate that thirst. There'll be no choice. And I want to be there when you do, Joseph. I want to be there to laugh in your face as you suck up the crimson nectar, and keep on laughing every night as the red hunger lures you into infinity."

And it *would* happen. Palmeri knew it as sure as he felt his own thirst. He hungered for the moment When he could rub dear Joseph's face in the muck of his own despair.

"I was about to finish saying Mass," Joseph said coolly. "Do you mind if I finish?"

Palmeri couldn't help laughing this time.

"Did you really think this charade would work? Did you really think you could celebrate Mass on *this*?"

He reached out and snatched the tablecloth from the altar, sending the Missal and the piece of bread to the floor and exposing the fouled surface of the marble.

"Did you really think you could effect the Transubstantiation here? Do you really believe any of that garbage? That the bread and wine actually take on the substance of—" he tried to say the name but it wouldn't form "—the Son's body and blood?"

One of the nest brothers, Frederick, stepped forward and leaned over the altar, smiling.

"Transubstantiation?" he said in his most unctuous voice, pulling the Pepsi can from Joseph's hands. "Does that mean that this is the blood of the Son?"

A whisper of warning slithered through Palmeri's mind. Something about the can, something about the way he found it difficult to bring its outline into focus . . .

"Brother Frederick, maybe you should—"

Frederick's grin broadened. "I've always wanted to sup on the blood of a deity."

The nest members hissed their laughter as Frederick raised the can and drank.

Palmeri was jolted by the explosion of intolerable brightness that burst from Frederick's mouth. The inside of his skull glowed beneath his scalp and shafts of pure white light shot from his ears, nose, eyes—every orifice in his head. The glow spread as it flowed down through his throat and chest and into his abdominal cavity, silhouetting his ribs before melting through his skin. Frederick was liquefying where he stood, his flesh steaming, softening, running like glowing molten lava.

No! This couldn't be happening! Not now when he had Joseph in his grasp!

Then the can fell from Frederick's dissolving fingers and landed on the altar top. Its contents splashed across the fouled surface, releasing another detonation of brilliance, this one more devastating than the first. The glare spread rapidly, extending over the upper surface and running down the sides, moving like a living thing, engulfing the entire altar, making it glow like a corpuscle of fire torn from the heart of the sun itself.

And with the light came blast-furnace heat that drove Palmeri back, back, back until he had to turn and follow the rest of his nest in a mad, headlong rush from Saint Anthony's into the cool, welcoming safety of the outer darkness.

XII

AS THE VAMPIRES FLED into the night, their Vichy toadies behind them, Zev stared in horrid fascination at the puddle of putrescence that was all that remained of the vampire Palmeri had called Frederick. He glanced at Carl and caught the look of dazed wonderment on his face. Zev touched the top of the altar—clean, shiny, every whorl of the marble surface clearly visible.

There was fearsome power here. Incalculable power. But instead of elating him, the realization only depressed him. How long had this been going on? Did it happen at every Mass? Why had he spent his entire life ignorant of this?

He turned to Father Joe.

"What happened?"

"I—I don't know."

"A miracle!" Carl said, running his palm over the altar top.

"A miracle and a meltdown," Father Joe said. He picked up the empty Pepsi can and looked into it. "You know, you go through the seminary, through your ordination, through countless Masses *believing* in the Transubstantiation. But after all these years . . . to actually *know* . . .

Zev saw him rub his finger along the inside of the can and taste it.! He grimaced.

"What's wrong?" Zev asked.

"Still tastes like sour barbarone . . . with a hint of Pepsi."

"Doesn't matter what it tastes like. As far as Palmeri and his friends are concerned, it's the real thing."

"No," said the priest with a small smile. "That's Coke."

And then they started laughing. It wasn't that funny, but Zev found himself roaring along with the other two. It was more a release of tension than anything else. His sides hurt. He had to lean against the altar to support himself.

It took the return of the Vichy to cure the laughter. They charged in carrying a heavy fire blanket. This time Father Joe did not stand by passively as they invaded his church. He stepped around the altar and met them head on.

He was great and terrible as he confronted them. His giant stature and raised fists cowed them for a few heartbeats. But then they must have remembered that they outnumbered him twelve to one and charged him. He swung a massive fist and caught the lead Vichy square on the jaw. The blow lifted him off his feet and he landed against another. Both went down.

Zev dropped to one knee and reached for the shotgun. He would use it this time, he would shoot these vermin, he swore it!

But then someone landed on his back and drove him to the floor. As he tried to get up he saw Father Joe, surrounded, swinging his fists, laying the Vichy out every time he connected. But there were too many. As the priest went down under the press of them, a heavy boot thudded against the side of Zev's head. He sank into darkness.

XIII

A THROBBING IN HIS head, stinging pain in his cheek, and a voice, sibilant yet harsh . . .

" . . . now, Joseph. Come on. Wake up. I don't want you to miss this!"

Palmeri's sallow features swam into view, hovering over him, grinning like a skull. Joe tried to move but found his wrists and arms tied. His right hand throbbed, felt twice its normal size; he must have broken it on a Vichy jaw. He lifted his head and saw that he was tied spread-eagle on the altar, and that the altar had been covered with the fire blanket,

"Melodramatic, I admit," Palmeri said, "but fitting, don't you think? I mean, you and I used to sacrifice our god symbolically here every weekday and multiple times on Sundays, so why shouldn't this serve as *your* sacrificial altar?"

Joe shut his eyes against a wave of nausea. This couldn't be happening.

"Thought you'd won, didn't you?" When Joe wouldn't answer him, Palmeri went on. "And even if you'd chased me out of here for good, what would you have accomplished? The world is ours now, Joseph. Feeders and cattle—that is the hierarchy. We are the feeders. And tonight you'll join us. But *he* won't. *Voila!*"

He stepped aside and made a flourish toward the balcony. Joe searched the dim, candlelit space of the nave, not sure what he was supposed to see. Then he picked out Zev's form and he groaned. The old man's feet were lashed to the balcony rail; he hung upside down, his reddened face and frightened eyes turned his way. Joe fell back and strained at the ropes but they wouldn't budge.

"Let him go!"

"What? And let all that good rich Jewish blood go to waste? Why, these people are the Chosen of God! They're a delicacy!"

"Bastard!"

If he could just get his hands on Palmeri, just for a minute.

"Tut-tut, Joseph. Not in the house of the Lord. The Jew should have been smart and run away like Carl."

Carl got away? Good. The poor guy would probably hate him-self, call himself a coward the rest of his life, but he'd done what he could. Better to live on than get strung up like Zev.

We're even, Carl.

"But don't worry about your rabbi. None of us will lay a fang on him. He hasn't earned the right to join us. We'll use the razor to bleed him. And when he's dead, he'll be dead for keeps. But not you, Joseph. Oh no, not you." His smile broadened. "You're mine."

Joe wanted to spit in Palmeri's face—not so much as an act of defiance as to hide the waves of terror surging through him—but there was no saliva to be had in his parched mouth. The thought of being undead made him weak. To spend eternity like . . . he looked at the rapt faces of Palmeri's fellow vampires as they clustered under Zev's suspended form . . . like *them?*

He *wouldn't* be like them! He wouldn't allow it!

But what if there was no choice? What if becoming undead top-pled a lifetime's worth of moral constraints, cut all the tethers on his human hungers, negated all his mortal concepts of how a life should be lived? Honor, justice, integrity, truth, decency, fairness, love—what if they became meaningless words instead of the footings for his life?

A thought struck him.

"A deal, Alberto," he said.

"You're hardly in a bargaining position, Joseph."

"I'm not? Answer me this: Do the undead ever kill each other? I mean, has one of them ever driven a stake through another's heart?"

"No. Of course not."

"Are you sure? You'd better be sure before you go through with your plans tonight. Because if I'm forced to become one of you, I'll be crossing over with just one thought in mind: to find you. And when I do I won't stake your heart, I'll stake your arms and legs to the pilings of the Point Pleasant boardwalk where you can watch the sun rise and feel it slowly crisp your skin to charcoal."

Palmeri's smile wavered. "Impossible. You'll be different. You'll want to thank me. You'll wonder why you ever resisted."

"You'd better sure of that, Alberto . . . for your sake. Because I'll have all eternity to track you down. And I'll find you, Alberto. I swear it on my own grave. Think on that."

"Do you think an empty threat is going to cow me?"

"We'll find out how empty it is, won't we? But here's the deal: Let Zev go and I'll let you be."

"You care that much for an old Jew?"

"He's something you never knew in life, and never will know: he's a friend—" *And he gave me back my soul.*

Palmeri leaned closer. His foul, nauseous breath wafted against Joe's face.

"A friend? How can you be friends with a dead man?" With that he straightened and turned toward the balcony. "Do him. *Now!*"

As Joe shouted out frantic pleas and protests, one of the vampires climbed up the rubble toward Zev. Zev did not struggle. Joe saw him close his eyes, waiting. As the vampire reached out with the straight razor, Joe bit back a sob of grief and rage and helplessness. He was about to squeeze his own eyes shut when he saw a flame arc through the air from one of the windows. It struck the floor with a crash of glass and a *wooomp!* of exploding flame.

Joe had only heard of such things, but he immediately realized that he had just seen his first Molotov cocktail in action. The splattering gasoline caught the clothes of a nearby vampire who began running in circles, screaming as it beat at its flaming clothes. But its cries were drowned by the roar of other voices, a hundred or more.

Joe looked around and saw people—men, women, teenagers—climbing in the windows, charging through the front doors. The women held crosses on high while the men wielded long wooden pikes—broom, rake, and shovel handles whittled to sharp points. Joe recognized most of the faces from the Sunday Masses he had said here for years.

Saint Anthony's parishioners were back to reclaim their church.

"Yes!" he shouted, not sure of whether to laugh or cry. But when he saw the rage in Palmeri's face, he laughed. "Too bad, Alberto!"

Palmeri made a lunge at his throat but cringed away as a woman with an upheld crucifix and a man with a pike charged the altar—Carl and a woman Joe recognized as Mary O'Hare.

"Told ya I wun't letcha down, din't I, Fadda?" Carl said, grinning and pulling out a red Swiss Army knife. He began sawing at the rope around Joe's right wrist. "Din't I?"

"That you did, Carl. I don't think I've ever been so glad to see anyone in my entire life. But how—?"

I told 'em. I run t'rough da parish, goin' house ta house. I told 'em dat Fadda Joe was in trouble an' dat we let him down before but we shoun't let him down again. He come back fa us, now we gotta go back fa him. Simple as dat. And den *dey* started runnin' house ta house, an' afore ya knowed it, we had ourselfs a little army. We come ta kick ass, Fadda, if you'll excuse da expression."

"Kick all the ass you can, Carl."

Joe glanced at Mary O'Hare's terror-glazed eyes as she swiveled around, looking this way and that; he saw how the crucifix trembled in her hand. She wasn't going to kick too much ass in her state, but she was *here*, dear God, she was here for him and for Saint Anthony's despite the terror that so obviously filled her. His heart swelled with love for these people and pride in their courage.

As soon as his arms were free, Joe sat up and took the knife from Carl. As he sawed at his leg ropes, he looked around the church.

The oldest and youngest members of the parishioner army were stationed at the windows and doors where they held crosses aloft, cutting off the vampires' escape, while all across the nave—chaos; screams, cries, and an occasional shot echoed through Saint Anthony's. The vampires were outnumbered three to one and seemed blinded and confused by all the crosses around them. Despite their superhuman strength, it appeared that some were indeed getting their asses kicked. A number were already writhing on the floor, impaled on pikes. As Joe watched, he saw a pair of the women, crucifixes held before them, backing a vampire into a corner. As it cowered there with its arms across its face, one of the men charged in with a sharpened rake handle held like a lance and ran it through.

But a number of parishioners lay in inert, bloody heaps on the floor, proof that the vampires and the Vichy were claiming their share of victims too.

Joe freed his feet and hopped off the altar. He looked around for Palmeri—he *wanted* Palmeri—but the vampire priest had lost himself in the melée. Joe glanced up at the balcony and saw that Zev was still hanging there, struggling to free himself. He started across the nave to help him.

XIV

ZEV HATED THAT HE should be hung up here like a salami in a deli window. He tried again to pull his upper body up far enough to reach his leg ropes but he couldn't get close. He had never been one for exercise; doing a sit-up flat on the floor would have been difficult, so what made him think he could do the equivalent maneuver hanging upside down by his feet? He dropped back, exhausted, and felt the blood rush to his head again. His vision swam, his ears pounded, he felt like the skin of his face was going to burst open. Much more of this and he'd have a stroke or worse maybe.

He watched the upside-down battle below and was glad to see the vampires getting the worst of it. These people—seeing Carl among them, Zev assumed they were part of Saint Anthony's parish—were ferocious, almost savage in their attacks on the vampires.

Months' worth of pent-up rage and fear was being released upon their tormentors in a single burst. It was almost frightening.

Suddenly he felt a hand on his foot. Someone was untying his knots. Thank you, Lord. Soon he would be on his feet again. As the cords came loose he decided he should at least attempt to participate in his own rescue.

Once more, Zev thought. *Once more I'll try.*

With a grunt he levered himself up, straining, stretching to grasp something, anything. A hand came out of the darkness and he reached for it. But Zev's relief turned to horror when he felt the cold clamminess of the thing that clutched him, that pulled him up and over the balcony rail with inhuman strength. His bowels threatened to evacuate when Palmeri's grinning face loomed not six inches from his own.

"It's not over yet, Jew," he said softly, his foul breath clogging Zev's nose and throat. "Not by a long shot!"

He felt Palmeri's free hand ram into his belly and grip his belt at the buckle, then the other hand grab a handful of his shirt at the neck. Before he could struggle or cry out, he was lifted free of the floor and hoisted over the balcony rail.

And the dybbuk's voice was in his ear.

"Joseph called you a friend, Jew. Let's see if he really meant it."

XV

JOE WAS HALFWAY ACROSS the floor of the nave when he heard Palmeri's voice echo above the madness.

"Stop them, Joseph! Stop them now or I drop your friend!"

Joe looked up and froze. Palmeri stood at the balcony rail, leaning over it, his eyes averted from the nave and all its newly arrived crosses. At the end of his outstretched arms was Zev, suspended in mid-air over the splintered remains of the pews, over a particularly large and ragged spire of wood that pointed directly at the middle of Zev's back. Zev's frightened eyes were flashing between Joe and the giant spike below.

Around him Joe heard the sounds of the melée drop a notch, then drop another as all eyes were drawn to the tableau on the balcony.

"A human can die impaled on a wooden stake just as well as a vampire!" Palmeri cried. "And just as quickly if it goes through his heart. But it can take hours of agony if it rips through his gut." Saint Anthony's grew silent as the fighting stopped and each faction backed away to a different side of the church, leaving Joe alone in the middle.

"What do you want, Alberto?"

"First I want all those crosses put away so that I can see!"

Joe looked to his right where his parishioners stood.

"Put them away," he told them. When a murmur of dissent arose, he added, "Don't put them down, just out of sight. Please."

Slowly, one by one at first, then in groups, the crosses and crucifixes were placed behind backs or tucked out of sight within coats.

To his left, the vampires hissed their relief and the Vichy cheered. The sound was like hot needles being forced under Joe's fingernails. Above, Palmeri turned his face to Joe and smiled.

"That's better."

"What do you want?" Joe asked, knowing with a sick crawling in his gut exactly what the answer would be.

"A trade," Palmeri said.

"Me for him, I suppose?" Joe said.

Palmeri's smile broadened. "Of course."

"No, Joe!" Zev cried.

Palmeri shook the old man roughly. Joe heard him say, "Quiet, Jew, or I'll snap your spine!" Then he looked down at Joe again. "The other thing is to tell your rabble to let my people go." He laughed and shook Zev again. "Hear that, Jew? A Biblical reference—Old Testament, no less!"

"All right," Joe said without hesitation.

The parishioners on his right gasped as one and cries of "No!"

and "You can't!" filled Saint Anthony's. A particularly loud voice nearby shouted, "He's only a lousy kike!"

Joe wheeled on the man and recognized Gene Harrington, a carpenter. He jerked a thumb back over his shoulder at the vampires and their servants.

"You sound like you'd be more at home with them, Gene."

Harrington backed up a step and looked at his feet.

"Sorry, Father," he said in a voice that hovered on the verge of a sob. "But we just got you back!"

"I'll be all right," Joe said softly.

And he meant it. Deep inside he had a feeling that he would come through this, that if he could trade himself for Zev and face Palmeri one-on-one, he could come out the victor, or at least battle him to a draw. Now that he was no longer tied up like some sacrificial lamb, now that he was free, with full use of his arms and legs again, he could not imagine dying at the hands of the likes of Palmeri.

Besides, one of the parishioners had given him a tiny crucifix. He had it closed in the palm of his hand.

But he had to get Zev out of danger first. That above all else. He looked up at Palmeri.

"All right, Alberto. I'm on my way up."

"Wait!" Palmeri said. "Someone search him."

Joe gritted his teeth as one of the Vichy, a blubbery, unwashed slob, came forward and searched his pockets. Joe thought he might get away with the crucifix but at the last moment he was made to open his hands. The Vichy grinned in Joe's face as he snatched the tiny cross from his palm—and shoved it into his pocket.

"He's clean now!" the slob said and gave Joe a shove toward the vestibule.

Joe hesitated. He was walking into the snake pit unarmed now. A glance at his parishioners told him he couldn't very well turn back now.

He continued on his way, clenching and unclenching his tense, sweaty fists as he walked. He still had a chance of coming out of this alive. He was too angry to die. He prayed that when he got within reach of the ex-priest the smoldering rage at how he had framed him when he'd been pastor, at what he'd done to Saint Anthony's since then would explode and give him the strength to tear Palmeri to pieces.

VAMPIRE SLAYERS

"No!" Zev shouted from above. "Forget about me! You've started something here and you've got to see it through!"

Joe ignored his friend.

"Coming, Alberto."

Father Joe's coming, Alberto. And he's pissed. Royally *pissed.*

XVI

ZEV CRANED HIS NECK around, watching Father Joe disappear beneath the balcony.

"Joe! Come back!"

Palmeri shook him again.

"Give it up, old Jew. Joseph never listened to anyone and he's not listening to you. He still believes in faith and virtue and honesty, in the power of goodness and truth over what he perceives as evil. He'll come up here ready to sacrifice himself for you, yet sure in his heart that he's going to win in the end. But he's wrong."

"No!" Zev said.

But in his heart he knew that Palmeri was right. How could Joe stand up against a creature with Palmeri's strength, who could hold Zev in the air like this for so long? Didn't his arms ever tire?

"Yes!" Palmeri hissed. "He's going to lose and we're going to win. We'll win for the same reason we'll always win. We don't let anything as silly and transient as sentiment stand in our way. If we'd been winning below and situations were reversed—if Joseph were holding one of my nest brothers over that wooden spike below—do you think I'd pause for a moment? For a second? Never! That's why this whole exercise by Joseph and these people is futile."

Futile . . . Zev thought. Like much of his life, it seemed. Like all of his future. Joe would die tonight and Zev would live on, a cross-wearing Jew, with the traditions of his past sacked and in flames, and nothing in his future but a vast, empty, limitless plain to wander alone.

There was a sound on the balcony stairs and Palmeri turned his head.

"Ah, Joseph," he said.

Zev couldn't see the priest but he shouted anyway.

"Go back Joe! Don't let him trick you!"

"Speaking of tricks," Palmeri said, leaning further over the balcony rail as an extra warning to Joe, "I hope you're not going to try anything foolish."

"No," said Joe's tired voice from somewhere behind Palmeri. "No tricks. Pull him in and let him go."

Zev could not let this happen. And suddenly he knew what he had to do. He twisted his body and grabbed the front of Palmeri's cassock while bringing his legs up and bracing his feet against one of the uprights of the brass balcony rail. As Palmeri turned his startled face toward him, Zev put all his strength into his legs for one convulsive backward push against the railing, pulling Palmeri with him. The vampire priest was overbalanced. Even his enormous strength could not help him once his feet came free of the floor. Zev saw his undead eyes widen with terror as his lower body slipped over the railing. As they fell free, Zev wrapped his arms around Palmeri and clutched his cold and surprisingly thin body tight against him.

"What goes through this old Jew goes through you!" he shouted into the vampire's ear.

For an instant he saw Joe's horrified face appear over the balcony's receding edge, heard Joe's faraway shout of "No!" mingle with Palmeri's nearer scream of the same word, then there was a spine-cracking jar and a tearing, wrenching pain beyond all comprehension in his chest. In an eyeblink he felt the sharp spire of wood rip through him and into Palmeri.

And then he felt no more.

As roaring blackness closed in he wondered if he'd done it, if this last desperate, foolish act had succeeded. He didn't want to die without finding out. He wanted to know—

But then he knew no more.

XVII

JOE SHOUTED INCOHERENTLY AS he hung over the rail and watched Zev's fall, gagged as he saw the bloody point of the pew remnant burst through the back of Palmeri's cassock directly below him. He saw Palmeri squirm and flop around like a speared fish, then go limp atop Zev's already inert form.

As cheers mixed with cries of horror and the sounds of renewed battle rose from the nave, Joe turned away from the balcony rail and dropped to his knees.

"Zev!" he cried aloud. "Good God, Zev!"

Forcing himself to his feet, he stumbled down the back stairs, through the vestibule, and into the nave. The vampires and the Vichy were on the run, as cowed and demoralized by their leader's death as the parishioners were buoyed by it. Slowly, steadily, they were falling before the relentless onslaught. But Joe paid them scant attention. He fought his way to where Zev lay impaled beneath Palmeri's already rotting corpse. He looked for a sign of life in his old friend's glazing eyes, a hint of a pulse in his throat under his beard, but there was nothing.

"Oh, Zev, you shouldn't have. You shouldn't have."

Suddenly he was surrounded by a cheering throng of Saint Anthony's parishioners.

"We did it, Fadda Joe!" Carl cried, his face and hands splattered with blood. "We killed 'em all! We got our church back!"

"Thanks to this man here," Joe said, pointing to Zev.

"No!" someone shouted. "Thanks to *you!*"

Amid the cheers, Joe shook his head and said nothing. Let them celebrate. They deserved it. They'd reclaimed a small piece of the planet as their own, a toehold and nothing more. A small victory of minimal significance in the war, but a victory nonetheless. They had their church back, at least for tonight. And they intended to keep it.

Good. But there would be one change. If they wanted their Father Joe to stick around they were going to have to agree to rename the church.

Saint Zev's.

Joe liked the sound of that.

Authors' Biographies

Manly Wade Wellman (1903–1986) got his start in the pulps, contributing science fiction and horror tales to *Weird Tales* and *Astounding Stories* in 1927. He is best known for his fantasy stories, especially those that involve paranormal investigators. While he wrote more than twenty adult novels, his largest body of work was in children's novels, with dozens of books published.

Brian Hodge's most recent novel is *Prototype*. He has since broadened his interests to include crime fiction with *Miles to Go Before I Weep*, and expansion of the *Thrillers 2* novelette. Several of his sixty-some stories have been corralled into his first collection, *The Convulsion Factory*, themed around urban decay and offering no answers save that cities should brush after every meal. Spare time is devoted to tribal ritual music, movies with astronomical body counts, and, cash permitting, wanderlust.

Carl Jacobi (1908–1997) was a mainstay of the pulp magazines of the 1920s and 30s, writing for *Weird Tales* and *Wonder Stories* and many others. Known for his ability to bring subtle characterizations to his weird fiction, Jacobi never wrote a novel, but concentrated entirely on the short form. Collections of his works include *Revelations in Black*, *Portraits in Moonlight*, and *Smoke of the Snake*.

August Derleth (1909–1971) is best known as the cofounder (with Donald Wandrei) of Arkham House Publishing, the primary publisher of H. P. Lovecraft. Other authors whose short fiction was published by them included Robert E. Howard and Clark Ashton Smith. But the editor of Arkham House also wrote hundreds of poems, short stories, and novels, including a series of "posthumous" collaborations with Lovecraft himself.

238

Richard Laymon has written more than twenty-five novels, including *Bite, Quake,* and *The Stake.* He also has written screenplays for Hollywood and several dozen short stories for such books as *Love in Vein II, Forbidden Acts,* and *Screamplays.* Born in Chicago, Illinois, he studied English literature in Oregon and was awarded his master's degree from Loyola University in Los Angeles, where he resides today.

James Kisner's other fiction has appeared in *The Year's 25 Finest Crime and Mystery Stories, Vampire Detectives,* and *Predators.* He lives in Evansville, Indiana.

Hugh B. Cave was a mainstay author of many pulp magazines in the 1940s and 50s. Later in his career he wrote several remarkable novels, including *The Cross on the Drum,* one of the few excellent novels examining the theme of voodoo. Other novels include *The Nebulon Horror, Disciples of Dread,* and *The Lower Deep.* His dozens of short stories have been collected in several anthologies, including *Murgunstrumm and Others, The Witching Lands,* and *Death Stalks the Night.*

Charles de Lint is a full-time writer and musician who makes his home in Ottawa, Canada, with his wife Mary Ann Harris, and artist and musician. His most-recent work is a collection of his short fiction entitled *Moonlight and Vines.* For more information about his work, visit his Web site at www.cyberus.ca/~cdl.

Tanya Huff was born in the Maritimes and now live and writes in rural Ontario. On her way there, she spent three years in the Canadian Naval Reserve and got a degree in radio and television arts, which the cat threw up on. Recent books include the novel *The Quartered Sea* and a single-author collection entitled *What Ho, Magic!*

While **Ed Gorman** is best known for his suspense novels, including *The Marilyn Tapes* and *Black River Falls,* he has also published six science fiction novels under pseudonyms. A full-time author, Ed lives in Cedar Rapids, Iowa, with his wife, children's author Carol Gorman, and three cats.

F. Paul Wilson's novel *The Keep* was made into a successful movie of the same name and also gave rise to several tangentially linked sequels, including *Reborn, The Tomb,* and *Nightworld.* His short fiction has appeared in *Night Visions IV, Predators, Weird Tales,* and *Analog.* He has also edited several anthologies, including *Freak Show* and *Diagnosis: Terminal.* He lives with his family in New Jersey.

COPYRIGHTS
AND PERMISSIONS